THE VOYAGE

(Book 2 in the Robot Army trilogy)

by

BETH SCHLUTER

W & B Publishers
USA

The Robot Army Trilogy, Part 2: The Voyage © All rights reserved by Beth Schluter

W & B Publishers

For information:
W & B Publishers
Post Office Box 193
Colfax, NC 27235
www.a-argusbooks.com

ISBN: 978-1-9429810-9-1
ISBN: 1-9429810-9-0

Book Cover designed by Dubya
Printed in the United States of America

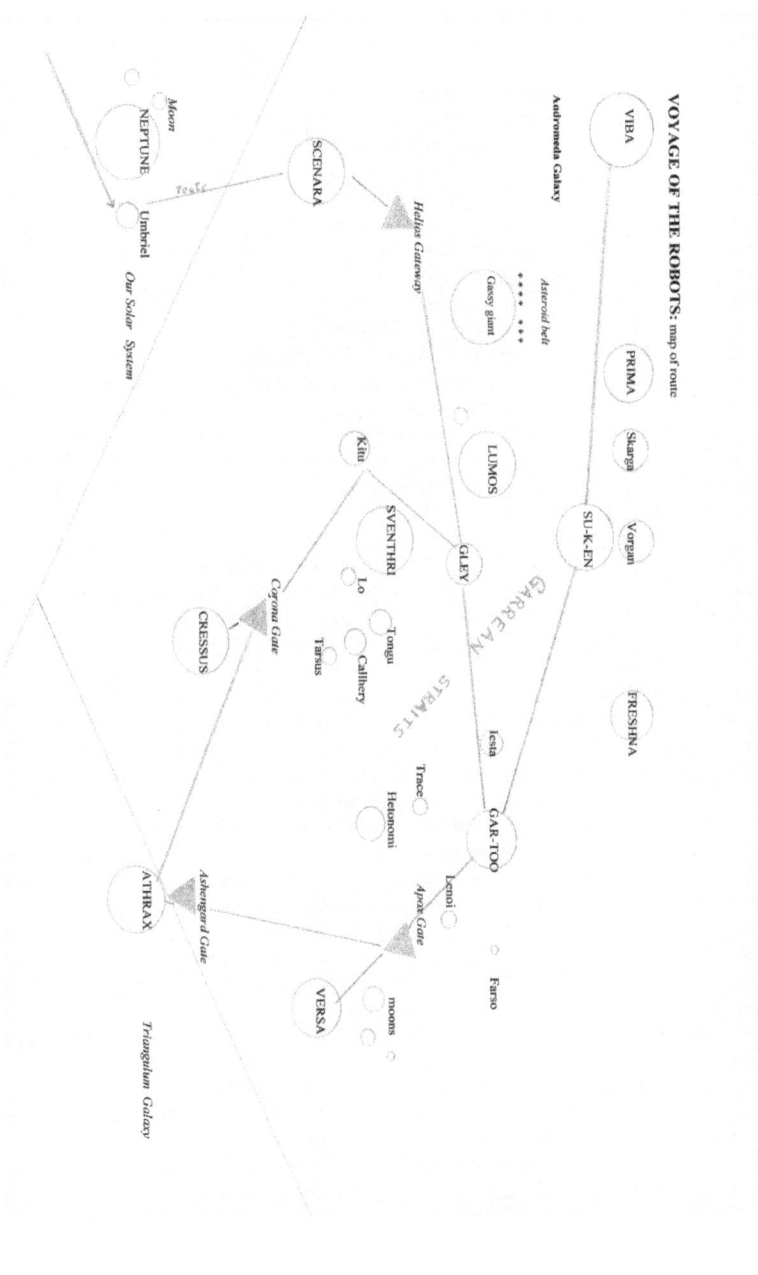

VOYAGE OF THE ROBOTS: map of route

Andromeda Galaxy

VIBA

PRIMA

Skarga

Vorgan

SU-K-EN

FRESHNA

SCENARA

Helius Gateway

Asteroid belt
**** ***

Gassy giant

LUMOS

GLEY

GARREAN

Iesta

STRAITS

GAR-TOO

Lenni

Farso

Moon

NEPTUNE

route

Umbriel

Our Solar System

Kitu

SVENTHRI

Lo

Tongu

Callhery

Tarsus

Corona Gate

CRESSUS

Trace

Hetonomi

ATHRAX

Ashengard Gate

Apok Gate

VERSA

moons

Triangulum Galaxy

Chapter 1

Warning

Lin felt the danger running through her body. All her senses warned her to act quickly as though all of the crew's lives depended upon it. She communicated telepathically with Argo, the AI fleet commander on the Starfinder mother ship. Argo and Lin had a strong telepathic connection and they trusted each other implicitly, even though Lin was only six years old.

"Argo! Danger ahead! Veer the ship away from it quickly! We have very little time!"

Argo heard Lin's message loud and clear even though he was on the bridge of the ship and Lin was laying in its depths in her own bedroom next to her mother Gale.

Argo scanned the sensors again, but there was no sign of anything in front of them!

"Say again Lin. I cannot see any danger. Where is it?"

The captain leapt to Argo's side on hearing the urgency in his voice. Argo related quickly to Captain Bull Carter what Lin had said. Bull looked ahead through the window on the bridge. The sensor had shown nothing and as far as Bull could see, there was nothing to be seen but stars for thousands of miles around.

Suddenly the sensors on the Starfinder began blaring an alert all over the ship. First officer Kian Furze reported urgently. "Hull breach Captain! In Sector five!"

Bull thought quickly where that was, he was quite new to the spaceship, having taken over from Captain Grey a few days earlier. Grey had retired after his long mission through space to find resources to save the Earth from its devastation, after an alien invasion forty five years previously. He had to travel for so long in space because the technology for faster space travel had only just been created by the Blues on board ship in the last few months. Now the Starfinder and its fleet could travel in a fraction of the time it used to take when Grey was in command.

Whilst Argo, an advanced AI, checked the stability of the ship, Bull, realising that Sector five was where the girl he was in love with was sleeping, rushed to hail Star on his mic.

"Star! Star! Are you there? There is a danger in your area somewhere, be on alert! ......Star, can you hear me?"

But there was no response at all from Star's room. Bull rushed out of the bridge to the beamer, where he could beam himself down to the sleeping quarters in Sector five, where Star was. As he left the beamer on the fourteenth level he nearly crashed headlong into Finch, who was on security duty near the engine rooms below and had rushed towards his girlfriend's room to check that she was alright when he heard the alarms sounding.

Finch and Star were lovers, both part of the ship's crew from Earth and they were friends of Bull's, so Bull was honour bound to never act on his love for Star, out of respect for his friendship with Finch.

"What's happening?" Finch asked worriedly as they both ran towards the sleeping quarters. "Is Star in danger?"

Bull replied that he'd not been able to hail Star when the alarms set off and that there was a hull breach in her sector somewhere. On hearing this news, Finch ran even faster towards his love, calling her name urgently.

"Star! Where are you? It's me, Finch. Star, can you hear me? " He called on his collar mic repeatedly, but still there was no answer.

***

The vast, blinding and sizzling energy cloud had engulfed Star completely, probing her thoughts and controlling her mind, looking for something it had never encountered before. It held her in its grip and she was unable to move or respond to her lover's calls. How he must be worrying about her she thought in her stricken state.

The sizzle of the energy hummed in her ears almost making her wish she was deaf. It was overpowering and intrusive. She tried to move her legs but her body would not respond. It held her in a vice-like grip. She tried to speak but her lips seemed fused shut. Anyone else might have totally panicked and given in, but Star was made of sterner stuff, she had been one of the Earth's Scavengers in her past, a vital role that helped her community to survive the devastation of her planet.

The ship's human crew, numbering only eight, were all survivors of the Apocalypse of over forty-five years previously. They had their lives turned around when a robot army landed on Earth last year and revitalised their world, returning it to its former beauty. The rest of the crew, numbering in their thousands, were all artificial intelligences from that very army that saved them. Argo was the supreme AI, possessing many skills, highly evolved and trustworthy he was the fleet commander now, based on board the Starfinder mother ship. Now the ship had been breached by this intrusive energy cloud. It had been invisible to all their sensor equipment, until too late – only Lin had felt its presence.

***

The two friends arrived at Star's bedroom door, guns in hand ready to defend her, but when they kicked open the door and entered the room they were shocked by what they saw. Half of the room was engulfed by a blinding energy cloud, sizzling and moving around Star, holding her in its grip. Her whole body seemed to glow with electrical energy. They ran towards her to try and wrest her from the energy field's grip, but as soon as they came near the spikes of electricity knocked them back viciously, stinging their bodies like sharpened knives!

"Star, can you move?" Finch asked urgently. But Star could not respond, it seemed. Her eyes stared at them, full of fear.

Bull again ventured close to the energy cloud but Star's eyes, the only thing she could move, glared in warning at him. Bull understood her well, having partnered her on their scavenging patrols in their past lives; they had made a good team. They complemented each other. He had fallen in love with Star over the last year, but could not act upon it due to her love for Finch, his best friend. Now both men felt helpless to rid her of this menace.

***

Blue 7's voice hailed the captain on his earpiece.

"Captain, we have lost control of the Starfinder, all systems are non-responsive to our commands. We are locked in position from when we suffered the hull breach, we are not moving!"

Bull responded quickly." Are the life support systems being maintained?"

The Blue replied that they were, but he had no control over them.

"Are the rest of the fleet affected by the same problem?" Bull added, thinking quickly.

"No, Captain. The fleet report no problems with their ships. What would you like to do, Captain?" Blue 7 enquired tentatively, awaiting the new captain's decision on how to resolve his first problem in his new career.

"Get one of the support ships to focus on our position to see if they can rid us of the problem. There seems to be some sort of energy field inside Star's bedroom, holding her prisoner. We can't get near to it from here. See if they can find the problem from the exterior. Captain out."

Blue 7 hailed the Silver commander in one of the fleet support ships to investigate how their ship was being held and to offer advice on moving the obstacle if possible. All the fleet support ships were piloted by Silver ranking AIs, below Argo and the Golds in skills, but still extremely skilled at manoeuvring their ships in times of battle. The Silver commander turned his ship around to head for the mother ship, but still keeping a safe distance from the danger. The rest of the fleet awaited just ahead, unmoving, ready to offer support when needed.

Silver 1 circumnavigated the mother ship from a safe distance, looking for the danger. On turning into the starboard quadrant the commander saw the problem clearly through his control window. A large energy field, like a sparkling cloud of electricity abutted the hull of the ship at that point, as though it was half in and half outside the ship at the same time. It was substantial in size, writhing along the hull of the ship. This would be a tricky operation to try to move it. He reported the details and awaited orders.

***

Resistance

Bull and Finch circled the energy mass, trying to work out how to release Star, but when they got too close to the object it retaliated by emitting a spike of electricity to warn them off. The shock stung their hands, making them drop their weapons. Star looked helplessly at them both and wanted them to keep at a safe distance. She didn't want either of them hurt.

Argo called the captain to the bridge to take reports from the fleet of the situation. Bull was torn between his duty to the fleet and his love for Star.

"You go, Bull, I'll stay with Star. They need you up there. I promise I'll keep a safe distance." Finch vowed . He could see how torn Bull was. Bull looked into Star's eyes and left the room, heading back towards the bridge. But his heart was back there, back where Star was held prisoner by this mass. On his way up he was updated by Argo as to what the Silver commander had seen.

Bull patched himself directly to Silver 1.
"Do you think you will be able to fire at the energy

mass without hitting the Starfinder?" Bull asked the pilot as soon as he reached the bridge. He watched the view of the mass on his monitor, relayed by the Silver commander from his ship's computer.

"Yes, Captain." The Silver replied. "I can shoot it at an angle that will avoid contact with the Starfinder."

"Then give it all you've got, Commander. We need that gone, fast!" Bull commanded, then he sat in his control position on the bridge, ready to add his own fire power once control had come back to the ship's systems.

Silver 1 brought in his ship from a steep angle to pulverise the energy mass and let loose his weapons. The missiles tore through space and smashed forcefully into the mass. Again the commander released more missiles to make sure of his target. As the explosions died down the Silver commander looked with horror at the effect his weapons had had on the energy mass. Far from destroying it the explosions had instead increased the volume of the energy field. It seemed to have absorbed the missiles' energy and added it to its own stores. He reported his findings to the bridge and was told to stand down until they could figure something else out.

***

Inside the ship, Star's body had jerked as the mass had been hit by the missiles. It had lifted her off the floor and held her aloft, while it continued to probe her mind.

Finch was fearing for her life and he felt so helpless, not knowing the best way to deal with the intruder. He was about to try to fire a blast gun at it when one of the Blues, the fleet's technical robots, walked into the room. He advised Finch not to aggravate the mass or it might retaliate in some way. Finch realised he was talking as if this was a living organism capable of reasoning.

"Are you suggesting we leave it be?" Finch asked in astonishment. He needed to do something to help her! But what could he do? "You talk as if this mass can be reasoned with! Why would you think that? It's just an energy field, isn't it?" Finch was confused and frustrated by the situation. "I must get to her somehow!"

The Blue saw his determination and offered an opinion. "We may be able to get closer to her, if it works.." He paused as if working it out in his head.

"What works? What are you talking about? Tell me! I'll try anything." Finch spoke with great urgency, willing there to be a solution.

"Well," the Blue offered reluctantly, "We have a metal casing that we use when we work with electrical equipment to protect us from damage..."

Finch interrupted in his confusion. "A metal casing? With electricity? Are you serious? I thought that metal conducts electricity, wouldn't it toast you?" Finch couldn't comprehend it at all.

The Blue continued. "No, not at all. If you are inside the casing you are protected. It is like a Faraday's cage, invented by a scientist in the nineteenth century . It protects the person inside the cage, the energy travels through the cage itself instead of your body. I could get to Star using the casing and move her away from it perhaps."

Finch was worried whether this would work or not, but it was all he had. "Okay, get me the suit and I'll go and get her. I need to try it at least."

But the Blue wasn't about to let Finch risk his life so he replied. "Oh no, sir! I can't let you use it, it would not work on you, it would not fit properly. I'll go. I'll get her out for you." At that he left to fetch the suit and put it on, not giving Finch time to argue about it. Finch looked at Star, who now had her eyes closed, as if asleep standing up, and he worried even more that he was losing her. *This has got to work!* he thought to himself.

***

Up on the bridge Bull looked at the increase in size of the energy field on his screen. Obviously trying to blast it away would do no good, but what else was there? He wished Captain Grey was here to offer his advice and expertise, he needed it right now. His thoughts were disturbed by a voice nearby.

"Captain? Is there anything we can do to help?" It was First Officer Kian Furze and his girlfriend, the XO Meera Khan; both previously of the military community who had joined the crew with the rest of them after passing the vigorous trials they had to partake in to crew the ship. They were brave and enthusiastic, but now the way to deal with the problem was apparently not with brute force.

Bull thanked the two crew members and briefed them on the situation. He pointed out that weapons wouldn't work right now but he was investigating other avenues to deal with the situation. He hoped they had ideas that would work.

Meera and Kian looked at each other trying to figure out the cause of the intrusion. Meera spoke up with a thought she had on her mind.

"Would you be able to think of a reason why the energy field has targeted Star? Is there anything special about the location of her room?"

Bull could not think of anything that was different in Star's bedroom to any of the others. " No, all the rooms down there are all of the same construction." Bull replied perplexed.

Meera looked again at Kian, then added. "Then, the reason it has targeted that area is because of Star. There is something about Star that it needs..." she continued, "Did the energy field try to grab you and Finch when you entered her room?"

Bull contemplated the idea. "No, it didn't try to grab us, but it stung us when we tried to get too close..." He thought carefully then added, "So you think it's Star herself that's the attraction? But why? I can't see the reason!"

Argo listened to the conversation and a thought occurred to him. "Bull, I am unable to sense what the energy field wants, but what about Lin? Perhaps she can communicate with it? After all, she was the only one to sense its presence."

Bull immediately hailed Gale, Lin's mother, on his control panel, hopeful that she could help in some way. "Gale? This is the captain, is Lin still with you?"

Gale responded immediately and announced that Lin was expecting his call. Bull told them to meet him down by Star's room as quickly as possible. Bull headed for the beamer, with Meera in tow, to offer her support if needed.

***

The Mass

Finch looked worriedly at the Blue as it entered the room encased in the metal caging. He could not envisage this working but they had to give it a go. The casing looked clumsy and ineffectual, but Blue 70 edged towards the sparkling cloud and looked at Finch before setting foot into the mass.

"What's the plan ?" Finch asked worriedly in case he should be supporting the robot in any way.

The Blue tried to look confident for Finch's sake, but the truth was he couldn't be sure this would work, being more concerned in case it harmed Star further. He held a wooden staff in his hand. "The plan is to get right behind Star and push her forward via this wooden prop , until she is clear of the field, then you can grab her and quickly take her away from the room."

Finch wished he hadn't agreed to this, but they didn't have another option at this point. He would try anything to free Star...

Blue 70 stepped into the glowing mass and the casing sizzled and glowed all around with each step he took further into the energy field. Star's eyes remained closed, so she was unaware of the Blue approaching. Finch tried to tell her what was happening so that she might prepare herself, but if she heard she did not show it. With every step the Blue took the closer he edged towards Star. He seemed unaffected by the electrical charges biting at his suit from all directions.

Eventually he arrived within an arm's length from Star and he reached out to touch her, but his hand could not make contact with her body at all, there seemed to be an invisible wall shielding her body from him. Blue 70 tried to reach her from all angles, but the result was the same each time. He was pushed away from her by an invisible force. She was completely engulfed within a shield. The Blue looked at Finch and shook his head. It was no good, the plan had failed!

As Finch and the Blue stood side by side discussing the turn of events they heard footsteps approaching. Lin and Gale entered the room and looked in awe at the scene in front of them, the captain followed closely behind, worry imprinted on his face.

Finch related to the trio what they had tried unsuccessfully to do and waited hopefully for them to suggest a new approach that would work.

Lin stood in front of the energy mass and closed her eyes. All stood in silence, watching, for what seemed like an eternity, but was in reality only minutes, before Lin told them all to go out of the room and wait for her. Bull was about to protest, but Gale shook her head and indicated for them all to follow her out into the corridor beyond.

Once alone with the mass Lin searched through her thoughts for an avenue to reach out to the intruder to be able to communicate with it. She felt a presence touch her mind, it was a sensation of conflicting thoughts battling out a debate, trying to reason out a new entity's purpose. Its conflict within itself was all consuming, it had encountered something it could not comprehend and was trying to find a reason for this entity's existence within Star. It seemed to serve no purpose to the energy mass, it could not comprehend the reason it was there. The mass had never encountered this in its existence in space and when it was identified as being part of this human the mass sought it out, to find answers why it was there.

Lin found herself confronting this entity as though it was a child trying to work out a puzzle, not wanting help from anyone, it wanted to resolve the problem by itself. But Lin could see it would never arrive at a conclusion without her interference, it had no experience of the situation to fall back on, to arrive at a conclusion. Lin tried to imprint her own feelings into the mass, but was swept aside repeatedly. Lin called for her mother to enter alone to join her. Gale came to stand by Lin and held her by the shoulders as they both looked towards the mass.

In the corridor outside, Bull thought hard about the reason Star was the mass' focus. She must possess something the mass hadn't encountered before for it to want to study her so intensely. Countless spaceships must have passed by this area of space in the past he reasoned. Had they been targeted in this way? Capt. Grey had certainly not encountered this problem when passing through this sector on his journey back to Earth, so Star had something different about her that interested the entity. He began to realise what it was...

In the bedroom Lin, and Gale were holding each other tightly, Gale stroking Lin's hair gently as she communicated with the mass, concentrating on emitting her feelings towards the cloud. She projected her feelings for her mother to the mass, but it was only marginally affecting the movement of the cloud. She realised what needed to be done at the same time as Bull. Bull entered the room with Finch in tow.

"It's her deep love for Finch." Bull stated quietly as he entered the room.

"Yes, I think so." Lin replied, releasing her mother from her grip. "I tried to project our love for each other to the mass and it did seem to affect it slightly, but Star's love for Finch is a different kind of love. He needs to be here to project his feelings for her to the mass."

Finch looked from one to the other then asked, "What can I do? Show me."

Lin took his hand and led him closer to the mass,

she held onto his hand and told him to think deeply of his love for Star, what she meant to him and she would project it to the entity."

Gale returned to Bull's side nearer the doorway and watched as the two others faced the energy field deep in concentration. Within a few minutes the energy mass sparkled more intensely and allowed Star's body to touch the ground once again, slowly her eyes opened and she latched onto Finch's gaze. But she was still held in its grip. She looked deep into his eyes and her heart ached for his comfort. All of a sudden the energy field engulfed both Finch and Lin as well!

Gale lurched forward to try to protect her daughter, but Bull held onto her arm and shook his head.

"No, leave them, I think the mass needs to complete the link between them all to understand."

Gale relaxed a little and watched as Finch, now inside the mass, energy glowing all around him, walked slowly towards Star. He was unhindered this time as he embraced her tightly in his arms. The mass released its tight grip on Star and immediately she responded by holding him tightly in her arms. Lin smiled and nodded her head, as though deep in communication with the entity. The energy field began to fill the room, edging closer and closer to engulf both Bull and Gale as well.

"Stay still" Bull whispered to Gale as the energy field began to envelop them.

The field intensified its glow on reaching Bull. It swirled around him as though curious, like a stranger inspecting every part of his being, it dazzled Bull's gaze as it swirled around him. It had left Gale's body entirely by now, concentrating on the three ex scavengers instead. Lin understood its intent and looked at the captain briefly before closing her eyes again.

All of a sudden the mass roiled around the room, between the three ex scavengers, swirling around their bodies from top to toe. Then abruptly it began to recede, further and further away towards the bulkhead, until it disappeared through the metal into space beyond.

Star fell exhausted into Finch's arms and he picked her up and laid her on the bed nearby. Whilst projecting their thoughts, Lin had realised how much Bull had meant to Star too and how Bull felt conflict in his feelings for Star. She felt sad that they were torn by their feelings, but she knew she couldn't mention it.

Star opened her eyes and spoke. "I could feel it probing my mind, asking me questions over and over about my feelings. It wanted to know what the feeling of love was that I felt for you, but it didn't understand, not until Lin brought us together."

Star looked past Finch at Lin in the background. "Thank you, Lin, I don't know if I'd ever have been freed without your help."

Lin smiled. "You're welcome. One day I'd like to be in love with someone just like you are. It must be a wonderful feeling."

Lin and Gale left the room and told the awaiting Meera that it was safe to enter now, all was well.

Chapter 2

Saturn

The Starfinder's immense and grey cylindrical form regrouped with the awaiting fleet and proceeded to continue on its mission to travel deeper into space. Its multiple layers had been added by the AIs, creating a structure, unrecognisable from NASA's original rocket form, set out into space all those decades ago. Its appendages speared out at sharp angles to its main body construction, housing a large robot construction wing and numerous powerful weaponry. It contained a viewing chamber in its higher layer, where its crew could view the galaxies it passed on its missions through space. To travel from one sector of the ship to another a being entered the beamer, which was a type of lift that could traverse the ship, both horizontically and vertically. Otherwise, a traveller could use the old fashioned metal stairwells that snaked through the ship at intervals.

***

Argo was concerned why the energy field had not been detected on their sensor, so he set the Blues a task of upgrading their sensor system to include identifying any energy masses in future. The Blues were happy to have something new to work on and set to work on their project straight away.

Guy walked into the lounge area where Kian and Meera were having breakfast, his headphones hung around his neck.

"Morning you two, have I missed anything?" he asked, rubbing his eyes to try and focus after his long sleep.

Meera looked at Kian, then back at Guy in disbelief.

"Are you serious?" she asked in astonishment. "Do you mean to say you have no idea what we have just been going through?" She held her spoonful of cereal inches from her face as if rooted to the spot since Guy's question.

"Been through? What are you talking about? I've been asleep, just woke up... what's going on?" Guy looked in confusion from one to the other, then Meera and Kian picked up their empty beakers and threw them at him , laughing at his ignorance. He ducked as the missiles came his way, completely ignorant of the events that had unfolded whilst he'd been asleep with his headphones on. When he finally heard what had happened he couldn't hide his embarrassment at being oblivious to it all.

"It's a good job you're not the security officer isn't it! " Kian retorted, still laughing. "I guess if we'd have needed a medic we would have to have waited until your dream was over?"

Guy's face filled with guilt.

***

In the bedroom, Star began to get dressed after her ordeal, as Finch waited anxiously beside her. He was worried of any long term effects on her body after the trauma she had undergone. He wasn't about to leave her side for a while in case she passed out. As she finished putting on her uniform Finch got up and held her in his arms once more. "You sure you feel ok?" he asked seriously, moving a wayward strand of raven hair from her eyes.

"Yes, I'm fine." Star replied softly, although the throbbing in her head told her otherwise. "Now, let's go and get some breakfast. I'm starving!"

The crew relaxed a while during their breakfast in the lounge, all making fun out of Guy's deep sleep, much to his dismay, but he took it on the chin and vowed not to fall asleep with headphones on again.

***

On the bridge the fleet commander and the captain reflected on the events that had unfolded. Bull's thoughts jumbled around in his head, the energy cloud had included him in the link, so there must have been some feeling for him from Star he reasoned, but how strong was it? He wished he knew. Bull had been torn between his duty and his feelings for Star and he was punishing himself for putting his crew at risk. What if they had been killed? The responsibility weighed heavily on his shoulders.

"Don't beat yourself up about it, Bull." Argo spoke gently as he checked the fleet reports, looking for any lapse in readiness for future encounters. He must ensure the whole fleet was a hundred percent ready for any eventuality.

"But I could have got people killed!" Bull retorted despondently. "I must focus on my responsibility as captain, the others are relying on me."

Argo turned to his captain to offer support. "They knew the odds, they had to try to help, whatever the outcome, and you had to ensure the ship's safety. You had to focus on the bigger picture, or we all might have died. It's the job you were given. They all understand that."

Argo clasped Bull gently on the shoulder in support, his tall frame looming large above Bull and Bull appreciated his presence beside him at that moment. He knew then that Grey would have done the same thing. Bull thought it would be wise to have a chat with Captain Grey about how he coped with problems, whilst he could still communicate with him, being that they had comms links with Earth whilst still in the Solar System. He could very well learn a few tips from him he thought.

***

Time passed quickly as they set on their journey to exit the Solar system, the planets passing by one by one as they ventured further.

The loudspeaker announced to the crew. "If you look through the portal you will see Saturn coming up in a few minutes, our second largest planet after Jupiter, which you saw recently."

The crew proceeded towards the viewing window, framing the galaxy around them near the upper deck, and looked in awe at the giant looming in their viewer. The spectrum of colours blending into each other with infinite precision, minute particles guided on an ever circulating pathway around the giant ball overwhelmed their view. It was so spectacular to see close up like this, they wondered how many other humans had enjoyed this experience before them.

Bull looked through his own window on the bridge, with Argo by his side, both marvelling at the sight in front of them.

"So many rings!" Bull observed, spellbound. "Do they have names, do you know?" he asked his fleet commander.

Argo replied instantly. "Oh yes. Some named after the person who discovered them. The first sector of rings is called Encke's division and the darker circle in the central area there is called Cassini's division, named after Giovanni Cassini who found more moons around Saturn, some rings were later named after famous people in the early 21st century , but a couple of other rings have to this date only been given letters to label them. Perhaps you would like to have your name on one?"

Bull thought about it. "Bull's ring? No, it doesn't really have that edge to it, does it!" Bull laughed. "So the smaller planets around it are moons then?"

Argo nodded in agreement.

The two continued watching with fascination for a while then Bull spotted a small dot in the distance.

"What's that over there, close to that moon?" Bull asked worriedly, pointing towards the object.

Argo zoomed the window magnification in on the object to reveal a small satellite in orbit around the planet. He accessed his database then replied. "Oh, it's a satellite from Earth, launched long ago in the late 21st century to investigate one of Saturn's moons. I believe it's one of the Seeker satellites, launched by the then space exploration company NASA. I think they were trying to investigate possible locations for terra forming a new Earth around here, but the alien war stopped all that.."

Bull thought about the people who had launched it, long dead now, but the satellite continued on regardless. "I wonder if they found what they were looking for with it?" Bull thought out loud. "If there is a possible life sustaining planet here?"

"I believe so." replied Argo encouragingly.

Bull looked at him grimly, he digested the information and wondered if the alien war had not happened, might he have lived out here with his family? Was Earth so over populated at that time that they needed to expand their territory? The thought troubled Bull deeply.

***

The planet moved slightly out of view as the Starfinder and the fleet passed by on their long mission into deep space. The vastness of it all was overwhelming and Bull felt so small and insignificant in the scheme of things as he travelled through it. He wondered how many other space travellers felt the same as him and would he meet any of them?

***

Stranded

Meera looked again at her screen, it was definitely there, worrisome; it shouldn't be! She informed the commander.

"Commander, I've discovered a craft in my viewer that shouldn't be that close to the asteroid field. I think it's being pulled in."

Commander Furze checked his sensors and informed the captain immediately. "Captain, the craft isn't manoeuvring away, it seems to be drawn towards the asteroid belt. Something's wrong. They have no control... I'm checking for life signs... Sir. There are five life signs on board."

Bull checked the screen to make sure there were no other craft in the vector, but he could see none. He called to the comms Blue. " Blue 7 see if you can hail the craft."

"Aye, Captain!" Blue 7 patched the message to the struggling craft. Seconds later he replied, "No visuals, Captain, but we have this..." He put the faint message on loudspeaker: "Please help.. weak. .need help.."

Bull received a report from Blue 9 detailing minimal oxygen supply on board the stricken ship, so the fleet commander decided to send out a rescue shuttle to bring the craft's crew on board. He sent two Argonauts and two Bronzes along with a shuttle to rescue the crew, with Guy, the ship's medic accompanying them.

"Be careful over there." warned the captain, "It may be a trap we are heading into; everyone on alert!" Bull and Argo watched as the small group headed towards the shuttle, Guy bringing up the rear with his medical equipment in tow on a carrier. "And Guy, stay on board the shuttle until the Golds tell you it's safe to board the spacecraft, we don't want to lose you!"

"Aye, Captain." Guy replied, "I don't want to lose me either!" He smiled as he entered the shuttle.

***

Argo and Bull looked on from the bridge as the shuttle headed slowly towards the stricken ship, avoiding the asteroids sweeping towards them.

"I've never encountered a ship like that before." The fleet commander stated whilst scanning the floundering ship for damage. "It seems to be losing its integrity, there are large gashes on the port side and vapour is escaping into the atmosphere. Their oxygen supply is almost depleted!"

Bull looked at the details on the scanner and began to worry that the ship might break up very quickly. "How

long do you think it's got?" Bull asked the fleet commander.

Argo shook his head and replied, "I really can't say.
We don't know how long it's been venting in this state...
But they must be as quick as possible transferring the
crew, just in case."

The urgency of the operation was reported to the
shuttle as it neared the stricken ship's docking bay. The
bay doors were wide open and small craft were strewn at
odd angles along its interior. All were smashed up! Bodies littered the space, floating around, still in their space-
suits.

"It looks like there's been a major skirmish here.."
Guy remarked as they landed the shuttle in a suitable gap
between the mish-mash of craft. " I'm glad I've got a
weapon with me!"

"Don't worry, we will protect you." The Gold closest to him smiled as activated the their ramp to open.
"Stay here until you are called for, the pilot will stay with
you."

Guy was relieved that he didn't need to venture inside the ship just yet, he was more than happy for the very
capable Argonauts to do the encountering! The Blue who
was piloting was a comfort as he was armed too. He felt
sure the Blue would protect him if needed.

The four AIs went through the airlock into the ship's
interior to search for the survivors. There was an alarm
blaring somewhere on the ship and the strobe lighting
ducts were hanging open here and there along the corridors, blinking their lights on and off intermittently. There
was evidence of random firing of weapons all around the
corridor they walked along.

Cables had been torn from some of the door mechanisms but the Bronze levered open the first door easily and they entered into the next corridor. Behind them, a figure shuffled, unseen, towards their own shuttle, heading for the ramp and creeping in.

Lights flashed on and off up the walkway and in the distance they saw a body lying on the floor ahead. When they arrived beside the prone figure they saw that the person was dead, a large hole evident in the chest area. It was a male with strange features, instead of a beard he had strands of what looked like thick skin strips hanging from his face where a beard might have been. His body was quite large, but not as tall as the Bronzes and Golds. His skin was quite orange with brown speckles on his hands and neck. His mane of russet hair was tied at the nape of the neck.

They continued along the corridor and found another male, also dead, shot in the head. Neither male seemed to have been armed.

Further along they drew alongside a sealed room full of scientific equipment, where they could see through the bulletproof window more bodies lying on the floor. These seemed to be a different species. They were all women and all had very long curly fair hair tied back in different styles. Their skin was tanned in appearance and on the face they all had a pattern of what looked like sequins attached around the eyes, presumably glued on , some of the women sported a different sequin pattern to the others. They were no taller than the average human.

The AIs interfaced with the door mechanism and entered. There seemed to be no wounds on any of them, it looked like they had suffocated thought the AIs. A hand moved in the corner of the room and a groan was heard from the woman lying there. Gold 5 went up to the woman and saw she was gasping for breath. He took out his oxygen mask from the medi-kit and put it on her face to help her breathe. Slowly she opened her eyes and looked in terror at the AI until he began to reassure her that they were there to rescue them. Next to her lay another female who was showing further signs of asphyxiation and the other Gold aided her to recovery with another mask. The Bronzes could not find anyone else alive in the room so they continued their search further into the ship.

The Golds took the two women survivors to the shuttle for Guy to help them further. They lay them down on the benches and Guy monitored their blood levels and looked after their oxygen needs. They both had passed out by the time they reached Guy. The unseen figure watched in silence, invisible to the naked eye. The Golds then went back into the dying ship to help find the other survivors with the Bronzes.

As they passed the room where they had rescued the two women, they met up with one of the Bronzes, who was carrying a male back towards the shuttle; the face looking like the ones that had been shot they saw earlier. He was alive but unconscious. The Bronze had found him on the bridge of the ship along with another survivor being tended to by the second Bronze. in the same area. That survivor was also a male, but the Bronze stated that he seemed to look like a Scenarian! He had been the one sending out the distress call. There was one more survivor to look for, so they spread out to look in different areas.

Suddenly the ship lurched, as though struck by something. They were being pulled further into the asteroid belt! The corridor walls seemed to groan and began to buckle around them! They hurried and the Gold punched a hole in the alarm system ensuring it would stop blaring its warning. It would be easier to hear a person's cries without it blaring away. The upper deck had a few more bodies of a mixture of males similar to the blonde survivors and females of the same species as the dead males found in the corridors, but all were dead, so they descended to another level.

On the lower deck the Gold spotted a life sign on his wrist heat sensor and found another female alive, a totally different species again! She was very slight and very beautiful, with white hair cut into interesting angles. She had some human features, but more like an elf instead, with pointed delicate ears and large expressive eyes. Her pupils were very large and took up a great deal of the eyeball, showing very little white. Her skin was very pale, almost shining. She was trying to crawl along the floor when they found her, but when she saw the AIs she collapsed completely as though she had fainted.

Carrying the survivor, now with an attached oxygen mask, the AIs rushed through the stricken ship as it began to grind and hiss in protest at its demise. The metal was buckling around them rapidly as they fled. In any minute the ship could blow up! They had to get out of there fast, so they rushed back up the stairway to the upper level and suddenly the Gold who was not carrying the female looked quickly at the other, sensing the danger they were in!

"Let's get out of here! Fast!" he shouted and in a flash he flew along the corridor having deployed his flight capability, with the second Gold, carrying the female following suit. They blasted the doors that were in their way to form a clear pathway for their flight out to the shuttle. As they entered the vast docking bay, the Gold called to the pilot on his mic to start the engines because they had to get out fast!

The shuttle was in the distance in front of them, a hundred paces away when the ship began to split in half. The pilot suddenly spun the shuttle around and sped out of the docking bay without waiting for the Golds!

***

"What are you doing?" Guy was distraught to find the pilot leaving the spaceship without the two Golds and any other survivors they may have found. "You can't leave yet! The Gold's aren't on board! Turn around! You've got to wait for them..."

Guy was incensed that the Blue could leave them behind and he could see in the distance through the shuttle window the whole ship breaking up behind them. He saw an almighty explosion rip apart the front part of the ship and turned his head away in distress over the loss of the two Golds.

After a few minutes the shuttle suddenly halted in position in space when they were only about a quarter of the way back to the Starfinder, Guy wondered what was going on. He ran to the window nearest the blown-up ship and watched it split into a million pieces in front of his eyes. He could only stare in disbelief.

Suddenly a bulkhead came down from the ceiling and shut them off from the rear ramp area. "What's going on?" Guy demanded urgently.

"Relax." The Blue replied calmly. "It's ok."

Guy couldn't believe it, how could he relax with all this going on? He felt the rear ramp mechanism operating to open the ramp doors beyond the bulkhead separating them. He stared at the bulkhead as he heard a heavy thump as something hit the metal. It was followed by another thump, then the grind of the ramp doors shutting again.

He stood transfixed, rooted to the spot as the bulkhead raised back up to the ceiling cavity. There in front of him by the ramp's closed doors stood the two Golds, one of which was holding a female.

"How the..?" Guy spluttered disbelievingly as the Gold placed the very pale female on the empty spare bench, oxygen mask in place over her face.

He remembered that the Golds could fly, but hadn't realised they could fly in outer space as well as in atmosphere. But what of the female? He couldn't fathom how she could have survived the vacuum.

The Gold told him how his own shield protected her whilst flying back to the shuttle and that the Blue would have known this and did the right thing in getting the shuttle out of there. Guy listened to all this wide eyed and was so impressed by this advanced being. He had a lot to learn, but at this point he really did have no idea how much more he was going to learn very soon!

***

Science

Guy scanned the body of the first curly-haired female in front of him and looked twice at the readings. It was incredible! Her heart rate was so fast it was a wonder she was living. It was pumping blood around her body at a tremendous rate! He scanned the other female of the same species and the results were the same for her too! *It must be a trait of their species* thought Guy, hoping that was the case.

Their features were very elegant, with upward slanting eyes and their skin was tanned in appearance. The sequins that formed patterns at their temples were different to each other and Guy could not see how they were attached at all. The small white-haired female nearby sat upright and looked around her in fear, wide eyed. Guy approached her in a calming voice, confident in her understanding due to their built-in translator chips, inserted at the start of their journey into space.

"It's all right. You are safe now, we rescued you from your ship. It blew up just a few minutes ago."

The female stared warily at them, but when she saw the other females, she jumped up to stand beside them and tried to stir them.

"Genai, wake up! Genai? Are you all right?" The elfin female cried in a panic at her friend, trying to shake her awake.

"It's all right, your friends will all recover, don't worry." Guy tried his best to calm her.

She looked again at the AIs, then at Guy. "What are you?" she asked warily, looking from one to the other.

Gold 7 related to her who they were and why they were here and how they had heard the distress call and went to rescue them. Guy introduced himself then she began to calm down a little.

"We have never seen your kind before, do you all come from different planets?" Guy asked gently.

The female paused then replied, but maintaining a stiff, wary stance, as if prepared to run at any moment.

"No, we are all, except for one, from the planet Su-K-En, we are, were, on a scientific mission, but we were swept into a kind of wormhole and arrived in this galaxy. Not long before it happened, we were attacked by several space craft, they were Sventhri pirates. They boarded our ship and began to kill our crew. Those who worked in the labs sealed themselves into their rooms, but the Sventhri destroyed our life support systems and we began to lose our oxygen supply. They destroyed all our means of escape and left us to die.... Is this all that remains of our crew?" The female glanced at her comrades despondently.

"I'm afraid so." Guy replied. The girl withdrew into herself at hearing this news and tears were forming in her eyes realising she would never see her friends again.

"Can you tell us more about yourselves, do you have a name?" Guy asked.

The girl paused again then added "My name is Da-Ee and I am a Su-ul. The two girls over there are scientists, Genai and Ursu, they are Endari. The male over there is the Commander, Kios, he is a K-Tu. The other male we rescued from a pod floating in space a while ago. He is Scenarian, his name is Kush, he was a fighter pilot, so he says."

Guy looked at the Golds then the Blue pilot spoke.

"Docking at the Starfinder, Sir."

***

Argo and Bull stood at the docking bay platform awaiting the arrival of the shuttle. They looked in amazement as the survivors were relayed out on hover boards, except for one, now walking alongside Guy. To the human crew they were extraordinary in appearance. Finch stood to one side, armed in case of trouble, with Star and a group of Silvers who made up the security force on board ship. The Su-ul looked alarmed at the weapons but Guy reassured her it was just a precaution. She stayed close to Guy just in case.

"Quite a mix of species here, Bull! Argo surmised as he watched the group head for sick bay with the security group in tow.

"I'd say!" remarked Bull. "Let's hope they're friendly!" he added briefly as he turned on his heel to be debriefed by the Golds. No one noticed the invisible figure sneaking out of the shuttle into the docking bay to hide.

***

"Science equipment, you say?" Bull queried the Gold in front of him. "Do you know what they were working on?" he asked hopefully.

"No, Captain. As you said, the priority was to get the survivors out as quickly as possible before the ship blew up, as it was we barely made it out in time." Gold 5 replied. "The ship had been attacked and the life support system was failing, they all almost suffocated. Others had been shot or hacked to pieces, presumably they tried to put up resistance, although I saw no weapons anywhere on board."

Bull was intrigued by this. It would be unusual for ships not to have some small arms on board ship for such eventualities. He definitely needed to have a chat with these beings once they were all awake. He hailed the medic for an update on the survivors and was told they needed rest for at least 12 hours before he could interrogate them. He also wanted to run physical tests on the group because their physique was unusual to say the least. So Bull would need to bide his time for now.

***

Finch and his Silver security team studied the sensor scrupulously for any signs of enemy craft in the vicinity. If they had attacked the Su-k-En ship recently they could still be in hiding somewhere. They could have been sucked in by the wormhole too. There were so many moons and asteroids to hide behind, it would be a difficult task using sensors alone.

Finch hailed the captain. "Captain, it's Finch. I think it would be advisable for a security detail to comb the area for signs of the enemy craft. They could well be hiding nearby. Do I have your permission to proceed, sir?" Finch found it incredibly odd to have to call Bull sir, but whilst on duty he deserved that respect.

Bull asked Argo's advice on the matter and the Fleet commander gave Finch his answer. " Lieutenant, I think it would be advisable to take some shuttles to comb the different vectors, but do not let them stray beyond ten clicks out. Keep in constant contact or we may waste time chasing after you. Commander out."

Bull added "Good luck.. stay safe! Watch for any anomalies you see in the stars, remember, there was mention of a wormhole, we don't want any of you swallowed by it by accident! Over and out!"

***

Search

The asteroid belt had several large structures to hide behind and the Silver veered in between the asteroids with great skill, avoiding contact with the large boulders in the assault course. In all the area covered in the allocated distance there was no vessel to be seen hiding. He rejoined the main group to his left, who were heading towards a moon's surface, looming large on his scanner. It was very pitted in its surface from all he could see from his viewer, with several large craters scattered on the surface where any number of spacecraft could hide! The squad separated out into different sectors to scan the surface of the moon, using heat sensors in the hope of catching engine heat signatures. But again it was a fruitless exercise, nothing was evident nearby so they returned to the Starfinder.

***

Silver 8's group had swept the area around the S-u-Ken ship debris in case the enemy had returned to salvage any metal. Large sections of the ship rolled out of control, crashing into each other, further twisting and breaking up the bulkhead fragments. As the Silver came past a large section of debris he saw something flashing in the distance, in amongst smaller items of debris. Silver 8 turned his ship towards it, a red light flashing on and off. Negotiating around fragments of floating coils and tubing, the Silver zoomed in on the object. He hailed the fleet commander and asked what he should do.

Argo asked for a brief description of the object and when he was satisfied with the reply he asked the Silver to retrieve it, perhaps it would turn out to be important.

Silver 8 approached the spinning structure. It was quite small, about the size of a small safe, a cuboid with a handle on a metallic frontage, the glowing red lights were attached to the top of it. He pressed the button that released the extendable arms on the front of the shuttle and extracted the object, inserting it into the shuttle bay cavity. He continued his survey of the area but found nothing of more interest so he headed back to the Starfinder.

None of the search squad had seen anything suspicious and all had now returned to the mother ship. Bull gave the order that the retrieved object be put in quarantine until they found out more about it. For that they would have to wait for their guests to recover.

***

Guy made several discoveries about the aliens in his care, their physiology was entirely different from humans, apart from the Scenarian, who was the same. As he was scanning one of the Endari she woke up, alarmed. She sat bolt upright in a flash and took in her surroundings quickly. She jumped to the other Endari.

"Genai! Genai! Wake up! We are in danger!" Ursu looked around at the others, who seemed to still be sleeping. Genai woke up agitated and jumped in a flash next to Ursu, holding onto her arm. Guy gently spoke to the girls and told them what had happened, meanwhile the Su-ul got up and stretched then walked over to the Endari.

"Chill, girls. It's ok. They did rescue us, I remember, I was half conscious. We are aboard their ship." She walked slowly over to them, a sad expression on her face.

"We are the only survivors." Da-Ee added sadly, looking around her. Shock registered on the girls' faces.

"What of the ship?" Ursu asked urgently.

Guy replied that it had blown into pieces just as they were rescued.

"Oh no!" Genai gasped in horror. "All our work! Our experiments gone to dust!" she leaned against the bed in tears. Ursu paused then asked "Was anything retrieved from the wreckage?"

Guy was intrigued and added. "Well, it's funny you should say that because a small container with flashing red lights on it was retrieved, but that's all."

The girls looked at each other, grinned, then laughed and hugged each other.

"That's all? That is all ?... That is everything to us! Everything!" the girls relaxed immediately.

"Was that your experimental work?" Da-Ee inquired hopefully. The girls nodded gleefully.

"Then all is not lost!" Da-Ee replied.

Guy hailed the captain to let him know the survivors were awake. In minutes Bull and Argo, accompanied by Finch were at the sick bay doors.

The Scenarian and the tall K-Tu male were now up and about also, taking in their surroundings.

Bull introduced himself and the others, and the K-Tu stepped forward and held a fist out.

"I am Kios, captain of the Su-i, the ship you found us on."

Bull was unsure what to do, but Argo led the way and held his fist out to touch the K-Tu's in greeting. Bull then did the same. The K-Tu lowered his fist and bowed his head slightly, the fleet commander and captain followed suit.

The rescue was discussed briefly and all were visibly relieved on hearing about the retrieved container, which held the results of their year-long experimental work. Argo spoke to the Scenarian, letting him know that he had been on Scenara a few years previously and met the King and Queen. He told how they had helped end the war with their fleet.

The Scenarian looked downhearted at this news and Argo was troubled as to why. The Scenarian spoke "Then you do not know, Scenara has fallen!"

Argo and Bull looked aghast at each other. "What happened?" Argo asked worriedly.

"About a year ago we began to experience huge tremors on our land, then three months ago the domed city fell into the depths of the planet, with all the inhabitants with it, the King and Queen included..."

Argo bent his head down low on hearing this, *Grey will be devastated,* he thought. Argo could hardly believe this, he remembered Queen Laifa fondly.

The Scenarian continued, "Prince Cruza was safe because he was patrolling space, searching for refuge for us with his fleet when it happened. When he saw the planet cracking up and the molten core beginning to rise to the surface to engulf the cities and towns, he landed and rescued as many people as he could. We watched in despair as the whole planet began to break apart until we could look no more..."

Argo thought about the beautiful scenery and the wondrous carvings and art works, now all gone, along with the wonderful people that had created them.

"What happened to the survivors?" Argo asked despondently.

"We had nowhere to go, we went to find another planet that would sustain life. Our neighbouring planets' climate did not suit our needs, so we travelled for a while, searching the galaxy until we found an inhabited planet called Versa. The people there were suspicious of us at first and we were made to feel unwelcome. They had different views to us and there were many clashes between our two peoples. We later occupied a part of the planet that had fewer people living there, but we were constantly raided by a group of outcasts. They took a lot of our supplies and some of our people were killed in skirmishes. So

Prince Cruza sent out some of his fleet to travel space to find a better place for us to make a new home.

"I was aboard one of the fleet ships sent to find somewhere when we were attacked by an unknown enemy. We did not see them until too late, they had a way of making themselves appear invisible to other ships. They had cut my ship into pieces with their weapons before we could react. Some of us managed to reach escape pods before the ship blew up entirely, but I lost communication with the others. I know at least two other crew members were also able to escape in a pod. When my pod ran out of fuel it drifted in space for a long time before the Su-i found me and gave me refuge."

The K-Tu continued their story. "We were initially on a scientific mission to find the properties of minerals and rocks on various planets and moons, even asteroids in the vicinity. But when Kush told us about the invisibility capability of the enemy ship, our scientists started to explore ways and means of creating a substance that would make things invisible. The Endari found eventually that some of the minerals we had, possessed some of the properties we needed to develop such a thing. It was by accident that they discovered that when those minerals were mixed with a liquid and fed with an electrical charge it produced an invisible coating. They had experimented with coating small objects with it in a liquid form and then charging it with electricity created the invisibility! The container you salvaged contains the mixture, but unfortunately all our notes are lost! It could take some time to re create it to use as a means of cloaking our ships."

Bull and Argo looked at each other and smiled. "Not as long as you may think!" Argo replied mysteriously.

Chapter 3

Differences

The humans amongst the crew gathered in the lounge area to meet the newcomers, full of curiosity, as this was to be their first encounter with alien beings. They were very different in appearance and Lin initially found them intimidating, keeping close to her mother, holding on to a balloon her mother, Gale, had given her at her birthday party a few days earlier.

Da-Ee was fascinated by Guy and clung on his every word whenever he spoke. She found an overwhelming urge to touch his face and poor Guy was embarrassed by her curiosity. He had spent the morning giving them a guided tour of the ship. Meera watched her move around Guy, oblivious to everyone else.

Meera whispered to Kian, her boyfriend, how Guy had found an admirer at last! But Kian shook his head, telling her that Da-Ee was the wrong sex for Guy to reciprocate the interest. Meera raised her eyebrows at hearing this, she had no idea about his sexuality before.

The Endari girls were fascinated by the drinks that Finch and Star were drinking out of the server. They asked to taste the coffee as they'd never seen it before. Finch offered his cup and Ursu took a sip, thought about it then swallowed with a grimace on her face. Genai was less elegant, as soon as she tasted the coffee she spat it out violently, wiping her tongue repeatedly with her hand. Finch and Star laughed, then asked them to chose a drink they liked from the machine.

The girls went over and asked for Suku. It came out, looking like purple liquid, with a foam on top. They sipped it and smiled with relief. They offered a sip to Finch and Star, which they warily took. Both of them had to spit it out straight away as it tasted disgusting to them, smelling of mushrooms. They all laughed and accepted how different their tastes were.

"Things could get interesting at meal times!" whispered Star to Finch and he began to imagine all sorts of grossness being consumed by the girls.

***

Bull was talking with Kios, the Ku-Tu, about his knowledge of space and found out interesting details about parts of the galaxy that had never been explored by Earth before. Argo was commiserating with Kush, the Scenarian about the demise of his planet when the Su-ul spotted Lin and Gale. Da-Ee went to approach Gale and her daughter.

Lin initially became frightened and grabbed her mother's hand and in doing so, lost her grip on the balloon. She watched, dismayed, as the balloon floated high up into the bulkhead ceiling above, too far to reach.

Da-Ee saw how upset the little girl was and said softly to her, coming down to her level "Don't worry, little girl, I will get it for you."

The humans stopped in mid-speech as they saw Da-Ee walk up to the wall and then started walking up the wall vertically, as if gravity didn't exist! On reaching the top of the bulkhead wall she then walked, upside down, along the ceiling until she retrieved the balloon. She then re traced her steps and handed the balloon to Lin, whose mouth was wide open in disbelief. The humans could not believe what they had just seen!

The Endaris smiled and Ursu said "I see none of you have seen a Su-ul before."

Bull recovered his composure and retorted "Is there anything else we should know?"

Suddenly the alarm blared on the intercom. Bull was hailed on his mic by the Blue from the bridge. "Captain, we are detecting craft approaching!"

Bull was immediately on his way towards the bridge when suddenly he was overtaken at great speed by the two Endari! They were travelling so fast he barely registered them! As he arrived on the bridge three minutes later the Endari were already there, composed, not even out of breath, looking on the scanners.

"I guess that's another thing I should know!" Bull muttered to himself as he checked the scanner.

"Visuals." Bull ordered the Blue. The screen appeared at the front of the bridge and there, headed towards them were four large grey spaceships, shaped like birds' wings.

Ursu suddenly exclaimed in horror. "Oh no! It's the Sventhri! They are pirates, they are the ones who attacked us before! They can beam on board if they are close enough, Captain! Flee! Before it's too late!"

But Argo and Bull weren't about to flee! Bull called the Blue for a weapons report on the alien craft.

The Blue scanned then replied to the captain "No match for us. sir!"

Suddenly hundreds of smaller craft flowed out of

the larger ships, spreading out towards the fleet!

Immediately Argo ordered the fleet to engage the alien craft and watch out for boarding attacks, knowing the AIs could look after themselves. The mother ship would hold back this time at a safe distance from being boarded. The AIs would be more than a match for any boarding attempts by the pirates!

The fleet ships swerved in and out of the pirate vessels, firing from all angles as they swept by, but the Sventhri began to try and blast their way through the small craft to head for the Starfinder. The Silvers now started to lay on the heavy artillery, aware that their shields could sustain any blasts that came their way. The Silver commander headed directly for the leading pirate ship to force it to alter course, pummelling it with several missiles as it headed towards him. His squadron attacked the smaller alien craft, decimating them easily. Unfortunately the pirate ship shield held and it continued to try and blast its way through. More fleet ships entered the fray, attacking from all directions, pounding the pirate shields until they began to falter.

Suddenly four Golds sped out of some of the fleet vessels, heading for each of the larger pirate ships, ready to attack through their weakened shield. They latched onto the hull of each ship and began to pulse their rays towards the cockpit area, aiming to disintegrate the control sector so the ships would be helpless.

In moments a pirate beamed onto one of the fleet attack ships, armed with a blood-curdling spiky blade that was half the height of the pirate! He held it diagonally in front of himself and went to launch an attack on the crew. He paused in surprise when he saw all the crew were robots, then launched an attack regardless. As soon as he came near the Bronze co-pilot he saw to his dismay how tall the robot was when he stood up to face the onslaught. As the pirate lifted his blade to attack, the Bronze emitted a ray from his palm and the pirate's weapon melted in his hands. He screamed in agony, dropping the melting metal at his feet, pausing only a split second before beaming himself back to his own ship. Unfortunately for him his ship was spiralling out of control and heading for a full on collision with another pirate ship that had been disabled by the Gold. In seconds the two ships collided and exploded, leaving the two remaining pirate ships nose-diving out of control towards the moon nearby.

The Endari girls leapt for joy and smacked their hands together. Bull laughed and said that was something they had in common! He showed them how to "high five" and they went around doing that to all the crew on the bridge, much to the dismay of the Blues.

***

Cloaking

Hours later, the Endari watched enthralled as the Blue placed their experiment into the cloning machine and produced a duplicate, possessing all the qualities of the original.

"Can we make a large enough batch to coat the ship?" inquired Genai excitedly.

The Blue replied that they could easily create enough of the liquid to coat the whole fleet, to which the girls stood there speechless.

So production started in earnest and the Blues managed to analyse the ingredients and mineral make-up of the liquid precisely enough to give the girls their formula back again. Within a few hours they landed the fleet on one of Uranus' more stable moons, Umbriel, so that the AIs and robots could coat all the ships with the new cloaking liquid. The Blues created the trigger for releasing the electrical charge that would instigate the cloaking at the touch of a button on the control panel. Soon the whole fleet would have yet another means of defence!

***

Whilst the AIs and robots were busying themselves with cloaking the ships, some of the crew decided to explore the immediate area around them. The Endaris wanted to see if there were any minerals of interest on the surface of this moon, others just wanted to explore and experience being out of the spaceship.

Bull told them not to wander too far away in case something went wrong. He sent a Gold along to escort them as a precaution.

Star and Finch were excited to try out their first space walk, as were Kian and Meera. Their helmets had built in recorders so that they could look back at their first space walk whenever they felt like reminiscing in the future! The others stayed on board ship, happy to let the others sate their curiosity.

The Endaris began taking samples of the moon's surface, gathering the small heaps of ice particles in their test tubes to take back on board ship to examine later.

Star and Finch felt strange trying to walk on the surface weighted down by their space shoes. It was a sensation that neither had experienced before, being quite different from their training. They headed towards a large crater nearby, followed by Meera and Kian.

The Gold watched from a short distance as they headed downwards into the sloping crater. He spoke to them on their internal headphones, telling them to keep their comms open so he would be able to check they were safe.

"Oh, look at this!" remarked Genai, heading excitedly towards a glistening rock nearby. "Look how it sparkles in the light of my torch!" she cooed, pulling her case open to place a piece of the rock into it. They combed the floor for more rocks in the ice and found another, which was totally different, very dark in colour, with a smooth surface. Ursu extracted it then held it in her hand, turning it over. She stopped suddenly, wide eyed, looking closely at the rock.

"Look, Genai! There is something on the other side... it looks like a picture of something!"

Genai grabbed the dark rock excitedly and looked closely at it in her torchlight. It did seem to have some sort of drawing on it. She put it in her case and looked for more, both girls very excited at the find.

***

Finch led the way along the iced-up rocky terrain down to the edge of the crater, but stopped momentarily as he looked towards the rim further along. He had caught sight of something ahead in his torchlight.

"Wait a minute." He spoke to the others following behind him. "What is that over there?" He pointed to a few yards further along the upper edge of the crater, then headed towards it with the others following behind, full of curiosity. When he stopped, the others saw what had caught his attention. It seemed to be a crude curving stairway carved out of the icy rock surface of the crater, leading down into its depths. The small group looked at each other wondering what to do. Finch pressed his intercom and spoke to the Gold escort.

"Gold 3 we have found a stairway leading down into the crater, we are going to follow it down." Finch uttered, hoping the others agreed.

"Hold on! I am coming with you!" Gold 3 answered, then quickly flew to their side at the top of the stairs.

The stairs looked as though they had been there for centuries, with the treads worn and uneven, but there was plenty of snow-like ice particles covering parts of them so it didn't look like they had been used for a long time. While the humans descended the stairway Gold 3 flew down into the depths of the crater, following the direction of the stairs. He shone his arm lights around him the further down he went as it became darker. He waited at the foot of the stairs for the others to catch up. Curiously, it became marginally warmer the deeper they ventured into the crater.

"Looks like people used to live here." the Gold remarked as the crew arrived beside him.

All had their helmet torches on and could see much better what was around them. The base of the crater was smooth, with carved columns standing like sentinels forming an arched walkway towards the side of the crater wall. They were created from a dark smooth stone and had drawings carved into each one. The drawings depicted sacrifices performed on altar stones, and when the group scanned the area around them they found such a stone, deeply cracked on one side of the crater. There were strange beings in the pictures, they looked half human and half animal. The Gold speculated that in ancient times beings must have used this place for sacrifices to their gods.

"But do you think they lived on this moon?" Star inquired, intrigued.

"Surely not, there's no breathable atmosphere and it's so cold!" Meera retorted.

The Gold didn't know of course, but replied that it could be possible that the moon had an atmosphere at some time in its past. He referred back to the images of the moon's surface as seen from space having contained ruts that meandered just like rivers would have done. Perhaps there were rivers here at one time. The others pondered over the possibility and wondered what had caused things to change.

Finch wandered further around the crater, looking for more signs of its previous use. Star followed behind, scanning the terrain around her. Meera studied the drawings on the pillars more closely, whilst Kian went to investigate the cracked altar stone. He rubbed away at the ice crystals covering it to see if it had more markings, but when he moved his gloved hand away he saw that his glove was soiled by something. He brought his glove closer to his light to see.

"Hey guys! Get over here!" Kian shouted in alarm. The company hopped over to him quickly, Gold 3 flying over. He held his glove out to show everyone, wide eyed.

"Have you hurt yourself? Is the suit compromised?" Meera demanded urgently, looking for a rip in his glove. Kian was white as a sheet, but shook his head.

"It's not my blood!" he managed to utter in his

shock. "It was on the altar stone here!" he pointed to the spot where he had brushed away the ice crystals, revealing a large quantity of blood, which pooled at the base of the altar.

The Gold quickly scanned around them then ordered urgently "Get out of here! Fast!"

Nobody argued.

The crew headed for the stairway as quickly as they could, looking around as they did so. It was too dark for their torches to penetrate enough of the darkness to see the whole crater. If they had been able to see, they would realise that a rock slab that formed a doorway, in the side of the crater, was slowly opening!

***

Close encounter

The Endaris had already returned to the ship with their collection of samples when the stragglers reached the surface above the crater once more. Gold 3 hailed one of the nearby fleet ships to pick them up urgently as there was imminent danger. He placed the AIs on alert, ready to defend the site from attackers. No sooner had the Gold spoken than there was a shuttle ramp opening in front of the crew with the shuttle co pilot urging them to board quickly. Argo ordered the closest fighter planes to give covering fire if necessary, to protect the shuttle as it lifted off from the surface.

Finch looked behind as the crew ascended the ramp safely. What he saw shocked him to the bone! From the deep crater they had just studied, there appeared a large mass of creatures armed with strange glowing scythes.

They were encased in an exo-skeleton of black, shining husks, making them look like huge six foot tall roaches on two legs and they seemed unaffected by the vacuum. Finch leapt onto the ramp and pressed the ramp door shut. The craft zoomed out of the area quickly and took the crew to a safer distance from the aliens, beyond the rest of the fleet.

Argo and Bull watched the viewer, horrified at the amassing army of strange beings surging out of the crater and running towards the fleet ships. Suddenly the aliens began firing their weapons at the AIs outside, who had been coating the ships. The AIs all locked their shields on and the silvery beams emitted by the aliens started to make their shields glow.

"They're penetrating our shields!" Bull gasped..

"Fire on the aliens!" Argo ordered the AIs immediately.

One by one, the AIs struck out with their lethal beams towards the gathered horde and they began to decimate the leading band of the army. But quite unexpectedly more beings, armed in a similar way began to surge out of several more craters around the fleet ships!

"There are too many of them." Argo realised quickly.

"Retreat to your ships and lift off the planet, there are too many of them!" Argo ordered his fleet.

Bull gave the order for the Blues to lift off as well and soon they had left the moon behind. They watched from their orbit around the moon to see if any aircraft was launched to pursue them, but none appeared.

Bull breathed a sigh of relief at their successful, if impromptu exit. At least none of their ships had been completely destroyed, but it was worrying that the aliens had weapons that had sufficient power to penetrate the AIs' shields! They would make a note in the log not to land on that moon ever again! Now they had to find somewhere else to park the fleet to continue the cloaking of the remaining ships as only a quarter of them had so far been cloaked.

***

They travelled along their route to exit the solar system and stopped at another moon they came across near Neptune after a few hours. Before they made a landing, this time they scanned the moon's surface carefully for any signs of inhabitants and also sent an advance party of Golds to assess the terrain beforehand. Apart from an area of erupting geysers in one sector, the Golds found a suitable spot to land the fleet ships that remained in need of cloaking. So, they landed once again.

The crew decided to remain on board this time and leave the moonwalk to the AIs and robots to complete the task of preparing the ships. They did not want to tempt fate and risk meeting unfriendly aliens again before leaving the Solar system.

The Endaris were keen to collect more samples, but Bull assured them that the AIs would do that for them and bring them to their lab for study. The Endaris were glad to have Professor Stark's laboratory at their disposal on board the Starfinder and they made good use of the equipment there, analysing their samples with great interest.

"Captain we have a little problem.." came the feeble call from the Bronze commander as the cloaking came to a close.

Bull transferred the call to visuals so he could see

the Bronze face to face. "What is it commander?" Bull asked, full of curiosity.

"When the robots were helping to paint the liquid onto the ships one of them, well, managed to get some on his lower body..." The Bronze commander stood to one side and a basic robot Checker came into view, well, half of him anyway, because all the lower half of him was invisible, along with half his face!

Bull looked at the Checker dumbfounded, then looked at Argo, who slowly came over to see Bull's screen.

"Oh no! It's Noblaczec again!" Argo groaned at the sight of the bane of his life and quickly withdrew to let the captain deal with it.

Bull tried to stop himself from laughing as he spoke. " Noblaczec. What do you have to say for yourself?" Bull awaited the feeble reply.

"Captain, it wasn't my fault, really. It was gravity's fault... Nobody told me I had to use a brush to cover the ship. I used a spray, but it all came back and floated onto my body! I can't get it off again. I'm sorry." Checker 159 looked crestfallen, with his half head hung low.

Bull, stifling his laughs, patched into the lab and asked the Endari if there was a way to remove the chemical, but they replied that they hadn't found one yet, but would work on it! Bull told 159 that he would have to go on cleaning duty for two days as punishment, until they found a way to get it removed. He winked at Argo after getting the information that Nobby hated cleaning duties. Nobby was dismissed in disgrace and as soon as he was off screen Bull laughed at his stupidity.

***

Captain Bull Carter listened with great interest at what the Blue had to say after he had entered his quarters for some sleep. Argo had accompanied the Blue, feeling the captain would want to have this information as soon as possible.

"So you are telling me that the Blues have made even greater improvements to our ships' engines?" Bull questioned the tech-Blue with incredulity. "So, then, what are we capable of doing now?" he asked the Blue, who stood to attention inside his quarters.

"Well, Captain, we can travel at better rates of speed now. Our normal cruise speed, which we have been using to travel through the Solar System these last few days, and then there's a range of hyper speeds which we can engage to travel ten times faster if you want to by-pass planets, or get ourselves out of danger quickly."

The Blue waited for Bull to absorb the information. Bull looked at Argo and smiled. He liked the sound of that very much! Apparently the Blues had made it their own personal goal to keep improving the ship's speed capability as much as possible. They were constantly applying it to all ships in the fleet. Bull congratulated the Blue on their achievement and asked if they could also try to improve the shields strength on the whole fleet when they had time. The Blue said they would try their best before he was dismissed .

Argo turned to Bull and told him of his plans after the ships had all been cloaked.

"Well, we will obviously be passing Scenara, or what's left of it as planned. We will check for any survivors and probably bring them on board. Then I think it should be wise for us to seek out the Scenara refugees at Versa and see if Prince Cruza needs our help to relocate their people. Apart from that, we will continue to search for planets that can sustain life and try to form alliances with other life forms that we might meet."

Bull agreed with Argo and the fleet commander left him to have some well earned rest. But before he went to bed Bull reported to Captain Grey how the mission was going before they left the Solar System. After today they would no longer be able to communicate with Earth until they laid new relay buoys into the next galaxy. They had intended to do that on their return to Earth as their last job.

Grey was obviously upset at the demise of Scenara and hoped Bull and Argo would be able to help them find a new home to settle in. He was pleased to hear of a possible alliance to be formed with the people of Su-K-En and listened with great interest on the cloaking technology that the Endaris had discovered. Stark was glad that his lab was being put to good use and wished them luck with their further experiments with their rock samples.

Bull found comfort in chatting to Grey about his responsibilities and the talk led Bull to have a better night's sleep for once.

Chapter 4

The colony

Sarf led his tribe's warriors down the craggy slopes of the vast mountains towards where his shuttles had been hidden all these years since their invasion of Earth. The colony had seen the Earth's natural canopy slowly return and they were curious to see how that had happened. They knew that their species had destroyed all the Earth's plant and animal life over forty-five years previously, so they wanted to know how it had recently begun to change.

They eventually arrived at one of their triangular shuttles, covered by debris to camouflage them years earlier, but now they were overshadowed by the additional cover of tree canopy which had sprouted everywhere in the Rockies where they had colonized. They had chosen this part of the Rockies because no humans had lived there and it was generally inaccessible to humans in any case. The deep ravines and rocky crags resembled their home planet of Viba, but here they weren't disturbed by ever increasing tremors and eruptions as on their home planet, which is why they had decided to stay here.

They were ugly creatures with slimy pale green skins sprouting tufts of sparse hair at intervals over their bodies. Their limbs were akin to a dog's legs, curving backwards at the joints and they walked with a lilting gait.

They had small glittering bloodshot eyes and their mouths were slits, covering sharp pointed teeth, that could grind down rock. To look at them was to feel revulsion.

***

Once up in the air they saw how much the terrain had altered since their arrival. The Earth and its plant and wildlife had returned to its former state. Sarf was not happy. Did this mean there were humans still alive? He would vow to make sure they did not stay that way if it meant disturbing his way of life! The shuttles zoomed low to keep out of the range of sensors should anyone be monitoring the planet.

Hovering over the land, dipping between the high ranges and the low plains, Sarf could see disturbing signs of change. A vehicle was cruising along a road far down below him with some people evidently inside, creating a strange noise. Sarf's pilot zoomed low, alongside the vehicle to confirm the Earthlings were still alive. They looked on in horror at Sarf's spacecraft as they hovered alongside them, matching their speed. The pilot fired at the vehicle and it blew up, scattering into pieces all across the road, spilling out its contents in the process. Sarf ordered the pilot to fire again at the bodies in the road to make sure they were dead.

Far in the distance another vehicle drove towards them, unaware of the danger they were headed into. A short time passed and they too were left scattered all over the road along with the truck they had travelled in. The plume of smoke rose up high into the skyline, inviting more people to come and head towards it to see what it was... In a nearby ravine a river flowed fast and deep, upon it were unsuspecting holidaymakers, enjoying the experience of kayaking through the passes for the first time since the war. Soon, they were too were also obliterated by Sarf's cruelty. Everywhere Sarf and his warriors saw human life they extinguished it, travelling further afield each time, away from their Rocky Mountain home.

***

Gold 19 re checked his screen and confirmed what he had initially thought. There were small explosions occurring on the planet below, in the Rocky mountains area. He zoomed in on the plume of smoke arising from a roadway in one spot and now could see the exploded vehicle with bodies strewn across the road. There didn't seem to be evidence of another vehicle nearby, so it had not been a collision. From the Grace space station high above the Earth, Gold 19 contacted the Silver ground troops below him and asked them to investigate the incident.

It took only ten minutes for Silver 80 to arrive at the scene from his station in nearby Vancouver. He saw the mutilation on the bodies, clear evidence of hostile intervention! He ordered the Mechs and Checkers in his area HQ to remove the bodies and debris and find out who they were.

The Silver headed further a field in his shuttle, looking for the hostiles, when he saw below evidence of more attacks. There were bodies and wreckage floating in the river below him and the stretch of road further ahead, beyond the craggy rock had vehicles strewn in the same situation as the one he had just left! Something was definitely going on! He hailed his squadron from Vancouver and ordered them to swoop the area to find any hostiles and capture them.

***

Twenty shuttles sped from the base towards the different sectors looking for hostiles. They swept an area from Vancouver up to Edmonton and down towards Oregon, Idaho and Montana searching for the perpetrators of these murders. On their sweep over the terrain some of the shuttles reported more signs of hostile attacks on civilians, resulting in the conclusion that these were aerial attacks due to the distances apart.

"We are looking for one or more alien aircraft." Silver 80 relayed to his squadron, hopeful that it was not a rogue faction of his own army that was creating this mayhem.

***

Katrina watched her tiny daughter run around the old golf course chasing her shadow. It was a beautiful sunny day and there were lots of families having a picnic in the Regional Park beside Eagle Lake near Minneapolis, enjoying their new-found freedom from life underground.

"Don't go too far!" Katrina called out to her daughter Tina. She was only four and was enjoying being out in this newly revived landscape. They had spent the post war years underground, with other families from the area, surviving in the high school nuclear shelter. It had been well thought out by the architects, supplied with its own vegetable patch and seeds, an underground water supply and wind powered energy. It had been stocked with enough food to last a period of five years and by the time it was depleted the occupants had established a steady food supply from their own produce. Even so, now it was redundant, happily so, as everyone enjoyed the new world the robot army had supplied.

"Don't worry, she's enjoying herself. I'm keeping an eye on her." her father Carl smiled, watching his daughter picking up some stray wild flowers in the grass.

Suddenly a great shadow cast over where they sat. All the picnickers gazed upwards and saw the two shuttles above them.

"I wonder what the robots are doing here?" Katrina spoke to her husband. "And why are they flying so low?" she enquired, puzzled.

Carl looked at the shuttles and suddenly a fear entered his body, making him go cold all over. He grabbed his wife's arm, lifting her up suddenly and began to run towards his daughter.

"Run!" he called to the others around him. "Tina! Tina! Come to daddy! Quickly!" he called in despair at his daughter, who stood rooted to the spot as she saw her worried father's face.

"Carl, what is it? What's the matter?" asked Katrina very worried now, running as fast as she could towards Tina with her husband.

Before Carl could answer a hail of missiles tore into the ground around them, catching some of the families unaware. The missiles continued to fire all around them as Carl grabbed his daughter and fled towards the old golf centre, his wife scrambling to keep up at his side. Loud explosions erupted in his wake, obscuring the first trail of disaster behind him as whole families were blown up by the hostile craft. Smoke from the explosions created some cover for the fleeing family.

Carl pulled his wife next to him behind a large toppled dumpster near the golf centre. They crouched down low hoping they would not be seen behind it.

"Who are they?" his frightened wife spluttered in shock. "Is it the robots? Have they turned against us?" she added in despair. Tina was crying uncontrollably in his arms.

"No, they are not the robots. They have a different insignia on their ships. These are alien!" Carl uttered in horror.

The explosions continued as the young family covered their ears to drown out the cries of the poor victims caught by the alien fire. A thud moved the dumpster next to them and Carl looked quickly over towards where a woman and a young boy scrambled to hide from the attack, their faces covered in blood from shrapnel hits.

Carl met the woman's gaze and his own terror was reflected back at him. The boy was so traumatised he couldn't cry any more. Carl realised that his own daughter had also stopped crying and he looked into her eyes worriedly. Her eyes were wide in shock, her whole body trembling and she held on tightly to her father for comfort, He kissed his daughter's forehead gently and held her tightly against his chest whispering to her "It's all right sweetie, Daddy's got you, it'll be all over soon!"

Suddenly, the whole clubhouse before them was torn apart by bombs. The force of the impact pushed the family to the ground and some more of the dumpsters fell onto their sides from the impact. One of them was slightly ajar on its side, so Carl pulled his family inside it and beckoned the frightened woman and boy to join them. The woman and boy sat there huddled together tightly, unsure what to do, fear in their eyes, but the woman suddenly decided to go for it and ran with her son into the dumpster to join the family. Missiles caused destruction all around them, drowning out the cries of the wounded and dying.

It seemed like a lifetime before the attack stopped, but was probably only minutes. All that could be heard was the popping and crackling of items in the building behind them being consumed by the fire and the occasional piece of building collapsing in on itself. Katrina looked over at Carl wondering what they should do, would it be safe to venture out, she wondered.

"You stay here. I'll go and see if it's safe to come out." Carl whispered to his family. Katrina held onto his arm and pleaded with him to take care and stay safe.

Carl slowly lifted the bent dumpster lid and crawled out from inside it. He stopped at the opening and looked to the sky to see if the alien craft was still around. There was no sign of them through the smoke trails, so he slowly got up, crouching to see the scene around him.

Where there had been young families happily enjoying the sunshine minutes before there was now a scene of utter carnage laid out in front of him. There were craters in the ground where missiles had dropped, and human remains lay strewn about the golf course everywhere. Smoke was clearing and he could see that where they had been sitting moments before, there now was blood and gore covering the ground!

Carl was almost sick at the sight of the body parts, but stopped himself when he heard a faint cry from the course in front of him. He told the rest to stay where they were that he would be back in a moment. Katrina was about to protest, but Carl was already on his way.

He weaved around the craters and tried to stay away from the worst of the carnage as he headed towards the faint cry. As he got closer he saw a picnic blanket covered in blood strewn amongst other debris in front of him. The sound came from under the blanket.

He was frightened to lift the material for fear of what he'd find. He shut his eyes and took a deep breath and began to lift a corner of the blanket. A woman's face was revealed below it, her face was almost shredded by shrapnel, blood seeping over her lips. She looked into his eyes and managed to utter "My baby...please help my baby.." before she passed out.

Carl looked at the grass around the blanket but could see no baby, nor could he see a buggy where a baby might be lying. He got up and scanned the surface for any sign, but there was none. He slowly got to his knees again to see if the woman could tell him more, but he realised she was already dead.

He thought that she might be lying with her baby, so he carefully lifted the rest of the blanket and fell backwards in horror at what he saw! This time he couldn't control himself and vomited violently! When he had lifted the blanket he saw that the pregnant woman had been torn in half by the missiles! The dead foetus lay next to her, torn from the womb!

Carl wiped his mouth on his sleeve and slowly made his way back to the hidden survivors.

***

The Hunt

The squadron found nothing but evidence of destruction in the wake of the alien craft everywhere. Soon they had to enlist the help of their colleagues in Chicago, Los Angeles and even Dallas to track down this unknown enemy of Earth. It was still uppermost in their minds that this could be the work of a rogue faction of AIs again, not to be dismissed until they had proof otherwise. Silver 80 contacted the Grace Space station and asked them to track the Silver shuttles on Earth as they swept the land searching for the enemy. They needed to know whether particular shuttles were found in the vicinity of the attacks as they happened. Gold 19 was surprised that the Silver thought it could still be rogue AIs, this late on in the series of events, but he would monitor the shuttles anyhow.

***

Mary, Bull's mother, and Reed were celebrating their honeymoon in New York, their first venture abroad in their entire lives. It was so much easier to travel now by shuttle, no longer having to spend hours travelling from airport to airport, like in the olden days, pre-war, they now made it to New York in under an hour.

It was exciting to see the renovations underway in the skyscrapers. A lot of the city was lost in the war, but now there was no need for such a vast amount of built up land because of the depleted number of people alive at the present time to occupy it. The couple had been to see a show on the renovated Broadway, as they had planned and the theatre was magnificent the way it had been built by the robots. The seating areas all included tables, laden with drinks and nibbles to enjoy during the show. Mary had never felt so spoiled in her life. A walk through Central Park was also planned for the next day and Mary wondered how big it was.

They looked at the holograms in New Times

Square, spewing news about the Starfinder mission in between adverts for new products and new shows sprouting up here and there. It had been great to be able to communicate with Bull on the Starfinder and give him the news of their marriage. Bull had not seemed surprised but was very happy for them and he had said the mission was going well that she had nothing to worry about. Life was good again.

***

Getting a hover taxi, they headed out to see the newly restored Statue of Liberty. Mary had heard a lot about it and had longed to see the views from the top of it. Reed helped Mary off the hover taxi and stepped onto Liberty Island. The statue was enormous! Reed pointed out some people near the top at the crown. Mary was sure she wouldn't be able to climb all those stairs, but Reed told her she was as fit as a fiddle!

After much pausing for breath and rubbing aching limbs, both of them finally reached the viewing area of the crown. Mary's eyes lit up with glee at seeing the tremendous view all around the statue. People below looked as small as ants. Reed looked at the mainland on the horizon, marvelling at the robots' expertise in renovating the lost structures. Mary looked at her new husband and felt a warmth enter her whole being. She had not been this happy in her entire life. She held his hand tight, squeezing it tenderly. He began to look down into her face when something caught his attention on the horizon.

Mary froze as she saw the concern on Reed's face. "What is it honey?" she asked worriedly. He was much taller than her and could see further. What he saw was obviously bothering him. She looked through the balcony to try and see what was happening. When she saw fire billowing up on the skyline she began to tense up. There... she saw it! This time she too had a clear view of what was happening.

On the horizon there flew two spacecraft, dropping firebombs on the city sprawl! Then there was the sound of gunfire being fired indiscriminately at the people below! Reed held Mary tight, "We've gotta get out of here!" he muttered hurriedly, "But where do we go? Where's safe?" he thought out loud. "Come on! Follow me!" he called Mary to descend the stairs as quickly as possible.

They were pushed from behind by the others who had seen the oncoming attack. Everyone was trying to flee as quickly as they could. Reed held on to Mary so she would not fall and eventually, after much jostling, they reached the ground.

Now bombs were falling across the Hudson river and the craft were heading their way!

People piled into every available hover taxi eager to flee the island, but Reed pulled Mary into a different direction! "Why aren't we leaving on the taxi?" asked Mary perplexed. "We won't be safe here!" she cried to Reed pleadingly.

"It's all right, I've got an idea!" Reed replied, urging her in the direction of the drainage grid a short distance from the base, just as one of the hover taxis, laden with people was blown up by a missile! Reed lifted the grating and lowered himself and Mary inside. Just at that point the Statue of Liberty exploded scattering fragments everywhere. They dived into the drain as it fell.

***

Scenara

In a matter of days, the Earth fleet had travelled the vast distance to the location of the planet Scenara, thanks to their newly accelerated engines. Argo and Bull looked in dismay at the pitiful sight that portrayed before them. The planet had two deep fissures that were splitting the sphere into three pieces. Out of the fissures the melted core of the planet oozed to the surface, engulfing the terrain around them. Volcanic eruptions were evident around the globe, spewing out plumes of ash and lava everywhere. Pieces of the planet were tearing away into the atmosphere to end up travelling in space for eternity. The beautiful domed cities were gone, swallowed by the melted core.

"Any signs of life?" Argo asked the Blues on the bridge, despairing at the sight of this once beautiful planet.

"We are continuing to scan, Commander." The Blue answered, "But the heat from the eruptions are making it difficult to deduce anything, sir!"

"What would you like to do, Commander?" asked Bull, knowing what the reply must be before he asked.

"Send down some shuttles to search for survivors and bring them on board." Argo replied. "Don't leave any Scenarians stranded." He uttered again.

The Blues sent the command straight away and within minutes all the fleet ships altered their trajectory to fly above the surface of Scenara to seek out life forms. From the lounge deck viewer Finch and Star watched in despair at the demise of this once beautiful planet.

"God! I hope this never happens to our Earth!" Star remarked, full of anguish for the poor people who had endured this.

"I know." Finch sympathised. "I don't think that will happen though." He hoped it was true, as he could not imagine how he would cope with such a thing. He held Star in his arms as they watched the fleet spread out around the globe, getting ever closer to the disaster zone.

Lin ran into the bridge with her mother, Gale, in tow.

"Hello Lin." Argo beamed at his little friend. "Is there something I can do for you?" he asked her fondly.

Lin looked at Argo with worry in her eyes. "There are families in trouble on the planet Argo! They are in danger. There's hot red stuff surrounding them. We need to get them out!"

Argo quickly asked her if she knew where they were, but Lin said she could only show him. Gale looked at Argo and said "Go! I trust you."

Argo picked up Lin in his strong arms from the beamer and ran for the nearest shuttle in the docking bay. They told the Blue to launch immediately for the planet's surface. Within minutes they were down near the planet's erupting surface, hovering along the failing terrain. There was no sign of life anywhere!

"Where do I go, Commander?" asked the Blue, looking towards Argo.

"Just keep going until Lin tells you otherwise." Argo replied. Argo looked at Lin as she stood next to him with her eyes closed.

"Turn around!" Lin yelled quickly. "They're behind us, further back!" she added.

The Blue turned the shuttle to face in the other direction and sped along avoiding the high eruptions of lava and rock from the volcanoes.

They came in a short while to an area surrounded by lava on all sides; a rocky crag formed into an island on the sizzling sea of danger. There, clinging to the rock were some people, but there was no way of landing the shuttle! Argo hailed Silver 10 for air support. Argo didn't hesitate. He told Lin to stay strapped into a seat and he opened the shuttle door.

He flew down towards the crag, much to the surprise of the desperate people. They held up their children towards him in despair, urging him to save their offspring. Argo told them calmly that he was there to save ALL of them and he grabbed three of the six children in his arms and flew up to the shuttle to deposit them safely into their strapped seats. He then sped back to the crag and soon the support shuttle was hovering next to him, aiding Argo with the rescue operation, another Gold, flying to support him. Bit by bit they both rescued all of the stranded people. Three families, each with two children aged under eight. They were so grateful for their rescue and informed Argo that there were other families still on the planet not far away.

The Blue continued on the search, guided by Lin , their support vessel following, until they found another group of people huddled at the edge of a bubbling lake a few kilometres away. This time the shuttles were able to land and the group rushed to board them , grateful at their arrival before they were to be engulfed in the lava flow that was heading their way. As the people strapped their children into their seats Argo heard a voice call him.

"Argo? Is it you? It is! Oh, how you arrived in time I'll never know!" The voice emerged from the crowd. A dishevelled woman in seared clothing, with a burn scar across her beautiful face came up to Argo.

Argo could only stare in wonder, stunned for a few moments because he thought her to be dead! He bowed to the ground in front of her.

"Your majesty!" Argo spoke reverently to the queen.

Queen Laifa bade him rise and then hugged him briefly before Argo spoke again. "We all thought you and King Khali perished in the domed city when it fell into the chasm as the planet began to deteriorate!"

The queen shook her head sadly, a tear emerging from her eye. "The king is certainly dead." the queen began, "But I was taking a morning ride on my horse when the domed city fell. I was saved by my location!" The queen turned aside and let her tears flow freely, remembering the last time she saw her beloved husband. It was too much to bear.

Argo tried to console her. "Your majesty, we have heard that your son Prince Cruza is alive and well and managed to rescue many of your people with his fleet. They found temporary refuge on the planet Versa."

The queen's spirit rose with this news and she managed a smile through her tears.

"My son? He is alive? Oh, thanks be to the gods! " she held Argo's hand and squeezed it on impulse, delighted at the news.

Argo related to her the story of the retrieval of the Su-k-en ship and how they heard the news from the Scenarian on board. The queen was promised she could speak to him when they were back on board the Starfinder.

***

New additions

All in all, Lin managed to help find over three hundred and fifty Scenarians clinging on to life at various locations on the planet. The other fleet ships had rescued a total of three thousand people additionally, and now they were all happily on board the Starfinder, being fed and re clothed and quarters being found for them all. Kush forced himself to look away as his home planet fell apart and he went to greet his fellow Scenarians.

In the lounge area he found, to his relief, hundreds of survivors in various states of health occupying the seats and table areas. He searched for any old friends that might have been rescued, then suddenly he caught sight of the queen's lady in waiting, Farsifa! So she had not perished in the domed city after all! He rushed over to the battered and torn figure where she sat at a table. He swept her into his arms.

"Farsifa! How wonderful to see you! But how is it you are here and not fallen with the domed city?" Kush asked perplexed.

Farsifa looked at Kush and it took a moment for her to register him. "Kush? It is you! But you were with the prince's fleet! Is the prince safe?" Farsifa asked desperately. They talked at length about the turn of events and Kush learned that the queen was rescued with Farsifa from the planet because they had been horse riding outside the city when it fell into the abyss. She had stayed close to Queen Laifa ever since, trying to keep her safe. Farsifa was pleased to hear that Prince Cruza had rescued many people and taken them to safety to Versa.

"But where is the queen now?" asked Kush.

Farsifa explained that Argo and the captain had taken her to a room they had set aside for her to get freshened up and sort out suitable garments for her to wear from the limited stores they had on board. The queen had allowed Farsifa to rest with the people instead of having to attend to her like she usually did.

"Oh I'm sure the robots will be able to create a fantastic wardrobe for her with their wonderful gadgetry!" explained Kush smiling at the thought. "How about you? Have they allocated you sleeping quarters yet?"

Farsifa replied that she had been told there was room for her next door to the queen so she could attend to her easily. She had been about to go and freshen up when Kush arrived. So Kush offered to accompany her to her quarters to show her the way, which she gladly accepted.

***

It took several hours for the Scenarians to settle into their temporary quarters, to get clothed and fed after their terrible ordeal. In the meantime Argo had sent out more shuttles to scan the planet's surface to look for any more survivors, but all they found was a little dog, sheltering next to his old home presumably his owners having died.

The Blue pilot stopped to pick him up and the bedraggled dog sat beside him in the cockpit all journey long! When they arrived at the Starfinder the Blue handed over the dog to Finch, who was waiting at the docking bay, ready to help with any survivors. Finch held him and stroked him gently and the dog reciprocated with a lick on

Finch's nose! Finch went up to the lounge to see if the animal belonged to any of the new passengers. A little girl came to stroke him and the dog wagged his tail enthusiastically. Her mother asked if she could look after it for she had lost her own. Finch gladly obliged, handing over the dog to the little girl.

"He's yours now sweetie, what are you going to call him?" Finch inquired smiling.

The little girl looked up at Finch and said "He's got a name already silly! He's called Chi Chi." She held the dog in her arms and fed it biscuits as her mother explained to Finch she was an Empath. Finch looked at the little girl, who looked to be about the same age as Lin and told her mother about Lin also being one.

"Ah! It's Lin that Jeia was talking to!" the mother explained that when they were waiting to be rescued with another family on a craggy outcrop, surrounded by lava, her daughter had communicated with someone called Lin and told her where we were. "That's how we got rescued! So Lin was the little girl on board the shuttle?" the mother asked and Finch nodded in reply. "Well, I'm sure Jeia will want to thank her once we've got sorted." Jeia's mother replied, smiling at the new little friend her daughter had cuddled up to on the lounge seat.

***

In the evening Argo and Bull held a welcome dinner for all the survivors and the crew mingled along with the K-Tu and the Endaris amongst the Scenarians. Not all the Scenarians had realised that the queen was in their midst, but when she entered the lounge, dressed in beautiful golden, regal attire, accompanied by her lady in waiting Farsifa, the Scenarians all bowed to their queen, glad to see her alive. Argo had also sent Guy to give the queen laser treatment for her facial burn, to help disguise it. She looked almost like new again.

The meal was a success and Bull realised that the Scenarians would make welcome allies to Earth, but the first priority would be to find them a new home!

"How on Earth did the queen get such beautiful garments in such a short time?" Star asked Bull quietly as they sipped their wine. Bull smiled and whispered towards Star that Captain Grey had provided the clothes. He had sent a large container of goods to give as gifts to the Scenarian royal family when they were due to visit the planet. Bull had decided to investigate the parcel after hearing of Scenara's demise and found the clothes amongst other things! Grey would be pleased at how useful his gift had become!

Star laughed at Bull's ingenuity and shared the information with Meera who sat next to her.

Da-Ee came over to their table and remarked at how well the Starfinder had coped with so many rescue missions. "Have you thought about becoming a full time rescue fleet?" joked Da-Ee to Bull and Argo. "It seems you excel at it !" she added, taking a swig out of a vile-looking green flask filled with liquid.

Bull realised that they had coped very well with many situations already, but he definitely wouldn't want to have to deal with disasters full time!

"I'd rather chew my boots!" laughed Bull, to which Star grimaced at the thought.

Chapter 5

Liberty

A section of the torch had landed with a thud above them, caving in the structure of the storm drain. Mary and Reed were knocked out by the impact as the Statue of Liberty was blown apart by Sarf's shuttle. Sarf laughed with glee as the enormous lady broke into large chunks, strewn everywhere around the island. The head had fallen into the Hudson river and sank out of sight.

Immediately, the Silvers were up in the air.

Sarf had made his first mistake, he had not bargained on the robot army being present to defend Earth and here in the metropolis were several Silver shuttles.

***

Having deposited their passengers safely on the ground, the Silvers set off to find and despatch the aliens. It was unfortunate that the shuttles had been used for ferrying people at that time, otherwise the Silvers would have been up in the air far sooner. Silver 60 led his squadron past Liberty island, fanning out in several directions to chase the alien craft.

Sarf's shuttles were smaller and faster than the Silvers' spearheads and could weave in and out between buildings, escaping the shuttles' tracker. The squadron leader cursed as the enemy craft dodged them, staying in occupied areas so the Silvers could not fire upon them.

As soon as Sarf's vessels reached an open area the Silvers fired their missiles, but Sarf's ships veered away at the last minute, rendering the missiles useless!

Further along the coast the craft fled, keeping low and close to populated areas. The Silvers pursued the two enemy craft , waiting for the opportunity to fire when they were out in the open. But try as they might, the Silvers could not match their speed and their missiles were constantly avoided at the last minute by Sarf's pilots. Now they were nearing Boston and Silver 60 hailed his colleagues in Nova Scotia to aid in the pursuit. Soon there were three more shuttles heading towards the enemy from the front, surely now that the enemy was surrounded they would soon be destroyed.

Sarf looked at his sensors and saw the group appear in front of their craft a few miles ahead; he soon realised he would be completely surrounded! They needed to get out of there fast! He spoke to the two pilots and their vehicles banked to the right... Silver 60 looked in confusion as Sarf's craft turned towards the ocean.

Why would they do that? They would know that they would perish for sure now they were an open target, surrounded on all sides! All the Silvers fired towards the two targets, now sure of their success, there was nowhere to hide any more. But they were wrong!

Silver 60 looked on in horror as the two enemy craft dived into the ocean and disappeared from their sensor! The Silvers wondered how long they could stay underwater and decided to sweep the ocean surface along the coastline waiting for them to surface again. But they waited for hours and there was still no sign of the enemy, perhaps they had perished? They sure hoped so! Eventually they returned to base to help clear up the mess left behind.

***

Unbeknown to the robot army Sarf's craft were completely submersible and were equally comfortable sailing through the ocean as long as they wanted. They headed across the ocean to find what else was happening in the world!

***

Mary opened her eyes, adjusting to the gloom of the underground drain. Something was weighing her down across her back! She looked around her to see what had happened and began to realise that something had fallen in on their drain hideout! Where was Reed? She hoped he was all right, but she couldn't see him in all the mess! She wiped the dust from her face and mouth and tried to call out his name. Her voice croaked to begin with, dust having dried up her mouth. She tried again and this time a sound did emerge, weak but audible, barely! There was no reply, so she tried to moisten her lips to try again.

"Reed! Reed can you hear me? Are you okay?" Mary called desperately into the darkness around her. A few pieces of debris fell from above into the space near her! She must get out before the whole drain fell on her, but she was pinned to the floor! She tried calling Reed again, but no reply!

She found a pipe on the floor near her hand and held onto it. It came loose into her hand, it had been severed from wherever it had been mounted. She lifted the pipe a little off the floor then banged it onto a metal brace beside her, making a loud clanging noise. She kept tapping the pipe in the hope someone would hear her. Dust filtered down all around her with the vibration.

Mary was worried about Reed. Where was he? "Oh, please don't let him be dead!" Mary sobbed out loud, beginning to panic at the thought. To her left she heard something shift, so she listened hard and called out again. "Reed! Reed! Is that you? I'm over here! I'm pinned to the ground by something."

Reed opened his eyes finally and held his head, blood was oozing down his forehead from a gash he had received in the collapse of the drain. He heard Mary's faint voice and quickly came to his senses. He tried to move, but a piece of rubble lay just above his head, wedged into position by a piece of girder. The girder had saved his life! If it weren't there the rubble would have fallen onto his head and killed him! He tried to slide along under the girder to free himself.

"I'm coming, Mary! I'm trying to get out from the rubble.. Are you all right?" Reed spoke worriedly to his new wife.

Mary breathed a sigh of relief on hearing his voice and in a few moments Reed had managed to crawl towards where she was pinned. He moved a few pieces of concrete slab from above them and soon there was daylight streaming down from a gap above.

He held Mary's hand and smiled "I guess it wasn't such a good idea to come down here after all, was it?" Reed managed as he made more space for his wife's head and shoulders. He looked above them both and realised they needed to move out pretty soon before the whole drain caved in on them.

"Mary, I'm going to try and climb up a bit to get help for you. I can see that girder is wedged by rubble too large for me to move. Will you be okay if I leave you just for a few minutes? I promise I'll hurry!" Reed looked into her eyes searchingly. Mary feared being alone in the tomb, but put on a brave face and replied "Yes, honey, you go ahead. I'll be fine."

Reed kissed her hand and started to climb upwards over the rubble towards the light.

***

Friends

After a few weeks of travelling together through space, the different species got on unusually well. The Endaris whizzed their way backwards and forwards along the ship at their super fast speed between their quarters and the lab, the passengers getting used to the gust of air passing them by in the corridors being either Ursu or Genai! The little dog Chi Chi loved to try to chase them along the corridors and Genai thought it great fun to give him the exercise! Kush was much happier now that his fellow Scenarians were away from the danger they faced on their ever diminishing planet. All that they wished for now was to find a new home for them all. He'd been pleased to speak with the queen and he knew Prince Cruza would be ecstatic to find her still alive.

Bull and Argo stood with Kian discussing the K-Tu that they had rescued from the Su-i. He had been the commander of the ship and therefore would know a great deal more about the other galaxies than any of the Starfinder crew did. They had all agreed that his help would be invaluable to them so they decided that Kios should be second to the captain to aid him in the journey to find Versa, amongst others. They all hoped that he would accept the role. Kian would remain the first officer, but would bow to Kios' knowledge should the need arise. After speaking to Kian they went to broach the subject with the K-Tu there and then.

***

Kios was alone, studying the Earth's solar system on the ship's data files at the lounge area holoscreen when the fleet commander and captain found him. They greeted the K-Tu then inquired,

"Have you seen our solar system before?" Argo asked the K-Tu with mild interest.

Kios smiled in greeting at seeing the two commanders. "Yes, but only from afar." Kios replied, turning to face the two. "I've often thought about venturing out to visit your system, but I've always been too busy on other projects. I'd been commissioned to lead the scientific research vessel through the Andromeda Galaxy for the past year. It is only because we were caught in a wormhole that we ended up here."

Argo and Bull sat next to him and discussed his knowledge of space at length and then broached the subject finally of him becoming second to the captain on this mission as he had superior knowledge of the system they were about to enter.

Kios looked at the two commanders with interest and thought briefly about it before agreeing, on condition that they are returned to their own planet when Bull's brief was completed.

Argo gave his word that they would do that gladly and so the three shook on it.

"This is an interesting custom you have, Captain." Kios smiled, acknowledging the handshake. "But I think you should know something about me first.." He paused, then got up from his seat. Bull and Argo looked in confusion, wondering what he was about to do. Bull wondered whether his hand should stray towards his weapons belt in case it was to be something unpleasant, but all at once his fears were replaced with total amazement as Kios transformed in front of his eyes and Bull found himself staring at a mirror image of himself! He gasped with surprise! The K-Tu was a shapeshifter! He couldn't believe it!

Just at that moment Finch walked into the lounge and did a double take! He immediately grabbed his weapon and pointed it at the two Bulls. "What's going on here?" Finch demanded angrily, unsure what was happening. Being security officer it was his job to be on top of things around the ship. The one thing he was sure of was that there should only be one Bull! The shapeshifter changed back to his K-Tu body immediately as Bull spoke to Finch.

"It's all right, Lieutenant. Kios was just showing us here his ability to change forms before taking on the role of second in command."

Finch visibly relaxed and lowered his weapon, then asked worriedly "But what about Kian? He's your first officer, what about him?"

Bull replied that Kian would remain in his role but that Kios was to aid the captain in his mission, given his vast knowledge of the space system they were entering. At that Finch relaxed and apologized for over-reacting and speaking out of turn, but Bull instead praised him for doing his job, after all, that was his duty.

***

The company went to get some drinks from the lounge machine and sat together at a table to get to know Kios a little better, Meera joined them as she entered the lounge a few minutes later. She had heard the news from her boyfriend, Kian, and she congratulated Kios on his new role. They realised how useful Kios's shape shifting could be in any future skirmishes and he was happy to tell them about many occasions when it certainly had been to their advantage.

Bull wondered why his fellow K-Tus on board the stricken ship hadn't used their abilities to cheat death. Instead they had been blasted as they stood, unarmed. Kios confided in the group that he had been troubled by that too. He had been thinking that it was indeed another of his own kind that had caught them unawares! The companions looked uneasily at each other and all came to the same thought... could the attacker be amongst them, still disguised ?

***

Help

Reed surfaced eventually to a scene of misery and death. People lay all around him with terrible injuries, some killed by the statue crushing them underneath its fallen pieces, others caught in the alien fire. He really had done the best thing in the circumstances, taking Mary and himself below ground to avoid death. But now he needed help for Mary, he couldn't help her on his own.

He looked around him and saw a cargo shuttle heading for the island with some people on board! He waved his arms frantically to catch the pilot's attention and was rewarded with the Blue pilot landing in a gap not far from him. Reed rushed to the Bronze commander within and saw that he had survivors of the bombings on board his shuttle, bandaged and bleeding they lay on the cargo holders. Reed explained to the Bronze the situation and the tall AI called the Blue pilot to aid him in rescuing Mary. The Blue, being smaller could get into gaps the Bronze couldn't, so they both followed Reed towards the drain where Mary lay trapped. Overhead, more cargo shuttles ferried the injured to the hospital for treatment, picking up the severely injured people still alive on the island as they passed.

The Bronze made it to the depths of the collapsed drain tunnel despite his height and immediately saw the metal and rubble pinning Mary down. The Blue picked up large pieces of concrete as though they were pieces of cardboard and flung them away from Mary. When the concrete rubble was all lifted, the Bronze then got his back under the metal girder that was part of the torch's structure that was pinning down Mary. It lifted easily under the Bronze's strength and Reed was able to slide Mary out from the girder's path. Immediately the Blue scanned Mary's body for injuries before moving her. Thanks be, Mary had suffered no broken bones, only cuts and bruises. The Blue lifted Mary up easily and carried her up, out of the tunnel, Reed and the Bronze following closely behind.

Once on board the shuttle, the Bronze covered Mary with a thermal sheet to keep her warm, as she lay huddled in Reed's arms. They looked at the array of injuries displayed on their fellow passengers and realised how lucky they had been, escaping severe injuries, unlike some they had on board.

Mary held Reed's hand tightly and thanked him for keeping them safe. He smiled and wiped a smear of dirt away from her cheek, then kissed it softly.

***

Soon the injured were at the hospital, being ferried to awaiting beds or chairs, depending on the treatment they required.

Mary and Reed felt stiff, but fine and after a check on their injuries they were allowed to leave soon after. They walked hand in hand through the debris strewn streets, which were already being tidied by some Mechs who had sprouted out of nowhere! *They certainly didn't mess around, these robots,* thought Reed.

They wandered along towards their hotel, wondering whether it would be still in one piece or not! Several buildings around them were still standing, untouched by bombs, but others had scars and pieces missing from their construction, the pieces lying scattered around the streets below.

The couple rounded a corner and looked at where their hotel was supposed to be and they breathed a sigh of relief at seeing that it was still intact! They smiled at each other and, with renewed vigour, headed for their accommodation.

***

Inside, the hotel lobby had been turned into a make-shift first aid centre, with people being served with cups of tea and biscuits as they sat receiving treatment. Mary recognised many waiters from the hotel restaurant amongst the first-aiders, helping to bandage or administer plasters to small cuts or wounds.

Mary felt she should help in some way, but Reed insisted she should get some rest herself after her trauma, so they boarded the lift and headed for their room on the thirtieth floor, overlooking the city.

The room was tidy and undisturbed by the events that had befallen the city; they were lucky!

Reed rang his friends in Phoenix, back home in the UK to see if there was any trouble there. Apparently no other country had encountered any attacks so Reed felt relieved. His friends worried about them both and asked if they were returning earlier because of the damage everywhere. Reed consulted with Mary and they both agreed to return home as soon as they could find a shuttle to take them. There was no point in staying in New York at the moment, as they didn't know if the attackers were intending to return to their episodes of destruction or not, and besides, the city didn't retain its appeal any more.

A few days later Mary and her husband were on board a shuttle headed back home to their home in the UK. Sadly, they had no way of knowing that the aliens were also making their way to their part of the world too!

***

Europe

The alien vessels had emerged from their oceanic journey at the coast of Portugal, ready to embark on another round of atrocities wherever they found humans!

They zoomed along the coastline seeking out settlements and were soon rewarded with the sight of humans near Lisbon. They fired at random into the crowds, killing without mercy, circling again and again to ensure all were dead. Nearby buildings were struck by missiles as Sarf's ships headed northwards towards Porto in northern Portugal, where here they repeated their campaign to kill as many humans as they could.

***

On board the Grace Space Station, orbiting Earth, the Gold commander, Gaea, hailed the Silvers below and warned them of the alien attacks' change of direction, as he followed the trail of explosions from his satellite screen covering Portugal and Spain. But before the Silvers could amass in enough numbers to surround the enemy, again the two ships fled to the cover of the ocean to continue their journey towards the Bay of Biscay!

The Silvers dropped bombs into the ocean where they thought the aliens might be, but there was no sign of the destruction of the ships! They preferred not to keep pummelling the ocean further with their bombs for fear of destroying all the work they had done in regenerating life in the oceans after their demise during the alien war.

The Silver Earth fleet amassed at every coastline around Spain, France and the UK that they could muster, in the hope of catching the aliens as they emerged out of their ocean sanctuary once more.

***

Sarf thought that the humans would try to catch them when they emerged on land again so as they neared the surface near La Rochelle in the Bay of Biscay Sarf decided to scan the land mass before flying out of the water once more. He was rewarded with the sight of several human aircraft (or so he thought) hovering over the coastline in front of him in France, so he retreated back into the water and headed further along the coast towards Britain.

As he emerged near the surface in the English Channel his craft was almost mowed down by a large ship powering through the channel just above him. Suddenly alarms blared above him from the vessel and the ship began to drop bombs into the water around his craft! His shuttle was buffeted by the blast nearby and his pilot quickly descended into deeper water to escape the explosions. Another hit the rear of his ship violently as they descended, causing the pilot to lose some of his steering capability. Sarf and his colleagues waited patiently at the bottom of the channel, waiting for the bombing to subside. The bombs continued to drop all around him, but they were comparatively safe from the depth they sat waiting.

***

After an hour, the ship above moved further along, so Sarf set his warriors to continue their journey, keeping to the safety of the sea bed to stay out of trouble as much as possible. They slowly advanced on the British coastline, with great difficulty, given their current steering problem; they were heading for the capital!

The old Thames estuary was soon in sight and Sarf's ships moved along, further and further into the river, closer and closer to London. They passed alongside where the old Thames Barrier used to be, now overwhelmed by the higher tides and lying redundant in the depths of the water, surrounded by the larger water mass that had eroded the land to either side for decades. The land that had been sacrificed to save the capital.

Then, there it was in front of them, newly restored! The Tower Bridge loomed in their sights, it was time to attack. The two ships shot out of the river at lightning speed, enough to confuse the enemy. They began firing straight away at all and everyone in their sights!

People fled out of the way and dived into shops and buildings and others into the underground. The Tower Bridge suffered damage to its steelwork, rendering one side useless as it hung out of balance above the water.

In seconds the Silvers were upon them. Warned by the Space station of impending disaster, they had been awaiting the enemy craft all around the capital. Now they homed in on Sarf and his warriors, pulverising them from all angles by their pulsars and missiles.

The alien craft finally were caught by the Silvers' supreme weaponry and the ships began to split and disintegrate into molten piles of metal, some large pieces falling into the Thames. Sarf abandoned his ship and tried to escape in a pod, but a Silver pulverised the pod into minute particles within seconds.

Sarf was no more! His ships and crew were evaporated into small droplets, never to bother the Earth again!

***

Gaea, the Gold commander knew something would have to be done to improve the speed capability of their ships here on Earth if they were to counter any further attacks of a similar nature in the future. So he organised the retrieval of data from the enemy craft deposited in the Thames to find out its capabilities, to enable them to modify their fleet to combat any further attacks by this foe in the future.

He gathered his Blue technical team on the Space station and authorised them to work on creating improvements to all their spacecraft here on Earth, to increase speed and also to improve the shields that were vital to keep ahead of the enemy, whoever they may turn out to be. He ordered that some of their craft needed to have submersible capability as well. Also he deemed it advisable to have a band of smaller, more agile craft to be able to follow the enemy in inner city situations for the future, so he set that as a project for the terra- based robots. They needed to be ready for any eventuality. They had to keep Earth safe.

***

The people re-emerged from their hideouts at seeing the aliens brought to their destruction and cheered loudly. The shuttles landed and the robots and AIs tended to the injured and dying, sweeping them on board to renew them at the domes nearby. These people deserved to live, they had suffered enough already. All over the streets, people helped each other to their feet and cared for the injured until they were taken by the AIs to be healed again.

***

Far away at the Rockies, the remaining section of the colony all felt the loss to their tribe, feeling their pain. They gathered together from all over the mountains and lamented, then planned their next move...

Chapter 6

Shapeshifter

Nobby moved along the cargo bay, now used to the stares from the other robots at the sight of his half body! As he prepared to lift a stack of crates, he thought he had heard some movement in a strange place, behind the cargo stack, so he edged his way around the containers to look, but , try as he might, he could not find the source of his curiosity, all that he saw were containers and an old empty cardboard box, So Nobby continued on his way to unload more supplies for the new Scenarian visitors.

Nobby took the toiletry supplies over to the lieutenant and handed them over, then a thought struck him. *A cardboard box? There are no cardboard boxes on the Starfinder! Only tough plastic containers are used for everything ! This was wrong!*

Far in the corner where Nobby had looked, the cardboard box moved, then moulded itself into a robot, it was a shapeshifter!

Nobby hesitated, trying to work it out and he decided he would have to investigate the box to see what it was, so he headed back towards where he had seen it a few metres further back in the cargo hold. Of course, the box was nowhere to be seen, but Nobby had not seen any other Checker carry it past him. Confused, Nobby went to ask the Checker commander about the box, but he looked blankly at Nobby and told him to stop dreaming and get back to work!

Nobby felt that something was amiss and he needed to tell someone who would listen to him... He decided to speak to the captain directly. He slipped past the commander and turned the corner towards the beamer to get up to the bridge. He would tell the captain in person, he knew he would listen to him.

**

Captain Bull Carter looked in amazement at the sight of the half robot body emerging from the beamer across the room from him, the rest of the crew laughed at the state of him, but Bull kept a straight face, as best as he could. "Noblaczec! How unusual to see you.. well, half of you.. here on the bridge. We don't usually see Checkers in here. Is something wrong?" Bull tried to look serious and the crew stifled their laughs.

Nobby hurried to stand—float—in front of the captain and spluttered his message to him with urgency. "Captain, please forgive the intrusion, but I have something to report that is preying on my mind." Nobby realised that the captain was now ready to listen so he continued. " I saw something unusual in the cargo bay just now, behind the containers. I thought I had heard movement in an unusual place so I went to investigate, but all I found were containers and an old cardboard box.... I returned to duties, but then it dawned on me that we do not have cardboard boxes on board ship, so I returned to look at it again. But when I returned, not two minutes later it was not there, and nobody had carried it past me or seen it! I thought you should know, Captain."

Nobby "stood" to attention as the captain began to look worried. He glanced towards his first officer then turned his attention back to Nobby. "Thank you, Noblaczec, you did the right thing notifying me. Please, come to tell me immediately you see anything else unusual happening, wherever it is."

At this Nobby saluted the captain and left, feeling proud of himself. The crew looked in confusion at the captain and wondered why he gave credence to Nobby's tale. Bull suddenly got up and handed over the bridge to the First officer and left. The crew all looked at each other wondering what was going on.

***

Bull headed straight for Argo's office, where he found the Fleet commander with Kios, looking at the charting of their proposed journey into the Andromeda galaxy.

"Commander, we may have a problem on board ship." began Bull urgently, relating to the commander the report Nobby had just given him. Argo turned slowly towards Bull, worry etched all over his face.

"So, you are thinking the same as I am. We have an intruder on board, a shapeshifter!" Argo sat down at his desk and bade Bull sit.

"We must warn our officers and give each other code words to check each other's identity." Bull thought out loud, already hailing Star and Finch on their uniform mic. The two lovers arranged coded words for each other and went to Gale's room to warn the mother and daughter to do the same.

***

Bull alerted his bridge crew also then called the Su-k-en crew and Guy to meet him back at the bridge where he then briefed them all on the situation.

"What about the rest of the Scenarians on board?" the First officer asked with concern.

"I'm afraid it would be impossible to get to all of them in time, all we can do is warn them of the intruder so they are aware of the danger." Bull replied quietly, as he headed towards security.

***

Finch was already on patrol around the ship with his team of AIs, ever watchful of anything suspicious since learning of the shape shifter's existence. But the cargo bay where they started their search was full of Checkers doing their duties, it would be nigh on impossible to check each one to see if one of them was the shapeshifter.

Finch hailed Kios on his mic and asked him whether a shapeshifter can alter his voice to sound like whoever he has changed into as well. Kios had replied that generally they could not, their voices tended to stay their own. So Finch at least had something to go on to aid in his search. He posted two of his officers at each exit to check the voice of any robot that needed to get by them.

***

Intruder

Star, now being off duty, paced the room in frustration. Despite Bull's idea of using code words to identify each other, it still meant that there was an alien at large on board ship. She didn't fancy becoming the object of this new intruder's attention like she was the last time, so she felt the need to leave her quarters as quickly as possible.

She re-attached her weapons belt and headed out of her bedroom. She saw that Lin was with Gale in their bedroom as she passed their open door, she stepped back apace and asked them if all was well. They seemed untroubled by the news of an intruder and they said they were fine, so Star continued her walk along the living quarters corridor.

A large group of Scenarians were gathered in the corridor discussing the news of the intruder, all were looking worriedly at each other. They eyed Star with suspicion as she approached and they all receded into their quarters to keep out of her way.

"Charming!" thought Star out loud as she passed further along the corridor, but she couldn't really blame them, seeing a person on their own like that. She would have probably done the same in their situation.

She headed for the beamer so she could reach the safety of the bridge, at least Bull and Argo would be there amongst the others. "Safety in numbers as they say!" Star muttered to herself. The beamer door opened and to her relief Bull stepped out.

"Oh thank god it's you!" Star sighed as Bull exited the beamer cubicle. "I was coming up to the bridge 'cos I'm so spooked after the last time! I thought it would be safer up there." Star remarked, full of relief at seeing her old friend. "Where were you headed?" she asked curiously.

Bull was coughing and rubbed his throat as though he had something stuck in it. He bent down to catch his breath and replied between coughs "To see you." Star was touched that Bull had been concerned about her.

"Well, I'm here now, we can go back up to the

bridge together, shall we?" Star asked. Bull continued to cough a little more and shook his head. "You go ahead, I'll follow in a minute, just getting a drink."

At that he left, headed down towards the galley, so Star entered the beamer and headed up to the bridge, several floors above.

As she exited the beamer cubicle there was a lot of commotion with AIs moving up and down, challenging everyone they met on their way along the corridor. However, they only glanced briefly her way and after speaking to her let her pass as she greeted them, giving her code. Outside the bridge exit doors stood two Bronze AIs on guard. Well, at least Argo and Bull seem on top of things here thought Star happily. She felt she had done the right thing coming up here. She approached the two guards and they asked for her code word.

"Hubbite." Star announced, then the guards let her aside to enter the bridge. She walked into the large room, full of holographic screens with the Blues sat below them. She scanned the room and saw Kian and Meera at their workstations, then suddenly she froze in horror and pulled her weapon out, pointing it at the captain's seat! All the robots on the bridge immediately pointed their weapons at her in response. Her eyes widened and she managed to blurt out "The captain's the shapeshifter!"

The Blues looked from one to the other confused, looked again at the captain, then at Star, unsure who to believe. "Star. It's me!" Bull spoke first, standing up from his seat. "What makes you think I'm the shapeshifter? I've been here all the time."

Star replied quickly "No! That's a lie! I've just been talking to the captain at the beamer on my floor, he came to look for me, to see that I was safe! He had a cough..."

The reality dawned on her immediately. A cough.. to disguise his voice? "What is your code word?" Star asked Bull quietly.

"Scavenger." Bull replied immediately. All weapons trained on the captain trained on Star instead. "Your code?" Bull asked softly.

"Hubbite." Star managed before sinking to her knees with the reality surging through her body like a virus that she had been alone with the shapeshifter! Bull immediately hailed the security leader and told him of the possible location of the shapeshifter. When he told Finch that the shapeshifter looked like him he was taken aback slightly. He didn't relish firing on his own friend, shapeshifter or not!

***

It was too much to bear! Again, she had been at the mercy of an alien intruder. Tears welled in her eyes involuntarily and Bull rushed over to her and lifted her and held her in his arms to comfort her. All weapons were stored back again. Meera and Kian eyed each other then continued with their tasks.

Bull called for a hot drink for Star and immediately Meera brought one over for her from the bridge server. Bull sat her down and handed her the coffee. Meera sat beside Star comforting her as Bull spoke to Argo about the possible reason the intruder had for being here.

"Well, so far he hasn't killed or injured anyone on board the Starfinder, as far as we can tell. If it's the same person who shot up the crew of the Su-i it's possible he's after the Endari's experimental work!" Bull deduced from the description of how the Endaris had sealed themselves in their lab previously, to avoid capture of their scientific work.

"If that is the case we'd better warn the lab and send a security team over there." Argo replied, seemingly in agreement with the captain.

Bull hailed the lab and Guy answered the com.

"Guy? What are you doing there?" Bull inquired, not expecting to hear his voice.

Guy explained that he'd been asked by Ursu to see one of the rock samples the girls were studying because it contained a medicinal compound.

Bull briefed Guy about the possibility of the shapeshifter coming their way and that he was sending a security team down to the lab area. Guy immediately related the news to the Endaris and despite their initial horror at the thought of encountering their colleagues' murderer, they were now set on avenging their friends' deaths by catching the perpetrator!

"But how will we know it's him?" Genai wondered out loud. The trio knew that only the Bronzes and the security crew were likely to enter the lab, so Ursu believed it would be as one of them that the intruder would disguise himself. They knew each other's code words, so they had to be prepared. The emergency button beneath the workstation was there to be pressed if the intruder were to enter and that would bring the security team to their rescue. All they had to do now was wait.

Ursu and Genai wished that they had Kios with them right now because he at least was armed; none of them had any weapons, but the girls had speed on their side.

***

Minutes passed and the outer lab door opened. Guy flashed a look at Ursu as a Bronze entered carrying a tray of test tubes. On his body was his ID number 12, which would also be his code, so Guy spoke to him.

"Ten, how many test tubes do you have there?" He awaited the reply with his clenched fists turning white with anticipation, finger poised below the alarm button.

The Bronze set down the test tubes on the far workstation and replied in a semi robotic voice "Forty, sir. I beg your pardon sir, but I'm number twelve." The Bronze turned to look at Guy, who apologised, then he went out again to fetch more supplies.

"Hmmm. I thought it was our intruder too.. Never mind, we'll get him eventually." Ursu commented to Guy softly.

A few minutes later Finch popped his head into the lab, giving his code, to ask if all was well and the trio nodded their heads, trying to act cool. Then Finch left again, saying they were patrolling the corridors outside if they needed help.

The robot came in again carrying more supplies, then started to place the rock samples onto the glass fronted storage containers along one wall.

Ursu and Genai were bored waiting for something to happen. They tried to busy themselves by looking at the sample under the magnoscopes again, counting the number of minerals in the stone. Suddenly a rock sample fell onto the floor behind them where the Bronze worked and a low curse was uttered by the clumsy robot.

Guy stopped in his tracks. He turned slowly towards the robot and spoke to him, "Everything all right, ten?" as the robot picked up the fallen rock and placed it back in the unit. The robot didn't reply, but simply nodded his head. The girls immediately latched on to Guy's clever test. The Bronze had not corrected Guy for getting his number wrong! They were sure it was the shapeshifter!

Genai and Ursu looked at Guy for guidance and Ursu headed towards the second emergency button nearby, but Guy stopped her. He indicated the robot had a panel behind his head that had an on off switch. Ursu had no hesitation, in a flash she had travelled the distance to the robot and switched off the button before you could say please! Her speed was their saviour.

As Genai pressed the emergency button the robot had frozen on the spot, unable to move. The fact that the intruder had turned himself into a robot was his downfall! He could not move at all!

Seconds later Finch and his men burst into the lab and saw Guy pointing to the stricken robot. As Finch was about to speak the real Bronze 12 entered the room laden with more supplies. He stopped short when he saw the replica of himself and realised the situation immediately. He watched as the security crew trained their guns on the shapeshifter and hailed the captain to see what he wanted done with the intruder.

Argo and Bull had no hesitation in coming to the same conclusion. They wanted no more conflict on board ship. "Put him in the airlock and give him a nice trip in space!" Bull replied menacingly.

So the Bronze lifted the intruder and did exactly that. At the air lock they deactivated his power switch and he turned to look at them, his eyes widening, before the airlock door shut on him. It was a K-Tu shapeshifter! They could not believe it! In minutes the ship was free of intruders once more, much to everyone's relief, especially to Star's.

Genai, Kios and the others were horrified to think of one of their own being responsible for all those deaths on board the Su-I. They just could not believe it!

***

Coserai

A few days after the shapeshifter had been flushed out of the airlock, the other K-Tu was aiding the captain and the fleet commander in moving the fleet towards the Helios gateway to the next part of the galaxy, where hopefully they would find Versa, the planet that sheltered the remaining Scenarians. Argo had not encountered a gateway before, so he was glad of Kios' input into dealing with it. Bull marvelled at seeing the strange glowing hole into deep space. The gate was enormous, the fleet would fit into its path tenfold at least, he estimated. Waves of blue and green light drew a viewer towards its centre, almost hypnotic to look at, like a pulsating aurora borealis. There was nothing but blackness in its centre, no stars glowed anywhere inside it, it was almost like Bull imagined that a black hole would appear.

The Blue spoke over the fleet tannoy *"Prepare to enter the gateway. Entering in ten, nine, eight..."* and so Blue 7 gave the countdown to the entry point, then all the fleet ships were sucked into the centre of the gate and vanished through it. The journey took only a short time, but during that time all that they could see through the ship's windows were flashes of light, like streaks passing them by. No sign of stars or planets, but a sensation of floating came over the crew as they sped through to the other part of the galaxy.

They emerged out of the gate as though a fly spat out from the mouth of a child. It was very disorientating after floating along in the quiet flow of the gate, to be now zooming out into normal space again, where stars and planets danced with moons in the dark. The crew's bodies felt heavier after exiting the gate and it took a while to acclimatise to the standard gravity once more.

They travelled through the new section of the galaxy, watching in awe the strange shapes twisted in the blackness of space, of gassy-coloured clouds of purples and red, writhing in twisted forms stretching through the black. They travelled on for days, passing large asteroid belts and gassy giant planets, which were incapable of sustaining life forms. Onwards through space, following Kios' planned trajectory.

From time to time curious lights, like dancing golden pinpoints swayed around the ships, joining them for a while on their passage through the void, like dolphins accompanying sailors through the seas. Observing, and calculating the essence of these passing tourists, then, abruptly, they would twinkle out again, to disappear from sight and merge with the stars.

***

In the distance, three planets could be seen in close proximity to each other, a large gassy giant with two smaller planets to either side. Kios said that the smaller two were moons of the gas giant Lumos, one of which was inhabited by small people, the Coserai.

"Are the Coserai hostile, or could we form an alliance with them?" asked Argo.

Kios thought for a moment before answering. "Well, they are friendly enough, but I can't think of a reason why they would make a good alliance. They are a primitive people, with very little technology, although they do seem to thrive very well. No wars have ever been heard of on their home planet."

Argo weighed the information, then decided it was worth the effort to visit these people anyway. What did they have to lose?

There was no means of hailing the people on the moon's surface because of their primitive lifestyle, so the fleet commander decided that he and the captain should pay a visit on Gley via shuttle instead of frightening them with a whole fleet. Finch's security team, including Star, accompanied them.

***

The shuttle headed for the nearest large inhabited area on Gley, which was beside a large lake. The moon's surface was varied; many parts of it were large orange plateaus with the occasional high rocky outcrop emerging at intervals out of the sandy terrain, other parts were lush, with grassy plains interspersed with pools and lakes, dotted with enormous trees, providing a heavy canopy to the lush areas below.

The Coserai villages were made of wooden structures topped with grassy roofs, interspersed with wooden pens containing animals similar to goats and pigs.

As they landed their shuttle, a large group of Coserai gathered to survey the vessel. None seemed alarmed, mostly they showed nothing but curiosity. They were dressed simply, in animal skin robes, tethered at the waist with plaited leather strips. They wore boots of leather also and many carried a stout staff, which may have been a walking aid, or used as a weapon.

The Coserai themselves resembled humans, but all were quite short; none seemed taller than five foot from what Bull could see. They had different hair colours, just as humans did, but they wore their hair slicked back with some kind of greasy substance and the females had flowers tied in their hair.

Bull and Argo descended the ramp, followed by the security team; none held their weapons however. Bull wanted to create a friendly impression.

"Greetings to the Coserai." Bull spoke loudly so all could hear him above the hubbub of the people gathered in front of them. They stopped their chatter to listen. "We come in peace. We have come from a galaxy nearby searching for friends and allies for our own planet Earth. We hope that you will become our allies should we need your help in the future. In return we offer you our support, should you ever need it."

The Coserai looked from Bull to the AIs and looked with interest at the artificial beings. One of the males spoke out in reply.

"Greetings to you people of Earth, we welcome you to Gley. But what are these beings that you have with you? They do not look like you." He pointed at the AIs, then Argo spoke, much to the surprise of the Coserai, who stepped back apace.

"Greetings. My name is Argo and I am the fleet commander and this is my captain." He indicated to Bull, then pointed to the Silvers behind him. "These are my fellow crew members, they help us fly our ships. We were created to help the people of Earth to travel across the galaxies to search for friends and allies. We were created to help mankind."

The Coserai took this information on board and some began to nod their heads in understanding. The male spoke again.

"I am Chu, the leader of my village, and this is my

woman Key," (indicating the dark haired woman next to him, wearing red flowers in her hair)." Here are my sons Tion and Tiju, they are good hunters." The sons strode forward next to their father, they seemed fully grown to adulthood but their father and mother seemed no older than them to Bull.

"Come, welcome to our village, let us have a feast to welcome you!" The leader indicated for the crew to follow him and the Coserai led the way to their nearby village, all now smiling and chatting amongst each other again.

***

The leader led them to a large dwelling in the centre of the village, where a spit was turned by a young woman outside the entrance to the house. On the spit was a large animal unlike any on Earth. Bull and Finch wondered what it would taste like and Star eyed the young woman as she turned the spit handle, she seemed very happy doing this tedious task, which was curious thought Star.

The dwelling was the leader's home and he led them inside as the villagers resumed their previous tasks before the arrival of the shuttle. Some were treating animal skins, others were tending to the animals and mending fences around the village. Others dried their nets by the lakeside, where an array of fishing boats were moored.

***

Inside the leader's house it was dimly lit by a few burning torches. The floor was covered with dried palm-like leaves and in places, rugs of animal skins were strewn along the perimeter of the round house. The leader sat on a raised throne and indicated for the others to sit on the skins in front of him.

In one corner of the room stood a raised area strewn with more animal pelts and bolstered by sacks of straw. This was seemingly the leader's bed.

Star tried to imagine sleeping in it but could only imagine it to be lumpy and itchy to say the least. In fact she began to itch at the thought, which led her to wonder if there were fleas in the straw. She shuddered at the thought.

Finch, Star and Bull sat on the rugs but the AIs remained standing, apologising to Chu for not being able to sit so low. The leader spoke quietly to his son sat next to him and the son left the room, returning shortly afterwards brandishing wooden benches, much to the crew's surprise.

Chu explained that his son had created these benches in his own house to sit on when his wife was unable to get up off the floor when heavily pregnant. He had thought of a way to raise her off the floor and created the bench for her. She liked it so much his son decided to make some more and he ended up with three benches in his house, but Chu's wife preferred to sit on the floor, so he didn't have any in his own house.

The AIs thanked the leader and gratefully sat on the benches provided for them.

The interior of the hut smelled of smoke from the fire, but it was very cosy and warm there. It reminded Bull of The Hub somehow. A woman entered the dwelling carrying drinks and proceeded to hand them out to the crew.

Argo pointed out to the Corserai that he and the other AIs did not eat or drink and thanked her for the offer. So the woman handed the drinks to Star, Bull and

Finch , then to the Corserai in the room.

Star looked at the dark liquid, wondering what it was. She envisioned a foul-tasting brew and held her breath before taking a sip. However, the drink was rather pleasant and tasted a bit like berries. She smiled at Finch as he looked at her for signs of how it tasted before trying it himself! When he saw her relief he downed it happily, only to regret it as soon as he swallowed it. His was a different drink, served only to the men and it tasted revolting to Bull and Finch. Bull almost choked on swallowing the vile liquid, but tried to smile to please Chu.

Chu saw his displeasure and chuckled. "I'm sorry, I should have warned you about your drink. Only the men drink it here. It tastes bad, but the effect afterwards is wonderful, it gives you strength and energy!"

Bull and Finch weren't too convinced and took his word for it, looking at each other trying not to vomit!

Star thought what a lucky escape she'd had!

***

Chu's village

Walking around the village, Bull and the others noticed that all the Coserai seemed very happy all the time, whatever they were doing. Bull wished that he could find that inner happiness somewhere. He looked at the simple dwellings, no luxuries to be seen anywhere, no modern technology, but all that didn't bother the Coserai in the slightest.

Chu's son took Bull, Finch and Star to where he normally tended the animals they kept for food, just over the edge of the village, closer to the lakeside. A large section had been fenced off for the beasts, encompassing part of the lake for the animals' water supply.

The animals resembled a cross between a cow and a horse, with tails rather like a cow's but heads more like horses, the bodies were stout like cows were but had horse-like hoofs. Very odd looking to the human onlookers. One of the animals suddenly turned on another over a patch of grass, butting its head against the other and preparing to rear up to attack. But quick as a flash, Chu's son Tiju leapt over the fence and held the animal's head, pulling it away from the other effortlessly! Bull and the others couldn't believe it! That would have required a great deal of strength and agility to do that and Tiju seemed to have plenty!

"How did you do that?" Star inquired, full of admiration for the show of strength.

"Do what? Pull the animal away? Oh, it happens a lot, we're used to it. You've just got to show them who's the master." Tiju laughed.

"But they are so big! It must require incredible strength to do that!" Star gushed in response.

"Well, I guess so, but we Coserai are all strong people." Tiju remarked, shrugging it off as though it was nothing.

Bull looked at him, intrigued. "Just how strong are you?" he asked. "I mean how much can you lift, do you think?"

Tiju thought about it briefly then answered. "I'm no stronger than anyone else in the village. We are all strong. I can lift you easily I would guess." he replied.

Bull indicated for Tiju to try and lift him. The man came up to Bull and hefted him easily over his shoulder, with not so much as a grunt! The crew stared with surprise, mouths agape. Bull was no lightweight, he was a muscular, solid man!

"Wow!" Finch and Star managed in tandem. Both thought how useful these people could be in times of trouble.

***

Later in the day the villagers all gathered in the circular space outside Chu's hut to eat. Tables had been arranged in the centre, near the spit, laden with fruit and cheeses, and chunks of the spit roast had been arranged onto a large platter in the centre. A row of villagers sat in a semi circle banging a rhythmic pattern on drums in one half of the circle and young women danced to the rhythm, dressed in feathered skirts with bands of flowers adorning their heads in front of them. Benches had been provided this time for the guests to sit at.

Chu himself sat on a raised platform in front of his house overseeing the festivities. His wife served him some of the food from the table before eating herself. Soon some sturdy children came to serve the guests with platters of food, then they went around the villagers with more offerings. When the drinks came around, Finch eyed the cup with suspicion, then smiled when he saw it was different to the previous drink.

Some of the dancers began to add to the rhythm with bell-like sounds from small husks they had in their hands being tapped against each other. It was a hypnotic rhythm and the crew enjoyed the welcome immensely. Men behind the drummers began to sing with the rhythm, an echoing chant rising and falling in pitch, adding to the hypnotic feel. The Coserai certainly enjoyed life, simple though it may be.

***

The feast lasted into the late evening, dances were interspersed with acrobatic feats by some of the village men and the crew were later invited to join in the dancing along with the rest. This was a welcome change from being stuck on the Starfinder. The humans relaxed to the sway of the rhythm and let all their inhibitions fade away. A feeling of well- being came over them and they felt they could stay there forever, enjoying the simple life.

As the evening drew to a close Chu came over to the crew to ask if they would like to stay on Gley for a while and bring the rest of their crew down in the morning to visit.

Argo thanked Chu and agreed to bring more crew down in the morning to visit awhile, but he didn't intend to scare Chu with the fact that there were thousands of crew, mostly all AIs, he would only bring the human contingent down for a visit he decided.

***

In the darkness of night the giant Lumos glowed, filling the horizon, overwhelming the night sky by its size. The second moon, Philar was an echo, further away, the far side of Lumos, apparently inhabited only by fierce creatures, so Kios told Argo later that evening. As evening drew to a close, the crew boarded their shuttle to return to the Starfinder and all felt very content with their encounter with the Coserai. It was comforting to know there were more friendly species in the world to ally themselves with.

***

"How was your visit?" Kush asked the captain as they returned on board the ship. Bull told him how they had been welcomed and shown around the village, but also how primitive the people on Gley were, having no modern technology, but seeming incredibly happy with their lot. Kush listened with interest, weighing up the news. He then asked the captain whether he thought it would be a good place for the Scenarians to settle down.

Bull debated how the people would fare with having such differences in their technological knowledge. *Would having the two species living together cause friction amongst this happy tribe?* He tended to think it would be wrong to inflict their technology on these primitive people. He needed to discuss the idea further with Argo, but in any event, the Scenarians on board ship would get to visit the planet the next day, along with the remainder of the living crew and passengers.

Chapter 7

A visit to Gley

As the Scenarians descended from the shuttles onto Gley, they noticed the simple huts that the Coserai lived in and marvelled at how primitive their lives were. The climate was pleasant here, which pleased the Scenarians. The tall trees surrounding the village offered dappled shade from the heat of the sun. The Coserai regarded these grey beings with interest, never having seen them before. They had met some other species in their time, but no Scenarians.

Argo led the Scenarians over to the Coserai village to greet the leader. As he arrived with the mass of people following in their wake, Chu emerged from his hut and smiled broadly.

"So many people! You must have a very big ship Commander." Chu enthused. Argo replied that they had many small ships and they had rescued the Scenarians from their devastated planet as it broke up into space a short time previously. He spoke about the many Scenarians that had perished, but that these were amongst some that had escaped to try and find a new home for themselves. Argo and his fleet were aiming to take the ones they had rescued to meet up with the others and try to find a new home for them all.

Chu listened to all this and wondered at the force

required to break up a whole planet. He began to worry about Gley and could that happen here. For the first time Argo saw worry etched on Chu's face.

"Was there a reason the planet broke apart?" Chu asked worriedly.

"Well, the Scenarians had been trying to defend their planet from warring invaders for decades and suffered relentless bombing from their enemies for much of that time. Perhaps the endless explosions started to have a detrimental effect on the planet. Who knows?" Argo replied.

Chu worried about this news, could they cope if they suffered such an attack? Were these invaders intent on invading other planets? This news was now a great worry to Chu. Never had his planet encountered any hostile intervention, but what if it were to start one day? They would be defenceless, Chu realised.

Argo saw the concern on Chu's face. "What are you worrying about?" Argo asked tentatively.

Chu asked to speak to Argo and Bull alone and bade the others to enjoy exploring their planet and take some refreshments in the village. His sons led the crew and its passengers to the food and drink that had been laid out for them.

In Chu's hut the trio sat down to talk. Chu expressed his fears about the invaders and how would they fare if such a thing happened. He knew that they had no defence against such an attack. The three talked at great length about the issue as the Scenarians and the others enjoyed their new scenery.

***

"It reminds me a little of the picnic area in the

woods near home." Meera spoke to Kian as they lay in a tranquil spot on lush green grass beside the lake. "It's so quiet there, just like it is here. No sound of anything but birds singing nearby."

Suddenly a large fish jumped up high out of the lake not far from them and splashed loudly back into the depths. Meera and Kian looked at each other and laughed. "Well, almost the same!" Meera added.

***

Ursu , Genai and Da-Ee strolled along the edge of the lake admiring the view and taking in the clean air. They saw the large fish leap out of the water and disappear again. Da-Ee screamed and jumped back in fright, never realising that creatures might live in the water. Ursu and Genai laughed at her innocence and made funny roaring noises, scuttling towards her with arms raised to depict some strange creatures. Da-Ee shuffled backwards out of their way, her face still in shock, but then she realised that it was silly and leapt in the air over their heads, landing behind them and swatting their rears for taunting her.

"Hey!" Genai grumbled. "No smacking!" and the girls all laughed in their mirth. As they continued their stroll Da-Ee made sure she had Ursu and Genai between her and the water's edge, just to be on the safe side!

***

The Scenarians were completely absorbed by the quaintness of the village and the attire of the people and some exchanged information with the Coserai people about their lifestyle. It soon became clear to the Coserai that these grey beings had many attributes that they could

never dream of. They spoke of trains and gliders and vehicles, of domes and elevators and suchlike. The Coserai
could not imagine what their lives must have been like.

One of the Scenarian women took out of her pocket
a holographer to show to her gathered hosts images of her
family and home. The Coserai stood back in amazement
as the hologram lit before them showing moving vehicles
gliding along a rail carrying people towards a large
domed structure. The woman and her family were shown
exiting a gliding vessel and entering a large palace, but
the woman was wearing extravagant gowns in this image,
she had a crown on her head, as did her husband!

The Coserai looked again at the ordinary looking
woman; here she wore no crown so they were confused.
Queen Laifa smiled and spoke as she switched off the
holographer. "Yes, in Scenara I was their Queen and my
husband.. King Khali. He has been killed in the fall of the
domed city."

The Scenarians and Coserai fell to a tangible silence
as they took in the fact that the Queen was amongst them,
but acting like any ordinary citizen.

"You are still our Queen, Your Highness," uttered a
Scenarian male, bowing to the queen. The others bowed
in his wake, then the Coserai did the same out of rever-
ence for her position and humility.

***

Decisions

The weather was warm and the scent of wild flowers filled the air. One of the Scenarians asked if they

could all camp out here on Gley rather than return to the ship for a few days. It would be wonderful to have room to run around and explore the land rather than be cooped up on board ship any longer than they had to.

"Somehow I thought that would be your intent." said Bull happily and he nodded to the Silvers posted by the shuttles. The Silvers went on board the shuttles and returned minutes later with a hoverboard laden with rucksack-type baggage from each shuttle. "We thought these might come in useful." Bull added as the Silvers began offloading the bags among the Scenarians.

One of the Silvers opened up a rucksack and out of it came a large pop-up tent for camping, along with a few supplies for bedding and cooking. The Silvers demonstrated how to set up the easy-tents, just with a shake the tent expanded out fully inflating into a dwelling for up to eight people at a time. The Scenarians and Coserai watched with interest how easy it was to set up, so they began to arrange the tents in a circle just a short distance from Chu's village, so as not to be underfoot.

The AIs unfolded tables and chairs outside each tent and handed out the bedrolls to each person. It looked like it was going to be almost a home away from home holiday, with small luxuries to make their camp comfortable. Very soon the Scenarians had finished setting up their little camp and had arranged the Queen's tent in a favourable position where she would be protected by the others. Farsifa would sleep in the same tent with her to tend to her needs, but it seemed Queen Laifa had decided to do some sorting out herself, putting things in the tent as she wanted, saving Farsifa the trouble, so she could explore like the others.

"Thank you captain for your thoughtfulness." Queen Laifa smiled at Bull as she emerged out of her completed tent. "It really is nice to be on solid ground again, if only for a short while!"

Farsifa emerged from the tent carrying a shawl for the queen, in case it got colder later.

***

Star sat under the shade of a tree for a break and the Endari girls came to sit with her. They watched the people chatting happily and strolling along the lakeside. Genai remarked how peaceful it was here, unlike her own planet, where people whizzed around busily from day to day. Star looked intently at the girls.

"Why do you have those sequiny things above your eyes?" asked Star, looking carefully at the differing patterns on Ursu and Genai's faces.

The girls smiled and Ursu replied.

"These? Well, they are neural interfacers, they help us zoom in on things far away in an instant, when we travel at our faster speed, we use them to avoid crashing into objects when travelling so fast. Each clan has a different pattern." Ursu smiled and Star seemed impressed. She was learning new things every day about these new passengers.

***

Bull watched as the groups strolled in the sunshine, talking excitedly as they explored this pretty part of the planet. You would never know from looking at them how much they had suffered not so long ago. His fair hair glinted in the sun's rays and he placed his jacket on the branch of the tree beside him, such was the warmth of the day. Star came to stand beside him, happy to be away from the ship and its memories for a while.

"How's my best scavenger?" Bull asked, smiling at her. It seemed like a lifetime since they were both out scavenging for their community. Those days, regretfully, were now over.

Star smiled back at the memory and sighed. "I think I'll leave the scavenging for Ursu and Genai," seeing the girls lifting yet another piece of rock from the water's edge to add to their collection.

"It looks like they'll soon have enough rocks to fill a mine!" she smiled, remembering the Hub, where she had grown up with Bull and Finch. Memories both happy and sad mingled in her thoughts.

Bull wanted to draw her out of her melancholy. "C'mon! Race you to the jetty!" Bull urged and began to run towards the lake shore further ahead, where the villagers moored a few fishing boats. Star paused for just a second to drop her jacket and ran as fast as she could to try and overtake Bull. "Cheat!" she called out, laughing. "You had a head start on me!"

***

Chu invited Queen Laifa to stroll with him along the lake to have a talk while her people enjoyed the relaxed atmosphere here on Gley. It had been a long time since the Scenarians had been able to walk and run about without the constant pounding of the movement of the earth below their feet. Here they could easily forget their cares. Gley had an aura of peace and tranquillity about it.

***

Bull beat Star to the jetty and waited as she gathered her breath from the exertion. *When was the last time*

I have run like that. she thought to herself. She couldn't even remember, it was so long ago.

"Feels good doesn't it?" Bull smiled at her. "It's been so long since we had any fun. I sometimes wish we could just forget about everything and just enjoy ourselves for once, but hey! Not everyone can be captain, eh?"

Star smiled back at him.

Yes it did feel good, even if she was out of practice in running. She made a mental note to work out a bit in the gym on board the Starfinder once they were on their way again. She looked in the distance towards the encampment to see if she could catch a glimpse of Finch, but the throng was quite large and he was swallowed up among the Scenarians. doing his duty as Security officer.

Ursu called out to them as they made their way along the shoreline collecting samples. "Hey! Captain, we've found a lot of exciting samples here on Gley, quite unusual. It's going to be interesting checking these out in the lab when we return!" Bull nodded and replied .

"Just make sure you leave some on the planet or you might overload our ship's baggage capability!" Bull smiled and turned towards Star, "Do you think she'll buy it?"

Star laughed and replied "No, not a chance! I'm afraid you're stuck with an ever growing sample of rocks in the ship's lab! You never know, she might find something useful one day!"

***

Bull sat at the edge of the jetty, dangling his feet above the water, so Star sat next to him, relaxed in his company. She picked up some sticks strewn on the jetty and began to break them up into smaller pieces, feeding the segments one by one into the water below.

"Let's see how far you can throw a stick." Bull challenged her, grabbing a handful of small ones nearby. Star gave him a cheeky look then took a piece and lobbed it with all her might into the distance. Sadly, it only went a couple of metres as the breeze blew it back towards her. She made a cross face then challenged Bull to do better. He raised his eyebrows, looking sidelong at her then prepared to throw his piece. She watched with a smug look on her face knowing it wouldn't get very far. He lobbed it with all his might and both looked surprised when the piece launched itself at least ten metres away to land on the water.

"How did you do that?" Star asked, astounded at the distance. Bull said he actually had no idea, but claimed it was skill. Star looked at him and a thought struck her.

"You threw a pebble didn't you!" looking at a few scattered around them on the jetty. She went to wallop him for cheating but Bull was too quick and caught her arms mid air to restrain her.

"No I didn't, I swear!" Bull protested, holding on to Star's arms as she struggled. He really hadn't, he protested, but also he had no idea how to explain how it happened.

"Tell you what," he released her arms carefully, holding out his own in protection, "I'll do it again and you can watch me do it. It was probably a fluke." he reasoned with her, still smiling.

Star watched as he picked up a stick and felt its weight. He let her hold it first to check there was no trick to it. When she was satisfied she handed it back to him.

"Satisfied?" he asked unnecessarily and when she

nodded he lobbed it across the water. Both watched as again his piece landed about ten metres away!

Star pounced on him, convinced that he had cheated in some way. She straddled his chest and playfully tried to beat him , but he was too strong for her, laughing at how useless it was to even try. He let her continue for a couple of minutes before turning her over on her back effortlessly and pinning her down, powerless to move. Bull caught her eyes and his love for her pricked his heart again, all the feelings he had for her overwhelmed him and he dipped his face to meet hers and almost kissed her, but moved away at the last moment, his lips inches from hers and released her. Star sat up and extracted some sticks from her hair as Bull sat beside her, looking away.

"I'm sorry, I shouldn't have done that." Bull muttered quietly to her, wishing he didn't feel so much for her.

"It's okay." Star replied, resting her hand on his shoulder lightly. As he turned to look at her she smiled then added "But you did cheat, I know it," and at that she gave a playful whack on the arm and made to run off. "Race you back to the village!" she yelled, giving herself a head start this time. Bull emptied the pebbles out of his cuff and ran after her, pushing the stick into the water.

***

From the throng around the encampment Finch looked away and wondered what he should do, his feelings churned at odds with each other in his heart. It was not a good feeling.

***

Confrontation

Later on, Argo fell in beside Bull as he enjoyed the evening air on the planet. The Coserai had welcomed the refugees, exceeding Bull's anticipation of friendship between the two races. Queen Laifa seemed to have impressed Chu with her charm, he thought, as he remembered their long stroll by the lake earlier.

He hadn't seen Star for a few hours now and he was glad that he didn't run into Finch as he was sure his feelings would have betrayed him. He felt such conflict feeling the way he did about his best friend's girlfriend and he wished he could forget her, but he didn't think there would ever be a chance of that.

"Penny for them? Isn't that what humans say?" Argo spoke, standing beside Bull, looking at the throng in front of them.

Bull looked towards Argo and wondered if he knew anything, but before he could say anything Argo continued.

"You know nothing good is going to come out of it, don't you? You're going to end up hurting the two people you love the most."

Bull was shocked, wondering how he knew the way he felt. "Am I that obvious?" he asked.

Argo replied that it was obvious to him how he felt, but soon others would also know if he didn't do something about it sharpish.

"How do you un-love someone? I've tried to think what I can do, but it's so hard." Bull sighed deeply, his heart throbbing in his chest.

Argo looked at him carefully, then uttered the words Bull needed to hear, before he went back among the crowd. "You need to keep a clear head for your job Bull, You will have to try and forget her, think about it! And be warned... Finch saw what happened, be careful."

***

As Argo left, Bull's heart stopped a beat and he fell backwards against a tree in despair. He clasped his hands into tight fists, willing the pain to disappear, but of course it wouldn't. He was glad that the night time helped hide his turmoil, he felt unable to hold a conversation with anyone right then, so he slowly got up, full of anguish, he needed to be on his own, to think what he would say to Finch. So he set off back towards the shuttle a few metres behind him. There would be nobody there but a Silver on sentry duty beside it, he could find time to think in there, away from the crowd.

***

The Silver saluted him as he approached and Bull climbed up the ramp and headed inside for solitude. He didn't bother activating the lights inside the shuttle, he wanted to be in the dark, where nobody could disturb him in his misery. He followed the emergency floor lights to guide him into the interior.

The blow hit Bull like a sledgehammer as soon as he walked into the room. It sent him reeling to the floor, caught unawares, and he lay there gasping for breath, but in a few seconds someone was pulling him back onto his feet and pounding him again. He felt the blood trickling down his mouth and tried to make out where his attacker was, but before he could adjust to the dimness of the interior a voice full of hatred bellowed beside him, as the attacker held onto Bull's shirt.

"How could you! How could you do this to me? I

thought you were my friend!" Finch spat his anger towards Bull like a man consumed. Bull put up no resistance as Finch laid into him again, he felt he deserved it after all. He thought he'd probably do the same if he were in Finch's boots.

"Aren't you gonna fight me for her? Why don't you fight, you bastard!" Finch tore at him, incensed by the betrayal that he assumed he had received.

Bull managed to splutter between blows. "Nothing happened Finch, nothing did! I wanted to kiss her, I can't help the way I feel, but I didn't. I don't want to hurt either of you! I'm sorry!" Bull fell to the floor from his blows, putting up no defence.

Finch leant back against the bulkhead, his hands stinging from his blows, he gasped for breath as he heard Bull's words. He stood above Bull breathing heavily.

Bull awaited the next bout of blows, but they did not come, instead he heard Finch's voice utter quietly before departing. "Well, you have, more than you'll ever know."

***

Bull lay there in the dark, not bothering to rise, his heart was breaking because of what he had done to both his friends. He never wanted this to happen, but it had and now he would have to face the consequences. How did people get past this he thought to himself. How do you shut off your feelings and pretend it never happened?

His mind raced with thoughts that were beyond his control and he wished for peace. His stomach churned and he lay there in the dark, wondering what to do when he heard footsteps coming up the ramp. Bull groaned at the thought of anyone seeing him in his misery, he had to get up. Every muscle ached as he tried to lift himself up and straighten himself out. Too late, the ramp lights came on, someone was coming into the shuttle!

***

"What the..?" Da-Ee exclaimed in horror as she saw the bloodied state of Bull. "Shall I fetch security captain?" Da-Ee quickly asked, turning on her heel to fetch help.

"No! No, please... just let me be... I'll be okay." Bull urged the Su-ul, trying to appear calm. The last thing he wanted was security to turn up. They were the ones who had done this!

He tried to stand up but slid sideways, disoriented. Da-Ee quickly ran to his side and helped him up. "Who did this to you?" Da- Ee grimaced at the sight of blood dripping from his forehead and cut lip as she propped him up on one of the seats.

"It doesn't matter, I deserved it!" Bull replied, wiping the blood from his eye.

"Here, let me patch you up." Da-Ee offered. "Let's get you away from the cockpit area to somewhere less obvious." She let him lean on her for support as she led him along to one of the rooms inside the shuttle.

They made it inside after a bit of effort and Da-Ee laid him on the couch while she ran to get the first aid box from back near the cockpit. Whilst there, she pushed the button to close up the ramp so they wouldn't be disturbed.

***

In the Senarian camp people were singing around the fire, enjoying their first night of open air freedom. Ursu and Genai were dancing to the music, along with Kios, Meera and Kian. Guy sat at the fire talking with one of the villagers about medicine.

"Where did Da-Ee go?" Genai asked, all of a sudden noticing her friend's absence.

Kios replied that she'd probably gone to chat up some poor unsuspecting guy as he'd often noticed her doing in the past.

"Oh, say no more!" Genai answered with a wink, smiling at the memory of Da-Ee's several past conquests.

***

Star got up from beside Guy and went to search for Finch, she hadn't seen him for quite a while. She asked one of his security team where he was and one of them pointed to the lakeside. Star wondered why he had gone there, so far from the others. She looked towards the lake and eventually saw a silhouette of someone that could be him, so she walked over to him. Why was he picking up something from the water she wondered, but as she got closer she realised that he was washing his hands in the water.

"Hey you. What's going on?" Star asked mildly as she came closer to him. " Why are you washing your hands?" Star looked at him, then realised, as her eyes adjusted to the night sky, that he looked very dishevelled, he had a streak of blood on his face! She looked down at his hands and saw how raw they looked. Her stomach went cold and she felt a shiver go through her body. She took a step back, horror spread over her face as she looked him in the eye. "What have you done?"

***

Broken

Star realised with a heavy heart that Finch had laid into Bull, his best friend, and all because of her! It distressed her so much to think she was the cause of the destruction of their friendship. She couldn't cope with being near Finch just then, she had to get away, she needed to be alone. She turned on her heel, taking one horrified look back at Finch, she shook her head in despair and ran into the night.

"Star! Wait! Don't go! I'm sorry!..." Finch began to head after her, but Argo's voice stopped him.

"Let her be, she needs to be alone right now." Argo took in Finch's appearance. "What have you done to him? Is he all right?"

Finch retorted angrily, "He'll live! It's only what he deserved."

Argo looked at him with a serious expression and Finch realised what was coming. "You leave me with no option. I can't have my officers brawling like this, report to the brig to cool off! I'll deal with you later!" Finch's eyes finally fell in recognition at what he had done. He had assaulted a superior officer whilst on duty. He knew how bad that was. He saluted Argo and headed to another shuttle, where his security team were based. Argo hailed them with the charges and as Finch approached the shuttle one of the Silvers took him to the brig on board, to be taken up to the Starfinder later.

***

Star wept silently in the dark, fearing for Bull and what Finch might have done. He must have seen them on the jetty, she figured, she should have told him nothing happened! Her feelings overwhelmed her and she leaned against the tall tree for support, sliding to sit at its base, leaning against its smooth scented bark. She soon became aware of a person nearby and turned her face to look. It was Tion, Chu's son, he had heard her sobbing in the dark. He came over and looked at her puzzled.

"Why is there water falling from your eyes?" Tion asked, perturbed.

Star was shocked by the statement, surely the Coserai cried now and again? The statement brought her out of her misery momentarily.

"Have you never cried when you're sad?" Star asked innocently.

"We are never sad, we are always happy." Tion replied simply. Star was taken aback, then added.

"What about when someone dies or has an accident, don't you cry then?" Star probed, beginning to forget about her own problems.

"When someone has an accident we heal them; when someone dies it is a welcome release from having lived so long. All of us welcome death after a long life." Tion smiled briefly.

It then occurred to Star that these people might live a little longer than humans and perhaps were glad to die when they were old and weary, so she asked.

"How old do people live to here on Gley?"

Tion replied "Well, my grandfather died when he was four hundred years old."

Star 's eyes widened with shock on hearing these words, when she found her voice again she asked Tion how old he was.

"Oh, I'm only two hundred and four and Tiju is two hundred and twelve." he beamed at her.

* * *

Da-Ee gently dabbed the blood away from Bull's face and put salve onto his cuts and bruises. His eye had swollen up, as had his cut lip. She reached for the ice crystals from the medi-pack and placed them in position over the swelling, holding them in place with her fingers. Bull moaned softly as it gently took effect. Da-Ee took in the torn appearance of his uniform and the blood stains coating his chest.

"Do you have extra uniforms on the shuttle?" Da-Ee asked quietly as she looked around the room.

"Should be some in the supply room.. over that way.." Bull replied, pointing, then grimacing in pain. Da-Ee placed Bull's hand on the ice crystals to replace her own as she made for the supply room on the left. She returned minutes later with a fresh blue and black uniform.

"Take your clothes off." Da-Ee ordered Bull, holding up the newly unwrapped uniform.

"Excuse me?" Bull remarked, abashed at her order.

"Well, you can't stay in that uniform, can you? You look like creke! The captain needs to keep up appearances, you know!" she bossed, without a hint of a smile on her face.

Bull had to face it, he did look a mess, so reluctantly he began to sit upright. Every muscle ached, his whole body felt broken and he winced in pain as he tried to unbutton the top section of his uniform. Da-Ee could see him struggling so she brushed his fingers aside and continued unbuttoning his uniform. She slid the sleeves down over his muscular arms, being careful not to hurt him.

"Stand up." she commanded and then proceeded to slide the remainder of his uniform down his body. Bull couldn't help but smile at how sensual it felt to have Da-

Ee undress him. Da-Ee caught the look on his broken face and piped up "Don't get too used to me tending to you. will you? It's just that men are so useless when they have any pain, they can't do anything for themselves!"

Bull tried to wipe the smile off his face, but seeing this tiny person telling him about men being unable to cope with pain was too much. Da-Ee glared at him and he sat back on the edge of the bed as she pulled the old uniform off before edging the new one onto his body.

Bull watched her as she carefully pulled the clean uniform on over his legs, smoothing out the fabric as she went. He stood up again to get the uniform on his upper torso; as soon as Da-Ee struggled to reach his upper body he sat back down again to help her out. Co-operating in this way he soon looked a little less battle worn. She pressed the captain's stripes onto his uniform having taken them off the old one and stepped back to look at him. Satisfied that he looked half decent she bade him lie back again so she could re apply the cold crystals to reduce the swelling. Bull allowed her to do the nursing, enjoying the attention she was giving him, but she wasn't Star.

Chapter 8

Eludium

Nobody could find the captain for days. Only Argo knew where he was, but Argo wasn't sharing that with anyone. He needed space and time to recover. Star spoke to the fleet commander about how she had heard about the longevity of the people on this planet and how odd it seemed that they never cried. Argo told her to keep it to herself for a while until he could find out more.

She asked if he knew how Bull was and Argo simply told her that he would soon be back to normal but that he thought it best to keep out of his way for a while. Star nodded and made her way back towards Lin and Gale, with whom she had been sharing a tent since the confrontation with Finch. She had kept out of his way since the fracas, unsure whether she could hold her tongue or not. In fact, she hadn't seen him since it happened. Maybe he had a right to feel betrayed, but laying into Bull was not the way to go about it!

***

Chu and Queen Laifa shared a drink outside his hut, chatting about her fallen planet and what it had been like. A few other Scenarians sat with them, talking about their homes and the people they had lost.

Chu seemed genuinely interested in what they had to say.

Argo observed the calmness and order around the people. Everyone seemed to be getting along together very well, he could sense that Chu was going to offer the Scenarians permanent refuge here on Gley. It was just a matter of time.

He pondered how that would work out, the two species being from such different points in their evolution and technology. Would the Scenarians force their lifestyle on these people? Or would they be prepared to take a step back and adapt their lifestyle to suit the Coserai? How did the Coserai feel about the differences, did it matter to them? Argo had a feeling that either way, things would pan out all right in the end.

***

Ursu and Genai were scanning some of the rock samples they had picked up on Gley, having set up a temporary workstation under the shade of a Goonai tree. The broad leaves made perfect cover from the hot sun during the day. Genai seemed overly excited about something she had found on the sample, so Argo headed towards her.

"Found something interesting ladies?" Argo smiled mildly at them as they were checking their sample over and over to make sure of something. Ursu looked up at him, excitedly and spoke with great enthusiasm about what they had found.

"Oh, Commander, it's fascinating! We checked all these different samples from Gley, the rocks, the plants and even the nasty drink the men have, and they all have it! It's wonderful, they all contain traces of Eludium, in varying degrees of course!"

Argo searched his inner database for the information he required, Eludium? His database ran through, then there it was, the answer. A recently discovered agent that prolongs life and promotes energy, found only in remote locations in the universe, It was always thought it was a mythical substance, but a scientist called Zen Eloud discovered its existence in a cave dwelling used by a holy sector of monks in the Andromeda galaxy years ago. The monks all lived for hundreds of years and were unscathed by illnesses and disease, despite living in harsh conditions.

Argo realised the implications of what he was hearing! This was why the Coserai lived such long and happy lives! If other species knew this, the planet would be a magnet for all sorts of invaders! He took the girls aside and pointed out the implications of what they were saying.

"So you're saying we've got to keep it a secret? From everybody?" Genai looked at Argo with great disappointment in her eyes. Their greatest discovery and they would have to keep it secret!

"That sucks!" Ursu added, with less refinement. Argo smiled, but he felt that they could be trusted to keep it to themselves, for now at least!

***

"Ah, Argo, there you are! I was wanting a word with you." Queen Laifa came towards him with Farsifa in tow, both looking very excited. He knew what was coming. As he had thought, Chu had indeed offered the Scenarians refuge here on Gley for as long as they wanted it, the only condition being that the Scenarians help the Coserai learn about their building technology.

Argo was surprised at that; only their building technology? Well, that was a small price to pay that was for sure. Argo followed the queen as they headed towards the elder to form a plan as to how the transition would take place, what they would need and what the robot army could provide.

***

After a few more days of recovery, Da-Ee woke Bull up with a cup of coffee, smiling at the sight of his less swollen face, his injuries had healed well with Da-Ee's salve.

Bull smiled at her, he couldn't have coped without her help and patience over the last few days and they had grown closer, both feeling a little isolated from the others. Sharing a bed with her was comforting—they had not made love—but she had tended him when he needed comfort and asked for nothing in return. They both took comfort in each other's presence.

"Are you ready to face the world yet?" Da-Ee asked, almost in a whisper as she lay beside him as he sipped his coffee. He looked at her and felt a warmth fill his whole being. Yes, he had felt the energy flow back into his bones and he was ready to take on what life had to dish out to him again. In fact, he felt better than he'd done for the past few years!

***

The comms board in the room buzzed and Bull answered the call. It was Argo's face looking over at him on the screen. Bull sat upright.

"Ah, Bull! I see you're alive then. How are we feeling today? Ready for some good news?" Argo beamed at him. Good news Bull could do with.

"Yes, Commander, fit and well, ready for anything. What is the news?"

Argo related to him the news of Chu's offer to the

Scenarians and Bull felt the weight of the world lift off his shoulders. He hadn't realised how much the responsibility for the people had weighed on him.

"That is welcome news indeed, Commander!" Bull replied. "I take it we are meeting to discuss the details?"

"Yes. I'll be on board in half an hour. I hope that gives you enough time..." Argo smiled coyly at him.

Bull realised how it must look to Argo, seeing him in bed, half naked with Da-Ee beside him. He began to splutter a defence, but Argo had disappeared from the screen before he had a chance! Da-Ee looked at him and spoke.

"Embarrassed are we, Captain?" she pulled the bedclothes off him and he was unsure what she was going to do, but she leapt out of bed and turned on the shower for him.

"Well, you heard the commander! You'd better get ready!" She flounced over to her clothes and picked them up off the floor and left the room, still undressed! Bull hoped nobody was about to see her emerging from his room in that state!

***

Transition

At the end of the week the Starfinder was preparing to set off again from Gley, leaving behind the Scenarian people to start their new life on their new planet. Argo had promised Queen Laifa that they would return with the remainder of the Scenarians once they had located them on Versa, where the prince had taken the other refugees.

The fleet had left behind a dome construction which

would begin the process of creating the materials needed for building homes for the Scenarians, along with any other items needed for their survival. A skeleton crew of Mechs, Blues and Bronzes were left behind to get things started and to operate the dome site. The Starfinder felt very empty again now that it was devoid of the thousands of Scenarian refugees.

***

The captain kept to the bridge as much as possible to avoid running into Star, and he had not seen Finch since the fight. Argo had told him that he had been spending time in the brig and suffered a demotion for his assault. It was better that he kept away from Finch , it would give him time to cool off he thought. Bull looked reasonably normal now, only a faint yellowing around his eye was visible from the fight and his cut lip had completely healed with the salve Da-Ee had used on him.

Meera and Kian, both working on the bridge as well, had not mentioned his injury, much to Bull's relief and he hoped that nobody else knew of the fight Finch and he had had.

Argo had told him that although Finch had been sent to the brig for the assault there didn't seem to be any gossip aboard ship about it, so perhaps nobody else got to hear of the fight. He certainly hoped so. Bull couldn't help but feel sorry for Finch's incarceration, but he thought it best to stay away from him for the time being.

***

Kios helped Argo plot his route—having more experience of space travel than he—and Argo had welcomed his co operation. Soon they had left Gley far behind, passing other distant planets and moons very soon after. The newly boosted engines made life much easier now.

"What do you think happened to the captain?" Meera whispered across to Kian at his console.

"Dunno, I guess he could have been in a fight ? But with whom I have no idea, do you? " Kian asked quietly. Meera shook her head and continued with her monitoring on her console.

Bull saw out of the corner of his eye the slight movement between them and he sighed heavily at the thought of being the object of their gossip. He really felt he needed to keep his feelings to himself in future.

***

After a few days had lapsed, Argo went to speak to Finch about the incident. Finch was still unable to understand how Bull had behaved with Star, considering they had been friends for so long. He asked Argo how he could reconcile that. Argo thought before answering, wondering how much he should reveal.

"What if you fell in love with Meera? What would you do? Kian is a friend of yours, is he not? Would you act upon your feelings?"

Finch dismissed the idea. "Of course not, he's a friend!"

"But what would you do if your feelings for Meera grew and grew each day, making the sight of her too painful to bear, seeing her daily with your friend, wishing you were him, unable to shake your feelings for her, no matter how hard you tried?... What would you do then?"

Argo looked at Finch and watched the anger dissipate slightly from his visage, being replaced with confusion and debate. He thought long and hard about it and could see how it would be difficult for Bull and he knew how much Star loved him; he had no need to be jealous of Bull. Star had told him repeatedly that nothing had happened , so maybe he owed Bull an apology?

Days later Finch was finding out the effects of having been demoted to a lower rank in the security team, he was replaced by Star!

***

After a few days out of the brig, Finch tried to hold Star before she prepared to dress in her uniform, but she flinched at his touch, still angry at his fight with Bull.

"Are you ever going to forgive me?" Finch spoke softly to her, wishing that he could hold her again in his arms. She had given him the cold shoulder for days now, turning her back to him in bed each night.

Star turned to look at him and saw the hurt in his eyes, she quickly looked away or she would melt into his arms and she felt he needed to think about what he had done.

"Give it time, perhaps." Star answered quietly as she buttoned up her jacket with her back to him as he lay on the bed behind her. She reached for her weapons belt and looked at him briefly before exiting the bedroom.

Finch thought about his actions and how Star had told him that nothing happened, just as Bull had said. Perhaps he did overreact, but he couldn't bear the thought of Star being with anyone else, especially not Bull, their friend. Friend, he thought about his friendship with Bull over the years, all the things they had done together. They had grown up together, defended each other from danger, laughed and played together as children, and now, it was ruined. He held his head in his hands and thought about how different things were now.

Finch had decided what he was going to do as he showered, he would go and see Bull, apologise. At least it would be a start.

***

Bull finished his coffee as he pored over the ship's data log. He heard the bridge beamer door whoosh open and turned his head expecting to see Argo enter. His heart missed a beat as he saw Finch standing there, looking over at him.

"This is not the place.." Bull began as Finch came closer to him, but Finch interrupted what he was saying.

"Can we go somewhere to talk, Captain?" Finch addressed Bull calmly.

Meera and Kian looked at each other then back at the two men, so it was Finch they both realised from Bull's reaction. Bull paused a second before answering, weighing up how calm Finch seemed.

"Sure, let's go to my office." Bull pointed at the doorway to the room next to the bridge. He led the way and waited for Finch to close the door behind them. He turned to face Bull, whose eyes locked on his without shame or fear.

"What did you want?" Bull managed to ask softly, looking at his old friend in the eye, unwavering.

Finch held his gaze for a few seconds before looking away and mustering up the courage to speak.

"I think I owe you an apology." Finch began quietly, "It's been preying on my mind how hasty I was to believe ill of you." He breathed out slowly, waiting for Bull's reaction. Bull couldn't believe that Finch was prepared to believe nothing happened between Star and himself. *Had something happened? No not really.* He had wanted it to, but stopped himself in time before making a mistake. Bull felt guilty all the same.

"You don't need to apologise." Bull replied. "I guess I might have done the same in your position, but really, nothing did happen."

Finch turned to look him in the eye, gazing steadily at his old friend. "But you wanted it to, didn't you?"

Bull couldn't deny this, it was true. "But I will never act on my feelings for Star I will promise you this." Bull replied truthfully. He didn't intend to come between them again, not if it hurt people this much.

Finch's head was downcast, digesting the promise.

"I will hold you to it." Finch replied as he left the room. Bull looked in his wake, wondering if he could keep that promise. He hoped he had the strength to!

***

Gar-Too

"Cloak Argo!" Lin's voice spoke urgently to the commander. Argo did not hesitate this time and ordered the cloaking of the whole fleet. Bull was about to question the reason why when in front of him on his screen he saw hundreds of Sventhri ships appear out of nowhere! They had cloaked just in time! The winged ships seemed to be on a mission as they were headed at high speed through the quadrant, not dithering around looking to pounce on some unsuspecting traveller. Bull wondered where they were headed , but hoped they were not going anywhere near Versa. That they did not need!

The fleet held back while the Sventhri ships stormed their way through the sector, waiting until they were out of sight before continuing on their way. The less they had to deal with the pirates the better, especially when they were travelling in such large numbers.

Argo thanked Lin for the warning and told her how with her help they had avoided the pirates just in time.

Lin was pleased and told him also that she could feel a Scenarian presence not too far away, but wasn't sure where. Argo was puzzled at this because Versa was still a long way off. But Argo had faith in Lin's senses so he ordered the fleet to look out for anything unusual on their sensors as they travelled.

***

"What are we looking for, Commander?" Bull inquired as Argo went to exit the bridge.

"Well, it could be anything, I suppose, Lin can sense some Scenarians not too far away, but she's not sure where. Let's just keep an eye out for the unexpected, I'd say." Argo replied.

Bull ordered the crew on the bridge to be vigilant for any unexpected craft nearby.

All eyes were trained on their sensors but there was no sight of anything just yet. The fleet spread out to cover as much of the sector as possible as they travelled on at normal speed, not wanting to miss anything. Nothing was spotted until the next day when they came within sight of a planet and two moons on the horizon.

Lin became convinced that Scenarians were down on the planet so Argo ordered some of the fleet to orbit the planet to search for any signs of Scenarian shuttles.

Argo asked Kios what he knew about the planet.

"Well it used to be highly populated at one time but in the last decade something happened to cause the inhabitants to leave to live elsewhere, it's now totally uninhabited, but I can't recall the reason why, I'm sorry." Kios replied.

In short order, Argo heard one of the Silvers report back from their sweep of the planet's surface.

"Commander, There seem to be large cities on the planet's surface but I can see no signs of anyone living in them."

Argo asked the Silver if there were any life signs on the planet at all and the Silver replied that there were many, but looked to be animal life forms. Argo thanked the fleet investigators and asked them to await orders. He looked to Bull and debated what to do.

"Well, we could take a look, just in case someone's left behind. I would also love to know why the people left there in the first place. There's no harm in looking. Let's take some shuttles down there to the main cities, as there only seem to be three." Bull mulled over the possibilities. Around the cities were vast expanses of greenery, but the rest of the planet was either water or high mountains.

***

Bull and Argo took the security team and the medic with them with a couple of shuttles and met up with the Silvers already in orbit around the planet, which was apparently called Gar-Too. Argo gave the Silvers locations on the planet to search for any people that needed help and Bull's shuttles took the other main city area.

As they approached the city they were surprised at the size of it, to have been abandoned like that. It was immense, with tall skyscrapers, mono rails, stone dwellings that were ornately carved and huge commercial centres that had contained myriad shops and cafes, all now deserted. The road system had almost been reclaimed by some type of weed growing there and the same weed seemed to coat the lower few metres of all the buildings as well. It made Bull realise how quickly plant life had taken over with the lack of people to maintain the city.

They landed the two shuttles on top of a tall wide building at the city's centre. Argo, Finch and Star led the security team ahead of Bull and Guy as they entered the roof exit to get to the lower ground to explore. The air smelled dank and musky, a bit like seaweed, and green algae had started to coat the inner walls of the building , the team observed as they descended through the rooms and corridors below.

It was eerily abandoned, with furniture still left behind where it had stood for a decade. An observer could easily imagine the people working here, selling their goods and living a good life. The splendour of the buildings dictated a rich economy and the floors were covered in marble.

It must have cost a lot to import, thought Bull.

***

As they descended the stairs to the lower levels, the room furnishings were in more disarray, some tumbled onto their sides, others heaped in one corner of the rooms and the windows were all broken. Bull puzzled as to what had happened here.

On the third floor the weed covered parts of the interior of the building too, spread out like a vine, entangling itself in every crevice as it stretched its tendrils along. Bull had never seen a plant like it and neither, more worryingly, had Argo.

"What do you think happened here?" Bull asked Argo.

"I don't know , but it looks like everyone left in a hurry!" Argo replied sadly.

Star had stopped ahead, looking down at something in the corner of the room, her gun draped across her chest.

"What is it?" Finch asked urgently and he looked towards where Star was focused. He saw it, entangled amongst other rubble piled in the corner, half covered by the weed, a child's doll, caked in dirt.

Star looked at Finch and spluttered sadly. "Do you think they got away all right? From whatever they were running from? "

Finch felt her sadness and replied lovingly. "Yes, I'm sure they did, they just didn't have the room to take everything with them, that's all."

They moved on through the weed-strewn corridors and then outside to the street level. The whole group stared in wonder at the weed-strewn and rubble-filled street, where once thousands walked the pavements to work each day, living an ordinary life, families, old and young, where were they all now?

***

Search

The Silvers from the second shuttle spread out in one direction and Star's team in another. It was eerily quiet, so Bull decided if they were to try and find anyone they should call out every now and then to see if anyone answered. The main thoroughfare was littered with debris, vehicles strewn on their sides, rusting away, battered and torn, it looked like some giant had come along and kicked them about. They were enveloped in the weed, which seemed to be actively moving as they walked through it!

Suddenly Finch ran towards a shop entrance, gun pointing ahead of him, he waved the team to spread out, something was moving inside the doorway. Argo zoomed in on it but there was no good angle from where he stood to see what it was.

Something crashed inside the shop as a clanking noise was heard. The security team stopped and Finch called out. "Come out of the shop, we are here to help you, don't be afraid."

They stood still, awaiting a reply, but seconds passed and no reply was forthcoming.

Star called this time, perhaps whoever it was would be less afraid of a girl's voice. But again no reply came. The clanking was heard again. The security team rushed forward silently, stepping carefully over the debris and weed until they were in the front of the shop.

Suddenly something barged past them shrieking, scarpering out of the shop into the street! They trained their guns on the evading being, then lowered their weapons laughing in relief. It was a boar-like creature, probably scavenging for food. It ran out of sight down the street.

***

They walked on for over an hour searching for any signs of people, but none were to be found anywhere, at least on ground level. In front of them stood a grand building around five stories tall. It looked like a museum or library to Bull, with its wide steps leading up into a large arch shaped doorway. Its lower windows were all smashed in, but the upper level had beautiful stained glass windows in them, all intact. *Why would the people want to leave such a beautiful city?* thought Bull. *It doesn't make sense.*

***

The team stood in front of the grand building, surveying the split roadway beyond it, to either side, wondering which way to go. Argo hailed the Silvers to see if they had any luck where they were. All of them reported the same findings, abandoned ornate buildings, the lower halves covered in the weed and debris strewn along all the weed-covered roadways. They reported seeing a couple of wild animals, but no people.

Argo began to report back his information to the others when Bull stopped him abruptly, raising his arm urgently.

"Listen!" Bull hissed urgently. All the party stopped still and listened, thinking he had heard someone call.

"I don't hear anything.." Star began, then she too paused as she heard it. A loud booming noise was heard in the distance and it sounded as though it was getting closer.

Argo flew up into the air straight away to have a better view. Immediately he called out to the others "Run! Get to the upper floors of that building now! Hurry!" The urgency in his tone made the others do as he commanded without question and as they began to ascend the stairs two at a time. Argo told his other teams elsewhere what was happening so they could be out of danger too.

***

The group ran up the stairs as fast as they could; it was hard because some debris was strewn across parts of the stairs. Finch was trying to imagine what the noise could be, it reminded him of something, but he couldn't remember what.

As Bull ascended the second floor stairwell he passed one of the broken windows and he looked out to see what was coming, but he couldn't see beyond the buildings across the road: they needed to get higher. Star stumbled on the third floor stairwell and as Finch grabbed her urgently by the arm to help her forward, he remembered what the noise reminded him of: a waterfall!

On the fourth floor stairwell they looked out through the open window and what they saw turned their blood cold! A mountain of water was rushing its way towards them, like a gigantic tsunami bulldozing through the city, engulfing everything in its path! They ran upwards to the top floor and out onto the rooftop, where they met up with Argo, who had flown down to join them.

"I guess we now know why the city was abandoned!" Bull gasped as they watched the powerful wall of water approach. They had made it to the safety of the upper part of the building just in time, as the water engulfed the magnificent building, leaving only the upper floors exposed above water level. The road that they had travelled on only minutes before was now under several metres of water. Debris floated all around the buildings, wreckage of cars, old furnishings and road signs, all tied in with the strangling weed.

The poor unfortunate boar had been caught by the water and it struggled in vain to swim to higher ground. Before Star could comment on how she felt sorry for the boar Argo had flown off the rooftop and headed towards the struggling creature! The team watched spellbound as Argo swooped down towards the boar as it struggled amongst the debris and in one swift motion he scooped up the creature out of the water.

They watched as Argo flew out of sight with the boar in his arms, not even struggling, the boar seemed to sense Argo was helping him. A few minutes later Argo re-emerged, minus the boar. Star wondered if the boar had fallen out of his arms. They watched as Argo came in to land beside them and before they could ask about the boar Argo blurted out "I've found our Scenarians!"

Finch, Star and Bull looked dumbfounded at Argo, they weren't expecting to hear that!

***

Rescue

Argo told the others that he had flown over the city to deposit the boar on high ground at the mountains nearby, and on his flight there he spotted a group of people on top of one of the tall buildings, they were Scenarians. Argo thought that he would be best taking one of the humans with him in case the Scenarians were afraid of him if he landed on the rooftop alone.

"Well, which one of you would like to go with me?" Argo asked, smiling. They all knew that it would involve flying in Argo's arms so they looked at each other briefly before Bull, much to the relief of the others, volunteered.

Argo told him to hold on tight and Bull was lifted into the air effortlessly by Argo.

***

The sudden movement at first made Bull's stomach lurch and he feared he would throw up all over his commander, but thankfully, the feeling passed quickly. Bull peered warily around the tops of the buildings. They looked like little islands in a sea of green weed, nothing like a beautiful city any more. Then, in the distance he saw the Scenarians, huddled on their rooftop, all watching them coming towards them. As the duo approached the rooftop, the Scenarians grouped together against the roof exit, ready to bolt below for safety if need be. None appeared armed. One lay slouched on the floor, tended to by a colleague.

"It's all right!" Bull called out, trying to reassure them. "We're here to rescue you." In a few seconds Bull and Argo had landed on the rooftop a few metres away from them. They eyed the two with suspicion, then one of them moved forward, a Scenarian male who looked to be around thirty-ish.

"You're Argo, aren't you?" The male approached after recognising the AI.

"Why, yes I am," Argo smiled. "I'm sorry I don't recognise you. You must have seen me on Scenara a few years back?" The Scenarian nodded and came closer.

"Yes, I remember seeing you in the palace with the King and Queen. You do know that they are now dead, fallen with the domed city when our planet started to break apart?" The young man looked saddened at the mention of the demise of his planet.

The man came to his senses and stretched an arm out in greeting. "I'm sorry, where's my manners? My name is Kuthri and these are my fellow crewmen and women, we were all sent by Prince Cruza, who survived, to find a habitable planet for us to live on after Scenara's downfall."

Argo let him continue before giving him the good news.

"Several shuttles were sent to find somewhere for us to start over again. We were one of them, we landed here a few months ago and unfortunately we landed our shuttle at ground level, so when the waters came and took us by surprise we lost all our means of escape. The shuttle has been totally wrecked. We have barely been able to survive since then, scavenging for things to eat from people's apartments in the top floors of the buildings. The lower floors were all wrecked. Our friend has begun to suffer breathing problems because of the damp air. We have not seen a single being, apart from the wild animals, since we arrived."

Bull asked about the waters, how long they flood for and how frequent. Kuthri replied that they flood for around ten days at a time, slowly receding in that period. Whilst they had been on the planet the floods had come three times.

"So there's very little gap between floods." Bull calculated thoughtfully.

Argo began to speak. "Well, I have some good news for you, Kuthri. your Queen is alive and well and she is living on Gley, not too far away, along with a few thousand of your people that we rescued from your planet not so long ago." Kuthri looked in disbelief and the others rushed forward for news of their comrades and their planet. Argo told them about the Coserai and how they had offered the Scenarians refuge on their beautiful planet and that Queen Laifa had accepted.

"If only my brother were alive to hear that news." Kuthri smiled sadly, thinking about his only brother who had also been on a mission to find a habitable planet for them all. They had found the wreckage of his ship months earlier whilst on their travels to find refuge. "He was fond of the queen's lady in waiting, Farsifa, I think they would have eventually married had they been given the chance!"

Bull piped up happily "Is your brother called Kush by any chance?" When Kuthri's face lit up on hearing his brother's name Bull continued, "Well, he is also alive and well, as is Farsifa, she stayed with the queen. We picked up Kush and his rescuers a while back, he'd been saved from his escape pod by a ship on a scientific mission. He and Farsifa are together on Gley!"

The Scenarians were delighted at the news and craved more information on who had survived. Argo told them that they had a data file on board their ship that could tell them all the names of survivors picked up by the Starfinder, once safely on board they could access it.

"So would you like us to take you on board our ship?" Bull asked with a smile. Of course all nodded their heads willingly.

Bull looked to Argo as to how it could be done. He told them he would fly to retrieve one of the shuttles to get them on board and then collect the rest of their team at the library rooftop. It was easier to land here because the roof was flat and large enough, but to retrieve the others Argo would have to drop a ladder for them to climb up to the shuttle. Afterwards he would rescue the stranded Silvers where they awaited on another rooftop, using the second shuttle. Bull breathed a sigh of relief at not having to fly in Argo's arms again, once was enough!

Chapter 9

Versa bound.

The Scenarians ate a hearty meal on board the Starfinder and were shown to their rooms by Star, eager to have more people back on her corridor again. It had felt lonely since the others had left. The Scenarian with the breathing problems was tended to by Guy at the ship's med lab. He would soon recover after receiving treatment, Guy had reported. They all were provided with clothing and they refreshed themselves in their quarters before seeking out information about the other survivors on their room computers. The crew of the Su-i went to greet the newcomers and caught up with Kush's brother to give him updates on how he was rescued. The Su-K-Enry were also glad to have more company on board again.

***

"My uncle is alive!" one of Kuthri's colleagues ex-claimed as he scanned the database. "And my niece and nephew too! I thought they had all perished in the domed city!" Feyyr looked excitedly at Kuthri.

"That's excellent news, my friend!" Kuthri re-marked, slapping him cheerfully on the back, sharing his joy. Kuthri was glad that Feyyr was no longer alone, his friend's parents had died when he was small and he had been raised by his uncle and aunt.

As the remaining Scenarians looked through the database they were cheered by the numbers rescued by the Starfinder crew, but apart from the queen and Farsifa they saw no other familiar names amongst the survivors. They were grateful that so many had made it. Now they had good news to give Prince Cruza when they would be reunited with him at Versa. They wondered if any other shuttles found other planets willing to take them as refugees, but they would have to wait to find out.

***

Bull ended his long day with a welcome shower and thought about the planet they had just escaped from. What had caused the waters to flood like they did? Obviously at one time there was no problem with the waters, the evidence was there for all to see. The city had not been built in a day. People had lived on Gar-Too for hundreds of years by the age of some of the buildings. He puzzled as to the reason why it had suddenly happened.

He had heard of tsunami's happening when earthquakes occurred under the oceans, but not occurring as regularly as these tsunamis seemed to and besides, none of the on-board computers recognised any tremors on the planet. It was indeed a mystery. He decided he would talk to Argo about his theories in the morning.

***

"Need company?" a small voice was heard from his main living room. A head peered around the doorway of the shower room, brandishing two dark eyes, sparkling at him seductively.

"Hey." Bull smiled at Da-Ee as she entered the room, holding two glasses and a bottle of bubbly; it was the only human drink Da-Ee liked. Bull finished towelling his torso dry then took the bottle from her and opened it. He poured them both a drink and they headed into the bedroom. Da-Ee was just the tonic Bull needed, she helped him relax and he was glad of her company. For the first time they made love.

***

Finch lay in the bed and held the cover open for Star to enter; he was so relieved that she had finally forgiven him for the incident with Bull now that he'd apologised to him. It was so good to have her in his arms again and he relished every moment as they made love in the candle-lit room. He vowed not to let his jealousy get the better of him again. Star had missed his touch and couldn't imagine being without him. She felt safe in his arms.

***

"What do you think?" Ursu asked Guy as she handed the data over to him. Guy looked carefully at the figures in front of him, he shook his head in disbelief.

"This can't be right!" Guy argued, waving the data in front of him.

"But it is. We've checked and double checked it, believe me! Both of us couldn't believe it either when we found out!" Genai added .

Guy thought of the ramifications of this information, the possibilities were incredible, and they'd been sworn to secrecy! This was going to be hard.

"Who else knows about it?" Guy asked in frustration. Genai told him that only they, Kios, Da-Ee and Argo knew and Argo had insisted they keep it to themselves. Guy thought about his reasons and he supposed he could sort of understand them. If any outsiders came to know this information the people on the planet could be in danger. Guy wondered if this would have the same effect on the Scenarians living on Gley too. After a time, could it happen to anyone? Could they all live to hundreds of years? He could not get his head around the information.

***

In the morning Argo and Bull pondered over the flooding at Gar-Too, discussing the probable causes of the excessive floods.

"It seems almost as though the planet has shifted out of its normal orbit." Argo surmised, thinking about the layout of the planet in connection to the moons Iesta and Farso.

"What could cause such a thing?" asked Bull.

Argo replied that it could have been that the planet had received a great impact or a magnetic pull, which caused it to alter its axis. "Other causes could be earthquakes and tremors, shifting plates under the oceans. But we felt none when we were there, although it doesn't mean to say they don't exist." He added thoughtfully.

"But wouldn't there be evidence of a large crater somewhere on the planet's surface if it had suffered such an impact?" Bull wondered again.

"Not necessarily. If the impact had been in the oceanic region it would be hidden from sight." Argo continued. "To find out we need to deep scan the ocean floors and that would take up our time. I would think you would rather use the time to get us to Versa more quickly, am I correct?"

Bull reluctantly nodded but he had not finished with the thought. "If we did find a large crater, we would know the reason why it floods. If that were the case is there anything that can be done to put it back on its correct axis again?"

Argo pondered the possibility and thought carefully before answering.

"I would say that there are a couple of possible ways to try. One is to hit it with such force in the opposite vector to counteract the move, the other is to blast the planet at strategic points which will alter the axis back to its original tilt. Either way, the ideas are fraught with danger, it could bring about the destruction of the planet!" Argo looked at Bull with an intense gaze, giving him the impression that he was not willing to chance it.

Bull decided he would leave the ideas for another moment in time, he had more pressing things to do right now.

"Set for hyper speed 3 for Versa." Bull commanded Kios and he sat back in the control area, wondering if it could be done one day.

***

Versa

As the fleet exited the Apox gate they saw Versa directly ahead of them, with three moons of differing sizes surrounding it. The planet was fairly barren in appearance from outer space, sporting large desert areas interspersed with high mountain ranges and canyons to the northern hemisphere. A deep fissure ran diagonally across the equatorial region. There were greener areas in the southern hemisphere, with large lakes and oceans surrounding the land mass. The planet didn't seem to have any large cities dominating the land anywhere, the inhabited areas tended to be smaller and reasonably close together, no more than around seventy kilometers apart in places. There seemed to be no signs of dwellings in the desert areas, perhaps they were too inhospitable for people to live there.

***

The Blues scanned the terrain that was inhabited for signs of Prince Cruza's fleet and eventually were rewarded with a sighting of the ships in the lower hemisphere, a few kilometres from the nearest town. He reported the findings to the captain and Bull zoomed in on the settlement.

"That's odd, they seem to have erected some sort of barricade around their settlement." Bull saw. "It looks like they have to protect themselves from something." He added worriedly.

Argo came and stood next to him, looking at the large screen in front of them, which showed the fleet ships formed into concentric circles with the Scenarians living within the centre of the circle in some kind of tents. A large wooden barricade had been erected around the exterior of the circle, presumably with armed men guarding the settlement.

"It looks like they have experienced some trouble here." Argo surmised sadly. "See if you can contact the fleet and let them know of our intention to visit, then let's get down there and see what's going on."

The Blue sent a message down to the fleet and spoke to a secretary of the prince, letting them know of their intention to visit, carrying a message from their queen.

Argo and a team of Silvers went down in one shuttle and Bull, the security team and the Endari girls went in another. The girls were determined to get more samples from each planet they visited!

"What do you think they are protecting themselves from?" asked Star, looking at the tall wooden barricade encircling their camp as they flew above it.

"I hope it's not some gigantic monsters!" Finch laughed, checking his weapons.

Bull looked closely through the window area as they came to land a few metres from the camp. He could see no signs of wild animals from above as they had approached the settlement, but that didn't mean there weren't any!

"Well, we'll soon find out!" Bull remarked seriously. He checked his own weapon just to make sure. The Endari girls looked at each other nervously, but decided they'd be safe enough with Argo and all the crew armed as they were. They grabbed their equipment cases and prepared to disembark.

The pilot gave the all clear for the ramp to be lowered, there was nothing on his scanner to warrant their concern at the moment! The Blue would stay with the shuttle to guard it. As they descended the ramp they saw several guards posted along the barricade pointing their weapons towards them.

"Not exactly welcoming, us are they?" Ursu remarked nervously. Bull watched Argo and the Silvers exit their shuttle a few metres away from them, none looking concerned about the reception committee. As they arrived within a couple of metres of the barricade, a guard called out over the palisade.

"Who are you and what is your business here?"

Argo spoke first, asking to speak to Prince Cruza, that they had a message for him from his mother Queen Laifa.

"Queen Laifa is dead!" another guard called out in response. Argo was undeterred and demanded to speak to the prince and to say it was Argo, a friend of Captain Grey, that wished to speak to him. A hushed murmur went around the palisade on hearing Grey's name, then suddenly a young man of about twenty-nine, dressed in a commander's uniform, but with a royal sash over his left shoulder appeared at the palisade platform.

"I am Prince Cruza." declared the Scenarian, looking suspiciously at the party. "I hear one of you claims to be Argo." The prince looked from one to the other.

Argo stepped forward. "Greetings your majesty, I am Argo."

Prince Cruza looked at him carefully as he bowed then he spoke."I'm told you have a message from Queen Laifa, but my mother is dead!" He kept his look of suspicion whist awaiting Argo's reply.

Argo placed the hologram on the floor in front of him and there in front of them all stood the image of Queen Laifa, alive and well! She spoke her message to her son;

"My dear son, it is true, I am alive and well, thanks to Argo and his crew. I was riding with Farsifa away from the domed city when it fell, so I was saved from certain death. I was rescued from the burning surface of Scenara by Argo and his crew. There are around three thousand of us here on Gley, awaiting you all to join us in a new life on this beautiful planet. The Coserai are charming and very welcoming and they look forward to your arrival. I

miss you greatly. Please listen to Argo, he will answer all your questions. Until your return, fare well.."

Prince Cruza finally dropped the tough exterior, a tear escaping from his eye and now, he responded in a more welcoming tone.

"Forgive me. I had no idea the Queen was still alive! I am pleased to meet you finally Argo, please come in to our humble settlement. We have to be careful here these days." He indicated the gateway in the palisade to his right, as it began to open to allow the group admittance.

Inside the circle there seemed to be thousands upon thousands of Scenarians living under canvas mainly. They looked at Argo's group as they entered the settlement. Prince Cruza came down from the walkway at the top of the palisade, accompanied by two guards. He held out a hand in greeting, which Argo took courteously. Argo introduced his companions before Prince Cruza led them to a seating area around a large fire inside the central area of the camp. He invited them to sit with him to share news.

"So long have I been afraid that the Queen died on Scenara as the city fell.. We were so sure all had perished there, but to have missed rescuing her, how can that be? We saw the city fall. It was all so quick, we thought none could have survived!" The prince pictured the crumbling dome fall into the abyss , finding the thought disconcerting.

"The queen understands that you had no reason to believe her alive, Your Highness." Argo informed the bewildered prince.

"But I formed a rescue party when the planet began to deteriorate! We searched for survivors for days before leaving for Versa with all that we could fit on board our fleet! Yet I find I left my mother to perish? How could I have done that...?" The prince, shaking his head, could not fathom how he could not have seen her and was devastated that he had left her to die with the planet.

Argo reassured the prince that he had done all he could do in the circumstances at the time, he wasn't to know of his mother's whereabouts. Argo described how they had recovered more people a few months previously from the planet, people who had hidden in the mountains by the lakes, to try and stay ahead of the molten core. That was where he had found the queen along with Farsifa and some families, trying to evade the lava.

The prince looked saddened at the fate he had unknowingly bestowed the people left behind and was torn over his part in it. Argo reassured him that all were alive and well and living on the beautiful planet called Gley. They awaited the prince and his people to join them there. The Coserai people who inhabited the planet had welcomed their company.

At this news the prince finally smiled. "They have been welcomed, and it is a beautiful planet, you say? Well, that is indeed good news! Goodness knows we could do with some of that! None of the shuttles I sent out to find refuge have been able to find any and some shuttles have been lost completely! Life has been hard here, we've had to suffer many raids by bandits initially and a few of our people died. We were attacked by wild animals at night on several occasions, that's why we had to erect the wall to protect us."

Bull reassured the prince that Gley was a safe place for them to live as long as they kept away from the horrible drink the men had there! The prince laughed and didn't notice the look Finch and Star gave each other at the mention of the drink.

"Well, your coming is very welcome indeed. How would you like to come hunting with me? We will find a large beast to put on the spit and we shall have a feast before we leave."

Finch and Bull looked at each other, both thinking the same, a hunt sounded like fun! It would give them a chance to hone up their skills again with a bow and arrow. They missed those days out scavenging with their bows. A real spit roast sounded much better than the mass produced meals on board ship!

"We're in!" Finch and Bull both uttered at the same time, smiling at the thought of the hunt.

"How about you, hon'?" Finch asked Star who was sat next to him. She also missed using her bow hunting skills and agreed eagerly. The Endari weren't keen and preferred to look for samples of the local minerals and asked permission to stay in the camp, which the prince readily agreed.

The robots would stay with the Scenarians to help them prepare for their journey back to Gley .

***

The Hunt

Bull and Argo were talking amongst themselves about the organisation of the relocation of the Scenarians when a voice interrupted them.

"Argo? Is that you? .... It IS you! I can't believe it. We meet again old friend." The Scenarian hurried up through the throng to join them, smiling broadly and held out his hand to greet Argo. Argo looked at Glian and smiled.

"Glian! How wonderful to see you here, alive and well! Is your wife here with you?" Argo asked with great interest.

"Yes, Kisha is here, we both were picked up by the prince when Scenara was evacuated. She still grieves over the loss of her brother and the queen." Glian's face took on a tinge of sadness before Argo gave him the news.

"Yes, it is very sad about King Khali, falling with the domed city, but I do have some good news. We rescued Queen Laifa along with a few thousand Scenarians a few months back. They are alive and well, awaiting you all to join them on the planet Gley, which we just left. We promised them that we would find you and bring you to join them. The people of Gley, called the Coserai, are very welcoming and the planet is beautiful. We also have a small group of Scenarians we rescued recently from Gar-Too up on the Starfinder, they will be coming down here shortly to see you all."

Glian beamed at the news and said they must come and see Kicha later on. He said that he was attending the prince on a hunt in a moment.

"Ah! Some of my crew are going on the hunt too. This is the captain, Bull Carter.." Argo introduced Bull, who nodded smiling at Glian. "He will be going, along with two of our security crew, Star and Finch, who are eager to draw a bow again apparently!"

"Will you be joining us on the hunt?" Glian asked Argo. But Argo declined, saying that it would probably be more of a massacre if he went! The trio laughed at the thought.

***

The hunting party set off shortly after, on foot, armed with a variety of weapons, Bull, Star and Finch preferring to use their bows again. Even after all this travel through space the three ex scavengers had proudly brought with them their previous scavenging weapons, just in case that one day they would be useful. Today was such a day! Some of Glian's group sported a range of spears and knives, the prince and a couple of his guards carried guns, straddled over their shoulders.

"With this array of weapons we should be sure of plenty of food for the feast tonight!" laughed Bull. Finch and Star agreed and wondered what kind of game they were hunting.

"A roast pig would hit the spot just right!" Finch drooled at the thought.

"Mmm, yes! Succulent pork, and crackling!" Bull enthused dreaming of the pig cooking over the spit.

"Hey, stop it, you two; you're making me hungry!" Star moaned light-heartedly. It was good to be friends again. They all hoped it would last.

***

Glian walked alongside the trio and spoke to them as they walked along, headed for some groups of trees in the distance.

"Well, there are wild boar here, that's for sure, and yes, they are delicious! We have caught some Dradnai in the past, they also have a certain appeal cooked on a spit."

"Dradnai? What are they?" Star asked.

"A native species, they roam in the wooded areas quite often, they are smaller than the pigs, about the size of a cat! They are scaly creatures with a feathered tail, they usually travel in groups, so a few of them can usually be counted on to grace our tables. Be warned though, they travel quite fast!" Glian replied.

"Are there any dangerous animals to beware of?" Finch inquired.

Glian replied that there were some wild cats and large furry animals that walk on two feet, but run on all fours, they have vicious claws and teeth and are twice the height of a Scenarian. They had attacked the settlement a few times when they first arrived here, hence the barricade . They had killed a few of Glian's people in attacks.

"They mostly travel at night, preferring to sleep in the day," Glian recounted. "The Versans call them Berei."

"I hope we don't encounter any of those!" Star retorted, grimacing at the thought.

Glian assured her that it was unlikely during the daytime.

***

They entered the wood from two angles, the prince's group worked their way forward from the left hand side and the others came from the right. They walked carefully over the low scrub, listening for sounds of movement. The wind was coming towards them so there was no danger of the animals latching onto their scent. The sound of a stream could be heard not far off. A watering hole was usually a good place to catch game thought Star, so they slowly headed that way.

The scavengers all had their bows drawn ready for any movement, but soon they heard the sound of a knife being lobbed through the air on the left flank. It was followed by a low squeal and a thunk as something fell ahead of the other crew. *Someone had caught an unsuspecting Dradnai,* thought Star.

Suddenly the ground was rustling furiously with animals running in all directions trying to get away from the hunters. Star unleashed her bow quickly and was rewarded with a second Dradnai for the feast.

Finch unleashed two arrows in quick succession and narrowly missed killing one, then had success with his second arrow. Bull managed to spear two Dradnai with the same arrow much to his surprise, but he pretended to Finch it was intended!

***

Very soon the remaining Dradnai had dispersed out of sight and all was quiet again. After retrieving their kill, the hunters continued forward slowly, right through the wooded area. Beyond, were open fields with low bushes scattered randomly. The river ran along the right side of the group, a few metres away. A few trees gave shelter now and then as they travelled on over the rough and bumpy terrain.

Bull spotted faint movement in the long grass ahead, he indicated to the others where he had seen the movement and all their eyes trained in that direction. They all heard snuffling and snorting softly emanating from the field and scrub ahead. A pig! They watched the movement of the grass and realised there was more than one. Bull saw that the prince's rifle was trained on the movement of one and Bull decided to focus on the other. All together Bull let his arrow loose at the same time as the prince fired his shot. The movement stopped.

The group walked over to the fallen prey, two wild boar caught cleanly, one shot by the prince and the other by Bull's arrow. They helped each other lift the carcasses onto the hoverboard, placing them next to the Dradnai.

Bull retrieved his arrow and cleaned it on the grass. They calculated that they would still need more to feed the whole fleet so they continued the hunt.

***

The terrain was becoming more difficult the further they went, with lots of craggy outcrops separating boggy scrubland. The ground underfoot was very wet, so they decided that the two groups should separate and meet back in a couple of hours.

They travelled quietly for half an hour looking for signs of movement but there was no sign because since the prince had fired his shot all the animals had retreated somewhere. Star wondered if any of them had retreated into the long grass further on, so she climbed up onto one of the tall rocky outcrops to look out over the fields full of the swaying long grass to see if she could spot any animals. Bull, Glian and Finch waited at the base of the rocks for the verdict. Star cupped her eyes to prevent the sun's glare blinding her view. She looked all around, taking a panoramic view of the terrain for miles in every direction.

Star saw the prince's group heading back towards the stream in the distance, but she couldn't see any signs of animals near them. She was about to look in another direction when suddenly something caught her eye! A head peered just above the long grass not far from the prince's group. It was behind them, stalking them! What was it? She strained her eyes to see, but it was very hard with the sunlight, but suddenly she caught a better glimpse! It was a predator, a big cat of some sort!

There was no time to warn the prince, they would not hear her call, the wind was in the wrong direction!

Star had to do something! She drew her bow and tracked the cat's movement through the grass, but it was very well camouflaged. She cursed and waited for it to spring out after its prey. In a few moments she was rewarded with the cat's leap into action. It was so fast! She had to get it right! There would be no room for error, somebody's life depended on it! Deep in concentration she let the arrow loose.

***

Bull and Finch watched her from the ground, bewildered by what was going on. Glian remarked that she must have seen her prey and gone for it, but Bull and Finch weren't sure, something was not right. The arrow sang on its path towards the prince's group. The prince turned his head and saw the arrow head straight for him! He didn't have time to react and he prepared to die. In a flash a large cat sprung in front of the prince, about to maul him when it was hit by the arrow! It fell in mid air to its death, struck in the head by the arrow Star had shot. Star released the breath she had held.

The prince could only stare in surprise and then relief, before praising Star's skill in saving his life. His bodyguards looked highly embarrassed, not to have seen the danger for themselves. The parties spent another hour hunting until they had caught enough wild boar to feed the thousands back at the camp, so they set back with their catch, heaving on the hoverboards.

***

The feast

Back at the camp the Scenarians cheered as they saw the large cat surrounded by pigs and Dradnai on the hoverboards approaching with the hunting party. It would seem the feast was on! The fires were well under way, ready for the spits. They had been bolstered up for hours to get to the right heat. Several people carried the kill over to prepare them for cooking and some people came over to the prince and his hunting party to give them drinks to refresh them after their outing.

***

Star had enjoyed her exercise and it felt good to know that her skills with the bow had not diminished. The prince had personally thanked her for saving his life and the prince's guards suffered humiliation at not seeing the danger themselves. But Star reassured them, stating that they would not have seen it coming through the long grass. It was only visible from above, where she stood.

When the group sat down to rest by the fires, drinking their refreshing juice, the Endari girls came over to see how they had got on. When Finch and Bull told them about Star's part in saving the prince's life they were impressed by Star's prowess with her bow. They wanted to know what each person had killed down to the very last detail! The men made sure to embellish the story to impress the girls further as they seemed so easily swayed by acts of courage!

Star simply smiled sweetly as the story got bigger and bigger. Star couldn't believe how gullible the girls seemed to be.

Star asked the girls what they had been doing whilst the hunt was going on and Ursu told her about the rock samples that they had collected to take back to the lab on board the ship later on. Genai said that the rocks didn't seem to display any particularly interesting properties as far as the eye could see, but it could be a different story under close scrutiny, she reckoned.

Bull managed to keep a straight face, he didn't give much credence to the idea that rocks might save the world one day!

Argo came over to the crew and congratulated Star after hearing of her skill with a bow saving the prince's life. All the Scenarians were talking about it so Argo reckoned. Star was getting a bit embarrassed with all the attention and she was now wishing that everyone would stop talking about it. Their rescued Scenarians from Gar-Too had rejoined their fellow companions here on the planet and the Prince was relieved to find them alive and well. They found friends that they thought had perished here on Versa, so they were greatly relieved as well.

***

As the night drew in and the torches were lit all around the camp, the mood turned to celebration as the Scenarians and their new companions gathered around the central fires where the meat was roasted to perfection. The barbecued aroma of spit roast meat filled the air and made everyone hungry! Servers carved the meat and arranged it on large platters on tables next to the roasts for everyone to help themselves. The guards on the palisades were taken plates of meat also while they guarded the perimeter, no one was going to miss out on the feast.

Some of the Scenarian women had prepared some fruit and roasted some vegetables also and they were piled high on plates around the tables for all to savour. The sweet smell of the roasted food filled the air as people danced and played instruments in the clearing next to the chairs. Several Scenarians danced happily, their bellies full of wonderful food. They had plenty to eat here on Versa, if only the natives had been friendlier they might have been happy to stay here. But, with the animal attacks and the early raids by bandits spoiling their sense of security they were happy to be moving to Gley in the morning.

***

The prince talked to Argo briefly during the evening, to let him know that, despite the faint hostility of the natives at the start of their stay, he wished to go and see the Versan chief before leaving the planet in the morning to thank him for letting them take refuge here. He felt it was only common courtesy after all. Argo said that he would accompany him if he liked and the prince welcomed the idea.

Halfway through the evening celebrations the prince's aide called for a few moments silence for the prince to speak. Everyone sat and awaited his announcement.

The prince thanked his people for being patient and supportive during their exit from Scenara. He praised them for their endurance and tenacity in the face of adversity and he promised them a better life once they were accepted on Gley. The people cheered at that thought. When the cheers had died down he raised a glass in toast for their fallen comrades, who would be remembered in all their hearts no matter where they were to live. When the toast was complete he asked for their patience once more as he had one more thing to do. All eyes were on the prince, wondering what he had to say. He stood in front of them and spoke.

"We have much to thank our new friends for. Captain Grey helped our people in time of need and Argo here has helped our people again when we needed aid," cheers went through the crowd at their mention, then the prince continued, "Today I personally have received the greatest help one could ask for, my own life was saved by one of Argo's crew..." A loud cheer went out again from the crowd as Prince Cruza asked Star to come forward. Highly embarrassed, Star got up from her seat and approached the prince. He turned to his aide, who had a wrapped gift to pass to the prince.

"Star, I am forever in you debt, as a token of my gratitude I would like to present you with a gift so that you may remember the day you saved a prince!" Prince Cruza passed the wrapped gift to Star and asked her to open it. Star was trembling with nervousness as she opened the wrapping carefully. All eyes were on her and the silence was tangible as she held her gift for all to see. A shining, beautifully engraved metal bow, very light and well balanced and on the metal a message was engraved on it *"To a shining star who saved a prince."*

The crowd stood and cheered enthusiastically as Star held her beautiful gift. She was humbled by the thought and muttered her thanks to the prince in embarrassment. She had never owned such a beautiful thing in her life, a tear welled up in her eye as she saw the gratitude of the people. Thankfully the music started up again at the prince's signal and a few people got up to dance again. Star bowed to the prince as she went back to Finch, overwhelmed by the generosity of these people.

Just as Finch was about to congratulate her an enormous roar filled the night. All the music and singing stopped immediately and the Scenarian soldiers all piled onto the palisade, weapons in hand.

"What's going on?" Finch muttered, looking towards the palisade. The roars intensified and seemed to surround them from all sides.

"I think the smell of the meat has attracted the Berei out of their sleep!" Star spoke as she rushed to the nearest stairway onto the palisade, new bow and quiver in hand. Bull and Finch rushed after her, grabbing their own bows that they had used during the hunt.

Below the exterior of the palisade was a sight to frighten anyone! The settlement was surrounded by scores of Berei, standing on two legs, stretching their clawed arms upwards to try and gain purchase on the palisade to pull at it. Their claws ripped into the wooden structure as they roared and snarled.

"They look hungry!" Finch remarked with eyebrows raised.

"No kidding!" Bull replied. "Shall we feed them?" He retorted jokingly.

An arrow whizzed past their visage as Star began her attack on the Berei. Not to be outdone, Bull and Finch launched their arrows one after the other in succession, each finding its target. The Scenarians threw spears at the Berei and some fell in their wake. Yet more Berei seemed to be running on all fours towards them from the woodland beyond, where they had hunted only hours before.

Argo watched with interest as his crew and the Scenarians were gaining ground on the animal onslaught. Bull saw him out of the corner of his eye just leaning on the top of the palisade watching the Berei fall!

"Are you enjoying yourself?" asked Bull sarcastically. "You sure you wouldn't like to help anytime soon?"

Argo continued leaning on the palisade looking down at the animals' death throes, shook his head and replied. "No, I think you're doing fine by yourselves, keep up the good work!"

Star smiled and shot another arrow into her tenth victim as Bull briefly digested what Argo had said. Bull then continued the attack, along with the Scenarian guards, the prince launching his own arrows a few metres further along the palisade. The companions thought it wouldn't seem fair somehow to use their guns to shoot these hungry bears down, so the guns stayed in their uniform holsters the whole time! It was much more of a challenge to use their bows and spears.

It took just over twenty minutes before the remaining Berei thought to retreat and give up on the attack. So many Berei lay dead at the circumference of the camp it was going to be interesting dealing with the bodies. The prince had an idea to take the kill over as gifts to the chief of Versa when he went to see him in the morning, then they could have their own feast to celebrate them leaving! That should cheer them up, thought the prince.

Chapter 10

Return to Gley

The Versan chief had indeed welcomed the gifts of the kill from Prince Cruza and thanked him graciously for coming to tell him of their departure. The prince got the impression that they were glad to see them go despite the chief's civility.

As the prince and his entourage left the settlement they observed the armed guards on the battlements around the chief's own settlement too. It seemed they had their own share of animal attacks here as well, yet they did not warn the Scenarians of this when they arrived on Versa!

***

It had not taken long for the Scenarians to pack their camp up with the help of the robots and their hover carriers and very soon all that was left of the camp was the sturdy palisade.

As the Scenarian fleet left the planet, the prince looked down upon it from space with a sense of relief, feeling his people would finally be at rest in their new home on Gley. They followed the robot fleet easily through space, passing the mysterious planet Gar-Too, where the seven other Scenarians had been rescued before.

On the return journey they were glad to see no sign

of the Sventhri pirates ships.

Bull wondered where the pirates had headed and hoped it was nowhere near where they were going! The journey was uneventful for a change and Ursu and Genai spent most of their time studying their rock samples in the lab, noting their properties and conducting experiments with the minerals found in the rocks.

Da-Ee spent more time with Bull, which he enjoyed. It helped him in terms of distracting him from his feelings for Star, although those feelings had not diminished. He learnt to control his feelings for her much better now that he spent time with Da-Ee.

The journey came to an end and Gley was finally in sight! The Scenarians were very excited at the thought of becoming reunited with their people once more. Kuthri couldn't wait to see his brother Kush and Feyyr was looking forward to seeing his remaining family at last.

The security team along with Argo headed towards their shuttle to go down to the planet. Bull had invited Gale and Lin to join them to give them a few hours respite from the spaceship for a change. Both were excited to be heading onto a planet.

They met up with Guy at the shuttle deck, who asked if he could join them as he would like to take samples of their dietary range. Argo agreed and they all set off, following the Scenarian fleet to land on the planet not too far from Chu's village.

***

Chu watched in awe as the large fleet came in to land on his planet. He had never before seen so many ships together. He looked towards Queen Laifa and smiled.

"Are these all your people, Your Highness?"

The queen replied that they were all that were left and that her son, the prince was amongst them.

"I shall be happy to meet your son." Chu responded, taking her by the arm to head for the landed fleet.

***

Queen Laifa's people rushed towards the fleet, eager to see loved ones again. As the ships' doors unfolded, the Scenarians were surrounded by cheering crowds as they descended the ramps onto Gley. Argo stood on the ramp looking at the displays of affection in front of him everywhere. He saw the prince rush towards his mother and embrace her tightly before bowing in front of her. He watched as Chu was introduced to the prince and Argo sensed that indeed they seemed genuinely happy to receive the Scenarians on their planet. Lin looked up at Argo and remarked at how happy the people all seemed to be.

Argo took a look towards the Scenarian settlement and saw the new dwellings that had begun to shoot up everywhere. It seemed the robots they had left behind had been working very hard using their cloning machine to create the materials required. He decided he would go down to have a look at them properly later.

The rest of his crew mingled among the crowd, greeting the people they remembered from last time. Guy started collecting samples of berries and fruits off trees nearby and began to compile a range of samples to study.

Soon Argo was approaching the prince and the queen, who were happily exchanging news in the company of Chu and his wife.

"Argo! Thank you so much for all that you have

done!" The queen beamed ecstatically at him. "We are indeed in your debt. Whenever your planet needs our help we will gladly give it!" The prince confirmed what his mother had said and shook his hand enthusiastically.

Argo thought of the mission Grey had given him, to find new technologies and allies for Earth in times of need. He realised that he had gone a long way to do this, with the cloaking device and with the revelation that Gley had produce that promoted longevity and happiness. He felt great relief that things were going well at last, with the Scenarians and the Su-K-Enry as possible new allies for Earth. Here, a hundred and seventy-five thousand more Scenarians stood on their new found home, a worthy planet for a remarkable people. He hoped when he returned the Su-i crew to Su-k-en there may be another alliance to be made there too? He smiled at the thought that Grey would be pleased to hear of their progress.

***

Gale and Lin wandered among the people and got caught up in their excitement. Everyone here seemed so happy to see them. One of the Coserai women approached the two, handing them some juice and a few snacks then went on to give some to others nearby. Gale sipped her drink and found it to be pleasant then she tried a few snacks and was impressed by how good they tasted.

The two sat beside a crowd which had gathered near the new Scenarian settlement's community hall. Banners of welcome adorned the trees around the parkland in front of the hall, which the Scenarians had created. Beautiful flower beds had been tended in a crescent shape, surrounded by benches formed into a wide circle. Solar lights had been erected around the perimeter of the parkland so that the Scenarians could enjoy the warm evenings outside as well as inside their hall. A walkway ran, edged by lights right up to the lake's edge, where the Scenarians had begun to build an impressive new jetty for the Coserai's boats.

The landscape had advanced greatly since their first arrival and had begun to take on a skeletal shape of a young town, with walkways joining the properties that had been built to either side of the parkland. The community hall stood in the centre between the housing thus far. A beautiful fountain had been created in the centre of the parkland, decorated with intricate patterns made from local stones in various colours. The Coserai had admired it greatly and they had asked the Scenarians if they could create one like it in the centre of Chu's village. Of course, they had agreed, as also they had agreed to create a new home for Chu's family , similar in the style of the Scenarian constructions, as he'd requested. Chu was very impressed with his new home and he decided that soon all his people would have homes like it if they so desired.

Argo inspected the nearest Scenarian property and found it well built and spacious. He was proud of the skills of his robot army.

Lin came up to him and stood beside him. She looked up at him, looking straight into his eyes. Her thoughts transferred into his. "This is a special place isn't it? It can help our people on Earth too."

Argo puzzled at what she meant and before he could ask her she replied. "Here is the means to end all illness and unhappiness in people's lives." Argo looked at her, wondering if she meant what he himself had suspected. Lin smiled and spoke once more before walking back to her mother. "Yes."

***

Science

Argo mused over the possibilities after hearing Lin's thoughts. Of course, Guy had asked for the samples, so he had suspected it too. Then there were the Endari girls and their discovery of Eludium, so things were moving on and Argo was content. He headed for the dome, to inspect the robots' progress with the re-building, but when he walked in he was surprised to find several Scenarians working there among the Blues.

He watched as they operated the machinery and fussed over controls on the myriad computers there, conferring with the Blues as though colleagues working together! A Blue spotted him and walked over to greet him.

"Commander, greetings! We have found lots of enthusiastic scientists and technicians amongst the Scenarians, eager to work for their community. They have taken to this work with full understanding! They are much more advanced in technology than we thought, they have even produced their own additions to our machinery, enabling us to produce goods at an advanced rate! It would be of my opinion that they are perfectly capable of running the dome without the Blues entirely, Commander!"

Argo smiled and saw that it was indeed true, everyone was fully occupied and involved in the process. Argo was impressed and left the building. Outside he met up with Bull, who seemed to be on his way inside the dome.

"Bull ? Were you looking for me?" Argo asked.

"No, Commander, actually I was going to see some of the scientists working inside the dome." Bull replied.

"Oh? And why would that be?" Argo inquired, intrigued.

Bull replied that he had asked Queen Laifa and the prince if there were any scientists amongst the people that had survived and he had found there to be several, of a variety of different disciplines. He told Argo what he had planned to do and that he was going to arrange a meeting with them as soon as possible.

Argo was impressed that Bull was aiming to attempt such a difficult plan and gave him his full support.

***

After all the greetings had been made, several hours later, the Scenarians had organised a party for everyone, with the Coserai as guests of honour at the parkland and community hall. Refreshments were laid on and music and dancing was to be on the agenda for the evening.

Star and Finch stood on duty in the parkland, sipping their drinks, watching all the action, everyone had a smile on their face.

"I guess we're a bit superfluous!" Star remarked, touching her gun lightly at her hip. "It doesn't look like there's going to be any trouble here, everyone's so happy!" Finch nodded, looking around at the people enjoying their reunion.

"Well, wait 'till the booze gets going! Then it might be a different story!" Finch laughed. Star smiled broadly then spotted Bull coming out of one of the Scenarian buildings with a group of them in tow. They looked to be deep in discussion.

"I wonder what that's all about?" Star mused nodding towards Bull's group.

"I dunno. But I saw him gathering groups of people together earlier too. They seemed to be chatting together earnestly about something."

Star was intrigued on hearing this. "I wonder what he's up to?" Star queried.

***

Lin walked up to Guy, who had sat down on one of the benches to sort through his case of samples that he'd collected from the surrounding area, a fruit cocktail by his side.

"Hi! Did you get plenty of soil samples as well as the vegetation?" Lin inquired earnestly, looking at his array of bottles and containers spread out on his case. Guy looked at Lin, confused, then spoke in reply.

"Soil? Why, yes, I think I've got a few samples from different locations. Why?"

Lin smiled as she looked him in the eye and responded. "You will need them to complete your experiments." Then she turned on her heel and returned to her mother, leaving Guy stunned and speechless.

***

The party was widely enjoyed by all, with families and friends reunited once more. Argo wondered how long it would be before the Scenarians had returned to their former way of life and brought all their technology into full use here on Gley. He hoped that Chu's people wouldn't find all this too overwhelming, but from the glimpses he'd had of the Coserai amongst the crowd enjoying the festivities he doubted that they would reject the changes, as long as the Scenarians respected the Coserai's wishes too.

He thought about Bull's plan and after talking with the scientists earlier in the meeting they attended together, he began to be persuaded that his idea might indeed work.

Time would tell! He had been impressed that the group of scientists had volunteered to come along to help put Bull's plan into action once they had left Gley.

They were reasonably sure that they would be able to manage the task without being away from Gley for too long. Indeed, many of the scientists concerned had no families amongst the Scenarian survivors here on Gley, so it would not be such a wrench for them to be away from their people for a month they reckoned, so Argo was more than happy to carry out the plan. The Blues would welcome their new venture he knew, they always loved a challenge and this would definitely be a worthwhile challenge!

***

Bull was eager for the evening to be over so that they could start their work in earnest in the morning. Once they left Gley they would be working overtime to ensure all the preparations necessary were underway. The scientists had assured him it was possible if they had enough power and energy in their weaponry. It was a matter of precise calculation, Professor Jin had said after he had showed Bull the technical instruments that they had on board their ships to carry out the work.

Bull had never seen such instruments before and he was pretty sure Argo hadn't either. Jin had demonstrated their use as simply as possible to Bull so that he had the gist of their capabilities. Bull had indeed been impressed and couldn't wait for the work to be done. Science was indeed a marvellous thing, he thought.

***

The calculations

The farewell from Gley was a brief one, after all, they hoped to return with their scientists that Bull had commandeered within a month or two. The Queen and Prince Cruza had wished them well on their mission and promised them another party when they returned!

***

The Starfinder and its fleet travelled again through the same sector in space for the umpteenth time, it seemed to the First officer Kian Furze. He had been party to Bull's plan on their return to the Starfinder and was excited, if not a bit sceptical on whether such a feat could be accomplished. Meera, the second officer also shared his doubts, but they hoped that, for the captain's sake, that it was possible.

Kios, the captain's second in command had met the idea with great interest and he had gone personally to the professors to discuss how it was to be done, he thought that perhaps the knowledge would be of value to him on his own journeys through space once he returned to his people. You never knew, travelling through the vastness of space what you would encounter one day.

Much activity was going on in the ship's labs, what with the Endari girls conducting experiments with their rocks and they still were trying to find a solution that would erase the invisibility cloaking material daubed all over Nobby. There was also Guy conducting his own experiments on the samples he took from Gley. Now there were also four new Scenarian scientists mapping out their scheme in another part of the lab area.

Professor Cer and Professor Jin were mapping out their plans for the specialized weaponry, whilst Professors Deann and Gurei were calculating angles of projectories for firing the new weapons to produce the maximum force needed to make a difference.

Ursu eyed the professors as she peered over her microscope, watching as they were engrossed in their calculations. She whispered over to her friend Genai, who was distilling samples next to her.

"Hey, do you know what's going on over there?" Genai didn't move her focus away from what she was doing and spoke quietly out of the corner of her mouth in reply.

"Some kind of weapon they're planning I think. I overheard two of them discussing nuclear fusion earlier." Ursu's mouth dropped, she didn't fancy being in close proximity to any nuclear weapons anytime soon! Unbeknown to the girls the professors had quickly dismissed the use of nuclear weapons for the use of sonic missiles instead, less intrusive.

Ursu walked over to get some test tubes, which were luckily closer to the place the professors were working! As she opened the container slowly to select the correct size tubes she surreptitiously eyed the screen that the two closest professors were working on . Unfortunately at that very moment Professor Deann happened to look her way.

"Is there something I can help you with?" Deann asked suspiciously, looking Ursu up and down as she awaited a response.

Ursu swallowed hard and quickly thought of a reply. "Just wondering how much longer you're going to need that space, that's all."

Deann raised her eyebrows and retorted disdainfully.

"Oh, and of course you need this precise location

because..?"

Ursu couldn't think of an answer, but Genai piped up from her workstation.

"We need to work on our solution that we've got in the cupboard under where you're working soon, that's all."

Genai smiled broadly at the professor and Ursu breathed again in relief, hurrying back to her spot with the test tubes.

Professor Deann looked put out and looked at the cupboard below, where there were indeed solutions stored, ready for examining.

"Oh. I see. Well we'll be here quite a while. Just let us know when you need them and we'll bring them over to you." Deann replied in a haughty manner before turning her back onto the girls.

Without her seeing, Genai made a rude sign as soon as her back was turned and Ursu laughed quietly.

***

Guy shook his head, grinning as he saw the sign and he looked at the two girls and gave them a "don't you be naughty!" look. They smiled broadly as they saw his response before continuing with their work. In a few minutes Bull walked into the lab and greeted everyone before heading towards Jin and his group, who were still in deep conference over their figures.

"How are things progressing? Do you need anything?" Bull asked helpfully. Jin turned to Bull and assured him that they were getting on fine and that they needed nothing as yet, but they'd let him know if they did. But Deann made a point of speaking to Bull.

"It's rather crowded in here, isn't it? Are you sure that there is no more workspace available?" Deann had one eye in Ursu's direction as she spoke. Bull picked up the hostility at once and eyed the girls before replying.

"Well, if you find it too distracting in here I could have you shuttled over to one of the fleet ships, where there is more space for you." Bull replied straight-faced.

Ursu and Genai stifled a laugh and held their heads low.

Professor Deann was momentarily speechless, having expected the Endaris to be moved instead, but replied, assuring Bull that they were sure they could work under such confined circumstances to be close at hand, should they need to work with him more closely. Bull smiled and turned on his heel, heading out of the lab, but giving the Endari girls a little wink on his way out.

■■■

Over the next few days the lab was heaving with samples being chipped away, heated, analysed, distilled, blasted with neutrons, mixed and re-heated over and over again by Guy and the girls whilst the Scenarians muttered and debated and recalculated before starting to assemble electronic equipment together in their corner of the lab, with the Blues bringing in materials they had concocted for them on their cloning machines on the lower decks. It was a hive of activity, each group trying to get on in their allocated space.

***

On the third day, Genai stood up from her workstation, looking in disbelief at her distillation beakers in front of her, checking again with the swabs what she thought had occurred.

"I did it!" Genai muttered to herself, disbelievingly, as Ursu looked on from her own work.

"You did? Did what?" Ursu asked hopefully.

"I found the removal agent! " Genai answered in complete amazement, as she rushed out of the lab with her sample. Ursu watched her go, a puzzled look on her face before muttering to herself.

"That's great, Gen, who are you going to remove?"

***

Un cloaking Nobby

Bull was relieved that Genai had found the solution to one of his problems and he put the Blues to work straight away at cloning the solution to mass produce it for use in defence for their own ships when confronted by cloaked enemy craft. It could be used to fire at the enemy to discover their cloaked whereabouts in battles in the future. First of all, a much relieved Nobby was to finally have the rest of his body back!

As the Blue applied the solution to Nobby's invisible parts he felt relief that he wouldn't be laughed at by the other AIs anymore. He had been an object of ridicule for so long that he had tried to keep a low profile since the accident by remaining on duty in the cargo bay, shifting and filling the containers as and when needed. Now he could escape the mundane duties down below and venture out to other parts of the ship once more. His confidence had taken a dent, but now that was about to change. He thought how happy Argo would be to find him out and about again!

***

A week later Nobby was indeed busy. He had been assigned a new duty along with the rest of his robot section. They had to take newly created canisters of the anti cloaking liquid from the cloning room to the various shuttles on board ship, so they could be ferried over to the rest of the fleet ships for installation. He felt it was an important job and he thought Argo would be proud of him again. Perhaps he should visit Argo again soon to report on his progress, thought Nobby.

***

The shipping out of the containers took over a week to complete and the extra supplies of canisters had to be stowed away ready for re-shipping once the ships' supplies had run out again. Also, the Blues had created a supply of canisters of the actual cloaking liquid itself, to store until needed on any new ships. Nobby was so busy he hadn't found the time to see Argo, much to Nobby's dismay. He hoped that once the job had been done there would be time.

He saw his section commander head towards him to check that all was being done properly. Nobby carefully stowed away the full canisters in the compartment, making sure to attach a label on each one as it came to him on the hover board. He'd never before been given the labelling task, it was an important job, so his colleague had said. He had told Nobby to make sure that the blue labels were used and not the red before putting the canisters in the compartment.

The Bronze cargo commander stood next to Nobby and watched him, before calmly asking him a question.

"Noblaczec. Exactly how many containers have you labelled and packed away here?" Nobby beamed with pride because he knew he had done more than the others.

"I have labelled and stacked three thousand and ten, Commander." Nobby stated with pride. The commander paused and asked him if this was the first day he'd done the labelling, to which Nobby replied it was. The commander looked at him briefly before replying.

"Well then, that's a good job, because now you will have to unload each one of the three thousand and ten canisters here and take off the blue labels and replace them with the correct labels.. THE RED LABELS!" The commander bellowed crossly in his face.

"But... But.." Nobby began to protest, to tell him that his colleague had told him to put the blue labels on, but the commander had already turned away and stormed down the corridor angrily, muttering crossly. Nobby re ran his vocal recording facility to catch the message his colleague had given him so he could protest. He found the correct section and re played it. He heard his colleague say clearly..

"Make sure you don't use the blue labels, use the red ones..."

Nobby's face fell, he was sure he'd remembered him say the opposite! Nobby looked at the enormous pile of canisters that he had stacked and labelled. This was going to be a nightmare, thought Nobby, then he reached for his first canister.

***

The fleet had been fitted with the anti cloaking canisters within the week, ready for deployment whenever needed . It seemed to Bull that things were working out well for the mission, in fact, far exceeding his expectations. The Endaris had worked hard and his Scenarian scientists said that they had their solution ready for him when they would arrive at their destination. In fact the Blues had constructed the prototype and were ready to test it. Kian was searching for a suitable target already as they headed through space. In twenty four hours he had the target in sight.

"Large asteroid at zero two eight degrees, Captain!"

Bull looked at the view of the asteroid on his screen. *Yes, it is certainly a large enough one,* thought Bull.

"Check for any spacecraft in the vicinity, Lieutenant." Bull ordered as he hailed the scientists in the lab. "Professor Jin, we have a target in sight for the deployment of the prototype, please come to the bridge."

Moments later the Scenarian scientist arrived at the bridge from the beamer, looking eager to test out the weapon. Professor Deann followed behind him.

"Sector clear of spacecraft, Captain." The lieutenant announced.

Jin and Deann stood next to the captain and looked at the image of the asteroid on his viewer.

"Yes, that is suitable for our purpose." Jin remarked.

"If you go over to the controller over there," Bull indicated the officer to his right. "You will be able to provide the officer with the precise location you wish to deploy the weapon. He will fire at the optimum moment."

Jin moved over to the Blue officer, who awaited his input, all the asteroid specifications displayed to the finest detail on his holoscreen in front of him. Jin and Deann scanned the details carefully and conferred amongst themselves before announcing to the officer the exact area selected for the deployment of the weapon. The lieutenant entered the data onto his computer and informed the Blue next to him that the details had been entered. The Blue then factored in the trajectory and waited for the optimum moment to fire the weapon.

"Weapon firing, Captain!" The Blue announced as he pressed the button in front of him. All eyes observed the flight of the sonic missile as it headed steadily towards its asteroid target. In a few seconds they saw the mass of debris projected out into space as the target was hit by an almighty sonic blast.

As the debris cleared away they looked once again at the large object moving through space. It seemed a different shape now, Jin and Deann looked at the updated information on the asteroid on the holoscreen in front of them. As they digested the information the Blue gave his result.

"The asteroid has moved on its axis by two degrees captain. Minimal damage." Jin and Deann smiled broadly and shook hands enthusiastically, obviously happy with the result.

"I take it you have accomplished what you hoped to achieve?" Bull asked the scientists hopefully. Jin turned and replied.

"Yes, Captain, I believe we have. We are ready to put into action your plan."

Bull smiled. He hoped that indeed this would work. It could make a huge difference to the people affected, but he would need to find them first!

Chapter 11

Return to Gar-Too

In a few hours they had arrived at their destination, ready to carry out Bull's ambitious plan. All the weapons needed were ready in position on the selected fleet ships, awaiting deployment to precise locations on the planet in front of them. It looked so inviting from space, with its large expanse of ocean and lush greenery on land, tall mountains and a sprinkle of empty cities here and there. But the hidden danger was well known. Bull knew its secret. Gar-Too was in distress and it needed saving.

The scientists looked through the magnitoscopes scanning the globe, searching for the precise location of the old impact site that had caused Gar-Too's oceans to form their frequent Tsunamis. There were no obvious scars on the land so it was sure to be in the depths of the oceans.

The instrument searched the layers of liquid to reach the bed of the oceans below. It took a long time to survey every aspect of the watery mass before Deann spotted the anomaly. She called her colleagues to view her findings.

They looked with interest at the large crater in the ocean floor. There was no doubt that this was indeed the impact site they were looking for. But Professor Cer looked perturbed, holding his chin and rubbing his index finger across his lips in thought.

"There's something not right about this." Cer began, thinking through the implications. His colleagues listened with interest. "This impact alone would not account for the regularity of the tsunamis, there is another factor that we need to consider. The magnetic pull of the moons."

The colleagues looked at the view of the planet in front of them. Then Deann zoomed in on the surrounding moons, looking carefully at the surface area. She turned to the captain and asked.

"Can we orbit the two moons to have a closer look?" The other professors nodded in recognition, agreeing with her train of thought,

"Of course! The moons! They could have been hit out of alignment too! " Jin enthused, looking closely at the viewer as the Starfinder headed closer to the nearest moon.

They orbited Iesta, looking for signs of impact and it was not long before they saw the enormous crater on one side showing that it also had been hit at some point! Perhaps around the same time, they thought, imagining an asteroid cluster crashing into the two orbs. This was another problem to factor in to their plan. They would have to counteract the impact on both Gar-Too and Iesta. They also needed to check out Farso, the second moon to look for any further signs of impact. It could be that all three satellites had been struck by the asteroids.

The bridge crew grew weary of the intense scrutiny of checking the moon for any signs of large enough craters on its surface. There were several craters on the barren Farso anyway, but they looked to have been there for several millennia, long before the first people had set foot on Gar-Too. It was a tedious task, but, to succeed, it had to be done properly. They had to know if it had been affected by a strike.

The magnitoscopes helped enormously, but straining the eyes looking through them constantly became a job instead, for the unweary robots on the bridge. At least they couldn't complain of eye strain!

***

At last, after hours of study, they had to conclude that Farso had not been impacted in the last century by anything substantial, that left the scientists with the task of adjusting their calculations to focus on the remaining moon, Iesta and Gar-Too itself.

After a long break for everyone, the time had arrived for the firing of missiles to correct the axial displacements caused by the impact of the large asteroids. The professors had selected the points of detonation for the missiles that would ensure the correct amount of force required to shift the two satellites back into position. They had decided that it would be best to deploy the weapons to their assigned targets simultaneously, which meant that two of the accompanying fleet ships would concentrate on Iesta and the Starfinder itself would focus on Gar-Too.

Bull was becoming nervous now that his plan was about to become reality. He worried that their intervention might have an even more detrimental effect on the planet than it already had suffered. It was a huge responsibility to decide to intervene in this way, but Bull knew that without anything being attempted to correct the fault it was a waste of a perfectly formed, habitable planet. And there were the displaced people to consider too, would they not prefer to return to their home planet given the opportunity? If it had happened to Earth, Bull felt sure that everyone would want to return if at all possible.

***

The fleet were arranged in position, separated into their assigned orbits around the two spheres. There was to be a concentration of force to be fired upon key points about the two. The countdown had begun as Finch, Star, and Da-Ee watched on the bridge to support Bull in his endeavour. Star noticed how close Da-Ee stood next to Bull, her fingers just touching his knee as he sat at the comms. He didn't seem to notice, but Finch had.

"Five...four...three...two...fire!" The countdown rang through all the fleet ships simultaneously and a barrage of missiles were launched on their prospective co-ordinates, each one containing a frightening destructive power in its own right. Were they about to destroy this wonderful vista or were they its salvation? Time would tell.

There was a deathly silence on the bridge as the missiles neared their targets, all eyes straining to focus on the flight of their emissaries!

"Brace yourselves!" One of the Blues called out from his workstation nearby. The Starfinder shuddered in the wake of the astronomical wave of energy that hit them on release of the missiles' force around the planets! Bulkheads on the bridge shuddered and creaked from the force of the sonic blast and anyone standing was caught off balance if they hadn't held on to anything. Da-Ee held onto Bull's shoulders as the wave tossed everyone about. Gale held on to Lin tightly as she hooked an arm around a support frame next to her in the medi lab. Star and the others all steadied themselves on whatever was nearby until the wave had passed.

A second wave of energy came in its wake and the crew were more prepared this time, holding on to items that could support them. When the waves had diminished the eyes on the bridge switched to focus on the targets. Had anything happened? Were they still intact or were they decimated by the blasts? All were questions on everyone's mind.

***

Jin and Cer looked at the data uploading on their holoscreen, the information coming in streams as the planet, hopefully, moved. All were waiting with bated breath for the result, for there was not much to see of any significant difference by looking at Gar-Too and Iesta from this distance. At least they looked intact.

Deann punched a few buttons on the computer and awaited confirmation, Gurei looking over her shoulder for the result. Instead of a roar of triumph from Deann, she despondently stepped aside for Jin to check the results on her feed. Iesta had moved, but not enough! It needed to move at least another two degrees to be back in the correct alignment! The four scientists began to argue the possibilities of what had gone wrong, completely ignoring queries from the crew on the bridge. They were in a world of their own, oblivious to outsiders.

Bull couldn't follow the gist of their conversation, science wasn't his strong point! He looked to Argo, who seemed to be following perfectly well what they were trying to figure out and what needed to be done. Suddenly they punched a few additional pieces of data into the computer and a roar of triumph was emitted by the Scenarians! They had figured it out by all accounts!

Gar-Too had moved the three degrees it needed to correct its axis. The data for Iesta had revealed the lack of two degrees of movement because they needed to factor in the different density of the moon into their calculations. Once they had factored it in, another blast of their weapons could be released to compensate and bring it to align correctly.

The minutes passed and Jin was ready with the data amendment. It was all entered into the missile launchers' computed trajectory and when the Starfinder was in the correct position once again, the missiles were let loose. They watched the K-Tons zooming in on their targets once more, like darts headed for the bull's eye, the contact point came closer until the impact sent an almighty blast wave headed towards the fleet once more.

"Brace for impact!" The Blue called on the tannoy once again and everyone on the bridge held on to whatever or whoever was close at hand. The wave shook the vessel, buffeting the fleet as it passed. The groans and creaks finally ended. The data began to download onto the console in front of Jin, the four scientists looking hopefully as the figures emerged. The crew held their breath in the hope all would be well.

Gurei whooped with joy and jumped from his seat smiling, clapping Jin's back , confirming the shift in its orbit as well!

All rose on the bridge to congratulate each other and Bull was elated that the plan had worked! Da-Ee jumped to embrace him, entwining her legs around his torso easily, his arms embraced her in response and he kissed her briefly on the lips as he twirled to one side in his joy. Star and Finch looked at each other with raised eyebrows, then a slow smile spread across their faces.

***

Inspection

They landed on Gar-Too a short distance from where they had rescued the seven Scenarians months previously. Just to be on the safe side they set the shuttles down on the flat roof of a tall building nearby.

The professors looked around from the rooftop at the vast expanse of the empty city with its weed-strewn streets and the smell of musty buildings. There was a clear tide mark if you looked closely at the buildings below of where the ocean had risen to envelop the city during its flooded period.

Finch wondered how long ago the Tsunami last swept over here as everything at the lower levels seemed so damp anyway.

Professor Jin wanted to set some gauges at intervals on the lower levels of the buildings to collect data over the coming weeks to ensure the tides had not returned since the axis had been righted. The information they gathered would feed back live to the Starfinder computer systems and they intended also in placing cameras randomly across the city's upper reaches, looking down onto the street level below for signs of water. There was no harm in observing from the safety of the Starfinder over the weeks it would take to return to Gley. Any signs of tidal surges would be seen on the ship's computers.

***

"How long do you think it would take to get the city back into a fit state to live in again?" asked Star, observing the debris and weeds covering the streets as she walked along them.

"I dunno, months I would reckon." Finch replied,

unsure of where anyone would start.

"I think a lot longer than that." said Bull, walking alongside them. "They would have to filter out the fresh-water supplies to the buildings after the infiltration of all that saltwater. I would guess that alone would take several weeks." He looked down the street at the high pile of rusted vehicles tossed into a recess in the corner of a building. The sea had caused a tangled mess everywhere. He could not imagine where to start.

"We could help.." offered Argo. They stopped in their tracks, looking at him expectantly.

"Help? In what way?" Kian asked, looking grimly at the tons of sediment they waded through on the street level.

"Well, we have the machinery to rid the cities of all its debris." Argo began, looking in all directions. "The Mechanoids would make short work of shifting the debris and the robots could incinerate this weed everywhere. It's not beyond us, as you know. It would just take time, that's all."

Bull thought about Argo's idea and liked the use of their time to renew this planet back to its former glory, but they would need to find out where the displaced people had fled and see if they wished to return to Gar-Too. He had an idea. He went over to Kian.

"Would you be able to hack into a computer system without knowing access codes etc.?" Bull asked his first officer, who looked at him full of intrigue.

"Well, yes, it's easily done, but why?" Kian asked, not really understanding how it could help.

"And would you be able to do this to a system that has no power?" Bull enquired further.

"Well, it is possible, using a portable energy pack

like this one." He replied, pulling out a pack from his shoulder bag.

Bull looked excited, then headed off along the street. "Come with me." He commanded Kian. "We'll be back in a while, you carry on setting your gauges, Professsor." Bull spoke before turning towards a large office block abandoned nearby.

***

On the fourth floor of the building, above the tidal line, the offices were left in limbo, abandoned as they had stood the last time people had worked here. Kian could see his need for an energy pack. Along the walls of a large room stood a line of holographic screen sites, with their respective computer hubs arranged below. Bull headed towards the computers with Kian in tow.

"I take it you want to access data from one of these computers, Captain?" Kian asked as he removed his bag from his shoulder.

Bull confirmed that was his plan, he wanted to see if there was any indication on any of the databases where the people of Gar-Too had decided to flee.

Kian pulled out a power pack and adapter and spliced it into the system, running his fingers over the main control hub to fire it up. In a few minutes, after much clicking and whirring, the computers all lit up, the screens glowing ethereally in the darkened room. Kian punched in some controls and a stream of binaries swam down the screens in front of them, searching for the required codes.

In a matter of minutes a voice blared across the room. "Evacuate! Evacuate! Imminent floods. Access your nearest shuttle now!" The computer voice repeated the message over and over until Kian punched in another code to stop it. Bull felt excited at the thought of being able to find out about their intended destination. He hoped that the community all decided to flee to the same location together, otherwise it would be a nightmare to track everyone down. Kian entered a command and waited.

Suddenly a figure appeared on the screen, dressed in a fine, pale lilac suit with colours attached to the left side of the chest, reminding Bull of military honour strips. The head was similar to a human, in that it had two eyes a nose and a mouth, with ears to either side, but the skull was larger, with three ridges protruding lightly either side of the skull, with hair growing in the area between the two sets of ridges. He had faint eyebrows and his hairline was shaped in a V, the point of which started just above his wide brow. He had a small goatee at his chin, superbly waxed into a v shape. All in all he looked like he should be a general or a prime minister or something similar. At least with their translator chips everyone now would be able to understand each other, no matter what planet they arrived at.

Bull was looking forward to finding out what he had to say. As he stood, unmoving on the screen, Bull found it rather disconcerting to look in his eyes, they were a vivid violet colour with a narrow ring of paler lilac around the circumference of the iris.

Kian looked at Bull before remarking "Scary!"

Bull however didn't find him scary, just interesting.

"Can we hear what he has to say?" inquired Bull hopefully.

Kian pressed a button and the man on the screen began to speak.

"It is with great sadness that this day has come, my people. The day when we all leave our beloved planet behind and seek a new life together on Cressus. I hope that one day we will have the technology to save our planet and return home once again. But for now, we must leave. Take with you only what is essential and valuable to you as space is limited on our shuttles. The shuttles will leave at noon tomorrow, before the forthcoming tsunami. A final warning will be given to escape in the shuttles before it strikes. I hope to greet you in person once we have arrived at our destination. Gar-Deen be with you! This is your president, Troi-Kah signing off."

The screen froze again, leaving Troi-Kah standing immobile once more.

"Cressus, eh? I wonder where that is?" puzzled Bull, but grateful that they now knew where the Gar-Toyans had all headed. Kian unplugged his power pack and the computer screens once again became transparent and dead. He re-packed his supplies into his bag as Bull waited, thinking about his next move.

***

Party time.

The return trip to Gley proved uneventful, but everyone was relieved to see by the data released from the gauges and cameras left on Gar-Too that there had been no further flooding in any of the three cities. It seemed their plan was working better than expected.

The professors had seemed more relaxed now that their work to design and deploy the weapons accurately had been completed, even Professor Deann had mellowed a little towards Ursu and Genai, even offering professional opinion on how to extract certain minerals on their samples more efficiently, with less power consumption. Genai had weighed up the information without comment to Deann, except to say she hadn't thought of doing it her way. But out of Deann's sight the girls amended their extraction methods and found the professor to be correct.

On arrival at Gley, the Coserai and Scenarians were true to their word and had a party prepared for their arrival and to celebrate the success of Bull's plan.

Argo was impressed to see a magnificent building had been erected overlooking the Scenarian town, which was fast becoming more like the towns he had seen on Scenara previously. Their ornate fascias reminiscent of the designs he remembered on his way to the palace at Scenara all that time ago. The queen came over to stand beside him and Argo bowed and smiled.

"I see you have spotted the new palace!" Queen Laifa commented after seeing him look at the magnificent building on the high ground overlooking the town. "It is not quite complete, but the main rooms have all been finished. Would you like to have a tour later?" The queen smiled, looking at Argo happily. Argo politely said that he'd be delighted to see it.

***

Meera could eat no more! She had been offered so much food and it seemed impolite to refuse and now she regretted it.

"I told you not to eat that last drumstick!" Kian laughed at the sight of her slightly green face.

"Come on, let's go and walk it off!" He added, pulling her up from her chair with both hands. Meera wasn't sure if she could walk under the weight of the food, but she got up, willing herself to try.

Zooming past the two like a bat out of hell, Genai sped towards Ursu at the far corner of the parkland, managing to avoid contact with anyone else in the crowd, even though she was travelling at such speed, she could have bulldozed anyone out of her way. The Scenarians and Coserai glanced in her direction as she arrived near Ursu, none of them had seen the Endaris do their speed walk until now. Da-Ee and Kios laughed at their expressions as they filled their glasses with more juice. Meera wished she had her energy right now!

***

Finch held Star in his arms as they danced along with others in the central area of the park, swaying gently to the soft music provided by the Scenarian musicians. It was a relief to be able to wear smart evening clothes instead of their uniforms for a change!

***

The Coserai marvelled at the instruments, the like of which they had never seen. Their own instruments were mainly drums, flutes, percussion instruments and something akin to a violin. These were far in advance of their wooden instruments, made out of a variety of light shiny materials which exuded a range of melodious sounds.

***

Next to Finch and Star danced Kicha and Glian, happy in their new, safer home. They appeared relaxed and it was as if all the worry lines on their faces had melted away with the happiness they now experienced.

They looked ten years younger the both of them.

***

Star saw Da-Ee towing Bull towards the dance floor. She was dressed in a stylish short black dress edged with shiny crystals of some sort. She looked quite beautiful all dressed up like that and a pang of jealousy stung Star's sub-conscious for a fleeting moment. She tried to look away and concentrate on her own beau, but found her eyes pulled back towards the couple as they danced slowly in each other's arms, smiling happily.

***

Gale was swinging Lin's arms back and forth to the music until a little girl of a similar age to Lin came to play with her. It was Jeia, sweeping her towards a group of children playing with balls on the grassy area of the park. Gale looked on happily at her child enjoying the freedom to run around. That was the only thing that bothered Gale, being on board ship wasn't a very good environment for a child to play like normal kids do.

She wondered how lonely Lin was, being without company of her own age to play with, in space, although Lin never complained, Gale felt she would benefit from having company of her own age on board. Gale tried the best she could to keep her entertained, but it wasn't the same as having someone younger to play with.

She knew that Lin missed Chaff a lot, even though they chatted via the comms when they were still in their own Solar System, but now that wasn't possible. She caught her twisting her friendship bracelet around her wrist the previous day, talking to it as though she was talking to Chaff herself. It wasn't healthy. Perhaps she should chat to Argo about it and see what he'd have to say.

The solar lights twinkled in the evening sky, giving the parkland a shimmering air in the warmth of the evening, bathing the dancers below in their glow. The central fountain was also lit up and some people sat around its surrounding low edging, dangling their fingers in the warm pool of shimmering water, embracing their loved ones as they enjoyed the evening. People still came around serving buffet food amongst the crowd and the atmosphere was jovial and calming at the same time.

Da-Ee and Bull had later gone for a stroll along the lakeside to find some alone time before they had to return to the party. They passed Kian and Meera, who were walking back towards the party after Meera had walked off her excess food intake! They nodded to each other as they passed and continued in their opposing directions.

Bull remembered how different things had been for him the last time he was by the lake with Star. What a fool he had been, he thought, and he remembered how Da-Ee had helped him afterwards, when he was left injured by Finch's attack, and here she was, helping him recover still! He looked her in the eyes and pulled her close to kiss her. He really did owe her a lot. Tonight she looked so pretty, he was a lucky man, he thought to himself. He forced himself to believe it. Otherwise he would fall apart.

***

At the palace Argo marvelled at the beautiful interior of the throne room, where the queen would receive her people if they had a problem. There was a main throne for her, all gilded ornately, and another throne alongside hers, less decorative slightly, which was for her son when he was receiving at the palace.

The walls were hung with magnificent materials, embroidered by the gifted fingers of the queen's ladies in waiting. They had created them as a surprise for her when it was learnt that the palace was to be built. The hangings depicted Scenarian scenes and animals as Argo had remembered from before, when he saw similar ones on Scenara. They were all embroidered with gold and silver threads.

The regal dining room was completed, a vast room where the queen could entertain guests from other lands, should they wish in the near future. Here she would also entertain Chu's people in repayment for their trust and friendship in allowing her people to live alongside them on Gley. The other completed rooms were the prince's rooms and the queen's rooms. Farsifa and her other ladies in waiting had accommodation next to the queen's, a floor below. The rest of the palace was still being constructed by the Scenarians themselves, with a helping hand from the Mechs and robots when needed.

The dome was kept fully occupied in producing all the materials they needed to restore the people to their previous comfortable lives. The building work was being carried out at an impressive pace. Argo was quite impressed. He would make sure to tell Captain Grey all about it when they returned to Earth. He wondered how the captain was managing now that he was living his life on the planet rather than in space. *At least his life would be calmer there*, thought Argo. *How wrong could he be!*

Chapter 12

On Earth

Sarf's people looked over at the horizon from their panoramic viewing point at the top of the Rocky Mountains. Their eyes scanned the distance for signs of humans. They sensed that their comrades had fallen and they were set on revenge! Only one shuttle remained for their people, hidden below in the deep ravine. The whole colony piled into the remaining shuttle, mainly mothers with children and a few elderly males left behind by Sarf's group of warriors. It didn't matter to them whether old or young, they all felt the need to avenge their fallen warriors. Grenia fired up the shuttle after placing her child safely in his harnessed seat behind her. She took a backward look at him before setting off into the skies with the remainder of the colony on board.

Each of the members of the colony had a grim determination to fight, even the youngest child was willing to fight to the death if need be. Grenia was fighting to control the altitude of the shuttle, having not flown one in decades. The ship flew too high at first and Grenia worried that they would be spotted too soon. She called for assistance from one of the elders behind her.

An elderly male with a limp approached slowly, trying to balance himself to reach the cockpit. After some effort, he reached her and sat in the co-pilot's seat. His warrior days were over, but he still remembered how to fly. He took over the controls as he let his supporting staff fall to the floor.

Over the mountains they flew, seeking out any humans they could destroy. They crossed over wide parklands and a few lakes, heading in the direction of Edmonton, where there would be easy prey. They saw the snaking form of the North Saskatchewan river in the distance and beyond it the new town that emerged from the ashes. People would likely be there, Grenia thought to herself, as they headed ever closer.

She saw vehicles hovering along the highways and began firing indiscriminately towards them. She saw the vehicles pile up and blow up into flames below her. She smirked with glee! She told the old man to fly low over the town so she could fire over the people below.

***

Up in the space station Gaea, the Gold in charge of the station spotted the signs of trouble very quickly.

***

People fled for shelter wherever they could as the hail of bullets tore into everything. Grenia fired a missile into the heart of the town and watched as the buildings blew up in a cloud of fire. Suddenly she was aware of another presence in the skies nearby. She turned her head in every direction looking for the aircraft. There it was! To her left, coming in fast.

***

Gaea had already alerted the Silvers of the danger, so they were ready this time!

The old man swerved to avoid its fire and swept

down low over the town in the hope it wouldn't fire at them there, in case they struck civilians in error. But, to his dismay, not only did the aircraft chase them but also two others came to join him! They were being herded away from the town. They continued firing as they went, trying to kill as many people as they could, but the people had now been alerted by the fleet's new alarms and had fled to cover. Grenia prepared to fire another missile, taking a look behind at her son to see if he was all right, then she fired the missile at the buildings in front of them.

The buildings exploded and debris flew everywhere, some even hit the shuttle as they passed by. The old man struggled to maintain control of the ship, careering towards a group of buildings down below. He pulled on the control just in time to avoid colliding with it, but in seconds they were surrounded by more aircraft. The old man looked at Grenia and both began firing everything they had in desperation, but it was to no avail! In a few seconds the robot craft had blown Grenia's shuttle to pieces and the last of their colony were evaporated into oblivion. Sarf's colony on Earth was no more.

***

The survivors in Edmonton eased out of their hiding places and saw the destruction of their newly built city. But they gathered their thoughts and made their way to help the injured and dying as best as they could. No one was going to kill their spirit; they had survived the long period since the big war and suffered many hardships. That had made them a tougher breed of people, in time the city would be whole again. They had faith in their protectors, this robot army that sprang from nowhere were here to help them and help them they did, a thousand fold.

***

Thousands of miles away Mary and Reed watched the screen as reports of an alien attack emerged from Canada. They watched, horrified as pictures were shown on the TV of the effect it had on the town of Edmonton and its people. There were witness accounts from the survivors of the random attack in the middle of an ordinary day. People had luckily heard the robot early warning siren blaring before the attack and many had been saved by this, helping them get to safety early on. However, some people were unable to flee and were caught in the attack. Others on the highway had been killed by a pile up caused by the aliens too. The body count had risen to forty five the reporter declared and there were nearly a hundred injured by falling debris.

"I hoped that all this was over." Mary stated sadly as she held Reed's hand as they sat on the settee at their home. "I hope Bull will be able to find the rest of these aliens and annihilate them all!" Mary added, although horrified at the thought of her son being in such danger.

"Don't you worry, he's got Argo on his side, remember? With the robot army they have in their fleet nobody is going to mess with them!" Reed replied incourageingly, hoping it was true.

"Do you think there will be more attacks?" Mary asked her husband worriedly.

"I shouldn't think so. The robots will be able to figure out where these aliens were hiding I'm sure, and when they do, that'll be the end of them!" he replied smiling. That he did believe.

***

Captain Grey looked worriedly at the screen. He had seen the report with Stark just moments before and he began to wonder if Bull and Argo were encountering difficulties on their journey too. He hoped that they had visited the Scenarians and formed an alliance with them. If Earth was going to suffer alien attacks like this in the future it was important to have allies if they needed them!

Just as Grey turned off the news report there was a knock on the door. There on his doorstep stood Gaea, the Gold in charge of the Space station above Earth.

***

Stark joined in on their conversation and agreed with what Gaea proposed totally. It was prudent to have Earth's home fleet increased to protect it from any further trouble whilst the Starfinder fleet travelled through the galaxies looking for allies. Gaea also proposed building two large warships to aid the Earth fleet in their battle when they finally discovered the alien home world. He wanted them kitted out with powerful weapons and shields and big enough to support a field hospital, kitted out with the latest technology.

Grey gave full permission for Gaea to organise the enlargement of the fleet immediately and the Blues had incorporated in their proposals a newer, faster engine for the advanced models of fighter planes for the new fleet's ships. It was also advised by Gaea to start laying a network of communication buoys past their solar system so that they could communicate with the Starfinder's fleet as soon as possible if any dangers were to arise. Grey felt a certain comfort in knowing that the robot army they had produced continued to have Earth's welfare at their hearts, so to speak!

***

Plotting.

Leaving Gley was a wrench for all the crew, it was like saying goodbye to their families all over again. They had made such good friendships here, but all of them hoped to return one day. The fact that they had formed an alliance with them helped enormously. Now they would need to form a system of communication between the two planets so they could hail them when needed. That was a simple task so the Blues reckoned and it was easily done on their journey, where a few satellites or buoys could be placed to relay information from one to the other across space.

***

Argo was pleased to have two new additions to his crew. At Gley, Professor Cer had introduced him to a colleague whose field was Hydroponics. Cer thought that the Starfinder could benefit from fresh produce grown on their own ship. They could not only grow food but plants that would have medicinal qualities could be cultivated there too.

More importantly, Cer's colleague, Professor Chase, had found an abundance of algae on Gley that could absorb carbon dioxide and if cultivated in large quantities on the ship it would help scrub the air on board ship and reduce the energy required by their current air scrubbers. Argo had welcomed the two to join their Science officers.

Ursu and Genai had got along with Cer quite well when he had been on board before, so they had no qualms about him joining them. They were grateful that it wasn't Deann returning!

***

Kios, it turned out, was familiar with the location of

Cressus and had given the fleet the proposed route to follow. He came across to Argo from his own desk, carrying a virtual chart to show him.

"I've mapped out the route we need to take to get to Cressus. We will need to head towards the Corona Gate near Tarsus first."

Argo looked at the route he had drawn, then looked worriedly at Kios and Bull. "But that's.." Argo was interrupted by Kios.

"Yes, it takes us past the Sventhri pirates' home world, I know. It's risky, but we do have our cloaking device now."

Kios looked at Bull, waiting for his response. Bull pondered over the options, going a different route would add months to their journey, so he didn't have any other option really.

"Ok. Let's do it!" Argo agreed reluctantly, wondering what kind of strife they heading for!

So they commenced the journey towards the Corona gate to reach Cressus to find the people of Gar-Too and give them the good news

***

Argo had been busy with the Blues, creating something top secret for days. Even Bull wasn't a party to the information what it was about! He never realised how sneaky Argo could be, but Bull wasn't too worried, Argo was always doing something in their best interests. The Blues had been sworn to secrecy, so no matter how Bull tried to find out, he drew a blank each time.

Argo knocked on the door of Gale and Lin's room, feeling pleased with himself. Gale answered the door and let him in. Lin was drawing as usual at her desk as he entered their lounge area. She looked up when Argo appeared and smiled.

"Hey! Argo! I wondered when I was going to see you! I know you've been plotting something, I can feel it, but you've hidden from me what it is. What's going on?" Lin asked with an air of mild suspicion on her face.

"You can't keep much from her, can you?" Argo laughed, looking over at Gale, who was nodding and smiling back. Argo went up to Lin and leant down to her level. "That's because it is a surprise! You wouldn't enjoy it as much if I hadn't made it a secret!" Argo added mischievously.

"Oh, go on, tell me!" Lin jumped up and down excitedly, then looked at her mum. "Do you know what it is, mum?" she asked hopefully. But Gale had no idea and shook her head.

"Come with me." Argo led her over to the doorway area then told her to close her eyes, which she did. "No peeking!" he added, looking at her carefully before opening the door. He looked around the door into the corridor and beckoned someone forward. Gale gasped in surprise and covered her mouth with her hand before she gave the game away!

"Now you can open your eyes!" Argo exclaimed with excitement.

Lin opened her eyes and looked on in complete shock! There, before her, stood a girl about her age, maybe slightly older, but she could see that she was a cybernetic girl, not a human girl. She had long fair hair and blue eyes and she wore jeans and a pink top and sported trainers on her feet which made her look very real. Lin could not hide her complete shock at seeing this girl, her mouth wide open in surprise. The girl stepped forward towards Lin and smiled.

"Hi Lin, my name is Fay and I want to be your friend. Would you like to play?" Fay held in her hands a lightweight beach ball in Lin's favourite colours. Lin took one look at her mum, who nodded happily, then Lin went over to Fay and hugged her excitedly.

"You bet!" Lin replied and the two playmates went off along the corridor to play ball.

Gale looked at Argo and thanked him profusely for creating this playmate for Lin; it would be such a help to her, now she would not be lonely any more. Argo was happy that Lin had accepted Fay so easily, she could just as easily have rejected her, but he was thankful that wasn't the case.

"Shall we go over to the lounge so you can have a break?" Argo asked. Gale hadn't had much time on her own on board the ship to socialise as she was always keeping an eye out for Lin, now it would be different. Argo told her that Fay would protect Lin if needed and that she would be safe with her. Gale was relieved and felt a renewed energy about her; she took Argo's arm and headed for the lounge area on the ship.

They passed the two girls playing ball in the community room a few doors down. Lin looked completely at ease with Fay, like they'd known each other for years. Gale realised that Fay resembled Chaff a little and wondered if that was deliberate on Argo's part. She waved as she passed, telling her where she was going if she needed her. Lin waved in response as she threw the ball towards her new friend.

***

Da-Ee

The flight to the Corona Gate would take a few
weeks, so the crew were able to relax a little for a short
time. The Blues made sure all the fleet were prepared
with plenty of weaponry should the Sventhri find them
and extra inspections of the outer hulls were carried out to
make sure the cloaking effect was complete.

Bull headed towards Da-Ee's quarters, leaving the
comms to Kios. He needed a break; he'd spent the last few
nights pondering over their least conspicuous route past
the Sventhri planet, in order to avoid detection as much as
possible should they have sensor capabilities he didn't
know about.

He knocked and opened Da-Ee's door, he'd never
actually been in her room before as she had always come
to him. He was mildly shocked by what he saw. The furniture extended not just over the floor area, but along the
walls and ceiling too! They must be bolted on thought
Bull. On the wall behind him sat Da-Ee, looking at her
tech-pad. He could never get used to her being able to do
that! The Blues must have helped her set it up, he realised.

He smiled as she walked down the wall towards
him, bringing her techie with her. She draped her arms
over his shoulders and planted a long kiss on his lips,
which he received with a welcome release of tension. She
was the best remedy he'd found for all his worries. This
felt good!

"What you been doing?" Bull asked, nodding towards the techie in her hand.

"Oh, this? Well, it's kind of a log book I suppose. I
jot down all my thoughts and experiences in here, all the

places we've been to, etc."

Bull raised an eyebrow, eyeing the techie again. "Oh, and am I in there by any chance? Have you recorded all your thoughts and experiences about me in there?" Bull teased.

Da-Ee ignored the question and put the techie away on her cupboard and went to get them some drinks. While she was in the kitchen area Bull activated the last page on the techie to sneak a peek. The words caught his attention:

" I have never felt this good before, Bull seems so different from other men I have been with. I think I am in love with him..."

Bull stopped there, stunned and placed the techie back. She looked at him as she returned holding the drinks and noticed the techie light fade out on the cupboard. She stood trembling at what he may have read, before walking towards him with the drinks. Instead he quickly turned towards the door.

"I'm sorry, Da-Ee, I have to go." Bull left the Su-ul looking lost in his wake.

***

Bull felt a storm churning in the pit of his stomach. He wished he hadn't read the words. He hadn't reckoned on her falling in love with him, he wasn't ready to go down that path, not yet! He almost collided with Finch in his hurry to get to his quarters. He apologised to Finch, but kept going unsure how to feel.

Finch watched him disappear towards his room and looked in the direction he had come from. Da-Ee's room was just down there! Finch realised that something was amiss between them and he wondered if he should speak to Da-Ee or not. He walked over towards her room, but he thought the better of it as he heard faint sobs coming from there. It was best for him not to interfere, perhaps Star should speak to her instead?

***

Star made her way from the lounge towards Da-Ee's room after Finch had spoken to her. She wasn't really friends with her, but she may need a friend right now, she thought practically. She knocked on Da-Ee's door and within a few seconds Da-Ee had rushed to open it, her face full of expectation. But when she saw Star her expression changed.

"I guess you were expecting someone else?" Star offered quietly.

"No, just hoping, come in." Da-Ee replied, wiping away a tear forming on her eye.

"Are you all right? You don't look too good." Star began clumsily. Da-Ee knew what she meant and straightened herself up.

"I'm ok. Bull and I had a difference of opinion, that's all." Da-Ee sat down on a nearby chair and indicated for Star to sit too.

"Is it something I can help you with?" Star offered kindly.

Da-Ee shook her head sadly. "No, I think we just need some space from each other for a while." Da-Ee replied, trying to sound more positive. "Would you like a drink?" Da-Ee asked politely.

Star thought she should stay a little longer to try and cheer her up. "That would be lovely, as long as it's not that awful Suku you girls drink! " Star remarked laughing.

Da-Ee managed a little laugh too "No Suku, would you like a coffee or a glass of wine?" Da-Ee asked brightly.

Star plumped for coffee and the two girls sat with their own drinks and had a chat, about everything but Bull.

***

Bull lay in his room; he'd spent the last few hours gazing at the ceiling from his bed. He was trying to work out how to deal with his issues. He enjoyed Da-Ee's company, she was fun to be with and she helped him forget about Star when he was with her, but as for anything more, he was nowhere near ready for that! He thought about how she would feel if he told her that he didn't want anything serious, would it offend her? Was there a way that he could say how he felt that wouldn't jeopardize his relationship with her? He pondered these thoughts over and over but got nowhere fast! He would have to tell her something, but what?

He poured himself a stiff drink to help him relax . Should he speak to her straight away, or should he wait? Thoughts became a jumble crashing together in his mind. Who could he talk to about it? Certainly not Finch, nor Star, what about Kian? No, he didn't want the rest of the crew knowing his business. His train of thought was disrupted by a quiet knock on his door.

Bull checked the door visuals to see who it was and he was surprised to see Da-Ee standing there with a bottle of champagne in her hand and an unreadable look in her eye.

"Can I come in?" Da-Ee asked softly. "I think we need to talk, don't you?"

Bull let her in and she went over to the table to set down the bottle.

"Are we celebrating something?" Bull asked, looking rather puzzled.

Da-Ee sauntered over to Bull and looked him in the eye. She touched his face gently with her fingers.

"Yes, we're celebrating starting again. A clean slate, no expectations, no complications, just fun." Da-Ee smiled and held his hands, pulling him closer to her, then kissed him slowly on the lips.

Bull looked into her eyes. "Are you sure? You know I can't offer you more just now."

Da-Ee silenced him with another kiss and he carried her over to the bed, relieved that she was clever enough to read him like a book.

***

Sventhri

The weeks had passed without trouble and now the two moons of Sventhri, Lo and Kitu, stood in their viewer, signalling the start of the major alert requiring full cloaking to travel through this sector of space. At any time, they could encounter the Sventhri pirates patrolling around their home world.

It had been a while since they saw the large fleet of Sventhri headed somewhere on a mission, probably to cause trouble for some poor unsuspecting planet somewhere. Bull hoped that they were still away, occupied with their fighting somewhere other than here! Their fleet had been large. Even cloaked, the Robot fleet would find it difficult to manoeuvre through such a company of spacecraft.

The Blues were on full alert for any craft passing through the area.

Bull's eyes were also trained on both his viewer and the sensor screen, and tension was mounting on the bridge the closer they got to Lo.

"I suggest we stay behind the moons as much as possible, Commander." Kios suggested, pointing to the planned route again. "We may avoid any sensors the Sventhri have if we keep to their dark sides as we pass."

Argo surveyed the data again and agreed. He didn't want to find out the hard way how many ships the Sventhri had defending their home world!.

***

"Spacecraft passing Kitu, Captain." Blue 7 reported calmly. "A single vessel, heading away from us, probably heading for the Corona Gate." The Blue tracked its course as it slowly travelled onwards.

"What type of craft is it?" Bull demanded, hoping it was not a fighter from their fleet.

"It looks to be a cargo ship, Captain. It is too large to be anything else, also it is travelling quite slow."

Bull breathed a sigh of relief.

***

They passed Lo, keeping to the dark side as they travelled at a steady pace. They didn't want to catch up with the cargo ship before it entered the gate. Lo seemed to be emitting gases into the atmosphere around it, which gave it a surreal greenish glow. It was like looking at thick pea soup from the Starfinder. Soon they emerged into the gap between the two moons and now they had a clearer view of Sventhri itself.

It wasn't a very large planet, but it seemed to have a lot of land covering the surface and only about a third of the surface was compiled of water. There were snow-capped mountains in the northern region which extended for quite some distance.

Bull zoomed in on the planet to see how populated it was. He saw several cities dotted across the globe and there seemed to be many smaller towns spread out across the wide expanse of land. Bull imagined that they could possibly amass a large fleet if required.

"A large number of craft are appearing from the planet surface, Captain!" Blue 7 announced urgently.

Bull worried that they had been seen on the planet's sensors.

The fleet kept an eye on the sensor screens to see the course the Sventhri were taking from their planet. In moments they realised that the pirates were not in pursuit, instead they were headed towards another system entirely! They were safe, for the moment!

***

Behind Kitu, the fleet were able to see several spacecraft moving around near the moon's surface, they were going backwards and forwards between the surface and a space station that they had constructed. It seemed the Sventhri were mining something on Kitu.

"Better not let the Endari girls see this!" Kian remarked with a smile. They passed the mining craft without problem and soon they were leaving Kitu and Sventhri behind. They had made it without detection!

Bull was relieved and thanked God for the cloaking gift the Endari girls had given them. Soon they had Sventhri far behind them and only the gate to look out for. People began to relax again. It would take several hours to reach the gate, so Bull left the comms to Kios briefly and went to see Argo.

***

"How do you think the Gar-Toyans managed to get past Sventhri so easily?" Bull asked Argo as he pored over Argo's charts in his room. "They obviously had to come this way to get to Cressus, so how did they avoid conflict with the pirates? Any ideas?"

Argo thought briefly. It was a good point. "Well, assuming that all the Sventhri were not away on holiday anywhere at the time they passed, I would say they must have had some sort of deterrent.." Argo paced the room, deep in thought.

"You mean they have superior weapons?" Bull asked, with a hint of excitement in his voice.

"A possibility." Argo replied. "On the other hand, they may have cloaking facilities like us. We won't know obviously until we meet them."

***

A couple of hours later, when Argo was looking over the flight plan on the bridge with Bull, the beamer opened unexpectedly. They looked around to see who it was. Argo gave a low groan as Nobby ambled towards them, grinning joyously. Bull smiled and said "He's all yours!" then turned to his console, pretending to be busy at something.

"Ah! Commander! I thought I'd find you here." Nobby gushed excitedly. Argo tried to fix a smile onto his features, and it appeared reluctantly, balanced lopsidedly on his face. Argo stayed beside the comms for comfort so he could pretend he was busy with something should Nobby exceed his welcome. Reluctant as he was to indulge Nobby, it usually turned out that Nobby was inadvertently useful in one way or another! Nobby came up closer, taking interest in all the knobs and buttons on the console.

"You have lots of controls here, Commander! It must be hard to remember them all!" Nobby's eyes swooped over the console, invading Argo's personal space uncomfortably. The bridge crew stifled a laugh with difficulty and Bull decided to move across the room to confer with Kian in case he got Nobby's attention too. Unfortunately Nobby took that as a sign to signal he could take a seat next to Argo and he promptly sat in Bull's comms seat! Argo winced before speaking.

"Noblaczec, what can I do for you?" he managed, calmly, with one eye on the console near Nobby.

"Oh, nothing Sir, I just came to tell you that I'm kept very busy now that the anti-cloaking liquid has brought me back to normal again! I've been fully occupied in ferrying the canisters of anti-cloaking liquid throughout the fleet . I'm sure it will be very useful to you, won't it?" Nobby beamed.

Argo tried to stay calm. "Well, that's very nice of you to come and tell me, now I'm sure you have lots to do as I have. I wouldn't like to prevent you from performing your important duties below." Argo indicated the beamer and stood up expectantly for Nobby to rise. Nobby did, but in doing so managed to put his full weight on some buttons on the console as he winched himself up out of the seat. Bull turned around quickly as he heard the unmistakable sound of something being deployed into space!

As Nobby headed for the beamer, unaware that he'd done anything, Bull and Argo quickly checked the console to see what he had inadvertently done. They breathed a sigh of relief when they saw that no missiles had been launched. However, Nobby had managed to deploy a self-detonating canister of anti cloaking spray into the space ahead of the fleet!

"Veer away from the trajectory of the spray quickly!" ordered Argo immediately. It was a good job that the fleet ships were nowhere near them at the time! Bull looked towards the beamer to give a piece of his mind to Nobby, but Nobby had already gone.

"Never, and I mean NEVER let that idiot near the comms again!" ordered Argo, shaking his head. "I'm beginning to wonder whether he should be shoved back into a cargo container for the duration of the mission, where he can't harm anything!" Argo added.

Suddenly Blue 9 called over to the commander.

"Commander, there's an anomaly on our viewer. I can't quite make it out." The Blue put the view onto the main screen for all to see. Bull and Argo saw empty space ahead at first and wondered what the Blue was fussing about. But then they saw it.

At first it appeared as a minute patch of grey in the blackness of space, but in front of their very eyes it became larger.

Kios looked afraid as he recognised the enormous ship unfolding in front of him!

"Alter course immediately! We're on a collision course with a cloaked ship!" Argo ordered quickly.

The Blue did as he was commanded and the ship was further revealed as they swung out of its way. Nobby's mistake had saved them all! The anti cloaking liquid had found its target inadvertently.

"Let's get out of here! All ahead full speed towards

the gate!" Argo commanded urgently as he read Kios' thoughts and in seconds the fleet had disappeared from the danger.

***

Gale felt a strange familiar feeling return to her thoughts and elsewhere on the ship, Lin sensed something too.

Chapter 13

Corona gate

"I just don't know how he does it!" Argo puzzled as he sat next to Bull at the comms. "I mean, how many times has that idiot saved people? It's uncanny. It seems as though he has an enchantment over him! I don't know how else to describe it!"

"Please tell me you're not going to let him know how he saved us today! We wouldn't hear the end of it!" Bull groaned at the thought of Nobby paying them another visit, "He could just as easily have started another war if he'd pressed the missile launch button instead! " Bull shook his head at the thought.

"God no! I wouldn't dream of it!" Argo laughed.

***

In a few more minutes they approached the Corona gate. Bull looked at it, enthralled. He found it hard to comprehend the technology behind such a thing and he wondered how these gates had come about. It was beyond him, that's for sure. He saw again the large circular gate with pulsating blue and green lights drawing voyagers into a centre of complete blackness, where no stars glowed. He remembered the odd sensation of floating they had all experienced whilst travelling through the Helios gate previously. He was sure this would be no different.

"Entering the gate in ten, nine, eight.." the loud-speaker echoed throughout the ship, warning the crew of the impending sensation of reduced gravity. Soon the fleet had been sucked into the gate and swallowed into its belly. Bull's stomach lurched in protest over the difference in gravity momentarily, before adjusting to its new sensation. The journey this time through the gate would be longer Kios told Bull, five days, so they would have to put up with the sensation of floating a lot longer. People tended to wander around the ship less, preferring to stay put as long as possible in their place of work. The robots however, faced no difference in their movement and carried on as normal.

***

Argo went over to Kios and asked him to come to his office. Kios followed him in and closed the door. Argo immediately asked him about the ship that they had inadvertently begun to uncloak back there. He wanted to know why Kios was so afraid of it.

Kios stood uneasily in front of the commander's desk as if trying to muster up the courage to speak.

"I recognised it immediately. You don't want to mess about with them; they're a very powerful and ancient species. They have altered the face of the galaxies in the past with their advanced weaponry. Nobody wants to get on their wrong side!" Kios still looked unnerved by the near miss.

"Who are they? What do you call them?" Argo inquired.

Kios looked ashen as he replied. "They are an ancient race called Y Gwylwyr, the Watchers. People believe that they are descendants of the Gods and it was they who formed the gates along the galaxies millions of years ago."

Argo looked at Kios and saw the real fear in his eyes. He thanked him and let him return to his duties.

***

Genai fired into the metal plate over and over again with different projectiles, the result was the same each time. It was incredible! No amount of pummelling caused a dent in this metal. She called the captain on her mic. "Captain, this is Genai down at the lab. Could you come down? I think we've found something very interesting."

Bull was intrigued with Genai's message and wondered what it could be. He knew it would have something to do with some of the rock samples they had hoarded down there! He hoped it would prove to be something useful.

"Well? What exciting new thing have you uncovered then?" Bull asked lightly as he entered the lab. Then he caught sight of all the weapons they had on the table. "Wow! You girls expecting a battle somewhere?"

Ursu laughed then brought him over to stand in prime position to view their experiment.

"See this?" Ursu pointed to a small metal plate the girls had constructed out of the ore in the rock samples somewhere. Bull looked unimpressed thus far, but nodded.

"Well, watch what happens when we attack it with a range of weapons." Ursu proudly announced.

Genai firstly pounded the metal plate behind the safety bar with normal bullets, nothing happened to the metal. She then hit it with a range of weapons, one after another, including a flame thrower, the robots' own ray beams and disintegrators. Each time the result was the same, the metal plate didn't have so much as a dent in it! Cer added that the metal actually seemed to absorb energy, therefore it would be useful in ship construction because it would enable the ships to prolong the effectiveness of their shields when attacked, by absorbing the energy instead.

Bull stared, trying to gauge the implications this new metal presented them with. It was, it seemed, indestructible! If they could get enough of this metal together they could form an indestructible fleet or even an indestructible army!

"Where did you get the ore for making the plate? Have you got some more here?" asked Bull excitedly. They would surely have to get enough samples of the ore to clone it in their dome machines he realised.

Genai's face fell.

"Well, that's the catch, really. We don't have any more samples of the ore because we had to leave in a hurry."

Bull looked at her expectantly to tell him where it was when it dawned on him very quickly that it was back on the moon near Uranus! That's where they were attacked by hoards of aliens with advanced weapons!

"Oh no! Not there! Not Umbriel!" groaned Bull.

Genai and Ursu nodded in unison with deflated expressions on their faces.

"Well, this time we could just take one shuttle down and be in and out with samples before they even know we were there!" Ursu suggested hopefully. Bull realised that was probably the only way they could do it. It was worth a shot. So, if Argo was willing, on their way back to Earth they would try it out, then they could work on creating this indestructible force!

A long while later the fleet emerged through the gate, spat out with great force from the blackness of the vortex. Suddenly a ship to ship alarm was blaring in the background!

"What is it?" Bull demanded urgently. Blue 7 replied.

"We have lost a quarter of the fleet captain!"

"What do you mean lost a quarter of the fleet?" Bull retorted impatiently.

"Well, only three quarters of the fleet have come out of the gate captain!" The Blue replied worriedly. Bull immediately hailed Argo.

Argo appeared on the bridge moments later, worry etched on his manly features. "How many have we lost?" Argo asked the Blue urgently.

"Three hundred ships commander." Bull and Argo looked at each other in shock.

"We can't just lose three hundred ships!" Bull cried out, at no one in particular. "Could they have already exited?" Bull inquired hopefully.

The Blue shook his head and replied that there were no ships on their sensors for billions of miles in any direction.

"Maybe they just haven't come through yet..." Bull managed hopefully, but he knew this was unlikely.

"Well, we could wait by the gate for a few hours more, but I think we would be wasting our time." Argo replied calmly.

"But we can't give up on them!" Bull argued. "We can't leave behind part of the fleet! We must do something."

Argo saw how this tore into Bull and he himself was at a loss at what could have happened.

"Has this sort of thing ever happened to you ?" Argo asked Kios hopefully.

"No, not to me personally, but I have heard of others who lost part of their convoy in a gate some years ago." He looked down at his console to hide his expression.

"And what happened to them?" Bull asked impatiently.

"I'm sorry, Captain, they were never seen again!" Kios replied sadly.

***

The news

Cressus appeared on the horizon, like a gigantic haze of blue. The planet was surrounded by swirling clouds of blue, twisting and coiling in opposing directions around the globe. There was no time to ponder over the demise of the fleet; they would have to sort that out once the people of Gar-Too had been informed about the news of their planet's restoration. Once they had hailed the Gar-Toyans, they planned on taking two ships to descend to the planet, carrying some members of the crew and the security force. Ursu and Genai were looking forward to gleaning new stocks of rock samples yet again and were keen to discover the merits of the planet.

Blue 7 managed to patch a line through to the planet below and was connected to the President's secretary. Argo greeted the woman and gave a brief statement , mentioning their wish to speak to the president of Gar-Too, that they brought good news. After some deliberation the secretary confirmed that two shuttles could come to meet their ambassador and their army commander on the planet, but they were to land on the far side of the camp out of sight of the city dwellers. The storm that was raging at the time would help hide their arrival they found later.

***

Lin looked at Gale as they sat strapped in as the ship descended into orbit around the planet. Fay was seated next to Lin.

"The people aren't happy here." Lin remarked to her mother. "There are lots of bad people here." she added. Gale held her hand tightly and looked at the rest of the crew.

Finch and Star checked their weapons to make sure they were prepared for a confrontation.

Argo came over to Gale. "Perhaps you and Lin had better stay on board until we can check how safe it is."

Gale nodded and looked to her daughter, thankful that she had the second sight.

"Inform the other ship of possible danger." Argo commanded the co-pilot.

***

They landed at an encampment clearly added next to the borders of a city nearby. Through the dust thrown up by the storm, they saw there were several spacecraft parked up in the distance that the Blue thought must belong to the Gar-Toyans. As the ramp was lowered on Argo's ship, the security force with Argo and Bull led the way forward. The rest of the human crew were told to wait on board until it was confirmed safe. They edged out over the ramp with guns trained in front of them and in the distance, through the swirling storm, they saw a large group of about twenty soldiers staggering towards them.

They were also armed.

A shout arose from the group of soldiers. "What is your business here?"

Argo looked at Bull and then stepped forward to speak, but the howling wind swirling around them made it difficult ,so he would have to shout.

"We come in peace! We seek the president and people of Gar-Too to give them good news." Argo shouted above the gale.

A single soldier and a civilian edged forward, the soldier carrying a weapon of some sort across his chest. He called for Argo and Bull to come forward to meet him, Bull checked that his gun was ready if he needed it. They ended up standing ten paces apart.

The dark haired soldier looked to be aged around forty, with a scar across his face. His uniform was looking battle worn, with several slashes across the leather jacket he wore. He looked in need of a wash and a shave. He had the same features that the Gar-Toyan president had on his face, the v shaped hairline, lilac eyes and ridges to either side of his head. He spoke first.

"You say you have news of Gar-Too? What do you know of it?" The man eyed Bull suspiciously.

Bull weighed him up and reckoned he'd had a few rough deals in his past and was therefore wary of him.

"My news is for the people of Gar-Too." said Argo. "Who are you?"

The man looked him up and down then looked him in the eye before replying.

"I am Krisus, commander in charge of the Gar-Toyan army and this is Helon, our ambassador, state your business." He kept a cool exterior and Bull felt he could easily overpower him in an instant should he wish to. He looked so battle experienced.

"My name is Argo, fleet commander from the fleet ship Starfinder from Earth and this is Captain Bull Carter. We happened by your planet some months ago and got caught up in its floods." Bull watched as recognition entered the man's face.

"So, the floods still flow then!" Krisus nodded without showing any emotion. Argo persevered.

"No. We, as a fleet felt it such a waste of a beautiful planet, to be ruined by these floods, so our scientists worked out a plan to stop them occurring again."

Krisus looked interested for the first time, so Argo continued and told him how they had righted the moon and Gar-Too and monitored the results to make sure the floods had permanently retreated. He said they were welcome to see their footage of Gar-Too's progress on board their ship if they wished. The ambassador looked at Krisus suspiciously.

"Why did you wish to tell us this?" asked Helon. Bull realised he was suspicious of their motives.

"We're here to let all the people of Gar-Too know that they can go back home! It is safe!" Argo replied as Bull smiled at both men. The look on Krisus' face was a picture.

"Then show us your proof." Helon demanded. Bull and Argo led them to the shuttle, as another soldier came to accompany them. They stood to one side of the screen, watching the Blue on board warily. On seeing the live feeds of his home with dry streets and the receded waters, Krisus dared to smile for the first time.

"How do we know this isn't just footage between the floods?" Helon asked. The Blue swept his fingers over the touch screen deftly and the Gar-Toyans watched as a time lapse period of one month was played out in accelerated speed of the streets of Gar-Too, with no sign of floods to be seen at all. Finally, Helon was convinced.

The ambassador looked from Bull to Argo as if weighing them up then said. "What is it you want from us in return? I'm sure you don't just do this out of the kindness of your hearts?"

Argo replied that they only wished to include the Gar-Toyans as allies for Earth should they need their help in the future. Helon looked to Krisus and the other soldier and they conferred briefly in private. After a few moments Helon came forward.

"This is a great thing that you have done for our people, but getting back to Gar-Too is not so simple. We have many problems, as you will see in our camp. I think we'd better show you. I will also need to speak with our president, Troi-Kah about your proposal."

***

As Krisus related the news to his comrades they threw fists into the air and cheered, relief clear on their faces. They invited Argo and Bull's party over to their encampment to meet their president, Troi Kah. Argo thought it wise not to let the others on board the ship join them just yet, until they knew what was awaiting them.

The encampment was sprawled for a couple of miles along the borders of the city and was a direct contrast to the buildings seen in the city itself. This was where the Gar-Toyans were allowed to live by the Cressus government. They had not been welcomed with open arms here it seemed, only tolerated, of sorts.

Troi Kah had been assured of safety for all his people here on Cressus but on their arrival it seemed that the

Cressians were only interested in the income they could command from their stay here. The government had re-neged on the initial deal of allowing the Gar-Toyans to integrate fully with the Cressians and permitting them to live within areas of the city.

The government patrolled their city limits with armed guards, only permitting a small group of Gar-Toyans to enter through the city gates at any one time, and that was only to purchase food. The prices kept going up each time they entered and soon the Gar-Toyans would be starved out of existence here. It was only a matter of time.

After meeting with the grateful president, who wel-comed the news of his beloved planet's restoration with great joy, Krisus then invited them to his shelter, a moulded dome-like tent structure, big enough for a dozen people to live in at any one time. It would give the ambas-sador and Troi-Kah time to confer about their intentions.

Krisus' tent was sparsely furnished with boxes for seats and inflated bedding in one section. A plank of wood stretched over two boxes served as a table in the centre. It only really provided respite from the storm rag-ing outside.

Bull wondered how low the temperature dropped to here. It was not really conducive to healthy living and the whole encampment was built of the same structures. In the corner of the tent sat three females, one of whom was lying on a bed covered in what looked like people's cloth-ing for extra warmth. Two children sat huddled together for warmth next to them. Star realised that the woman was ill with a fever.

"She has a fever, what's wrong with her?" Star asked Krisus directly.

He looked over at the woman sadly. "That is my wife, Omera, and my children Reyton and Reysha. My wife fell ill two days ago, but we have no medicines here and the Cressians will not provide us with any. I think they would like us all to die off one by one!" Krisus replied sadly.

"But that's barbaric!" Bull retorted angrily. "Have you tried reasoning with these people?"

Krisus replied that they had, with no effect and that in the beginning groups of them tried to sneak into the city to get medical supplies, but were met by armed guards and none of them returned alive. Several times they had skirmishes with the local people and had to defend themselves from attacks on their camp. It was suffer your lot or move elsewhere!

Argo asked Krisus if they had medics and Krisus replied that although there were several, they had no medicines at all. They had tried to do their best but it was impossible without supplies. Theirs had run out years ago.

Argo asked permission to bring the others, which included their ship's medics into the camp. Krisus readily agreed, so Argo hailed Guy on his mic and asked him to bring the others over. He sent one of Finch's team over to guide them to where they were.

***

Star watched as the two women bathed the woman's head in damp cloths and held her hand, taking it in turns. The two children looked frightened at the sight of their mother being ill.

In a few minutes the rest of the shuttle crew arrived at Krisus' shelter, escorted by a guard.

***

The illness

The Gar-Toyans looked suspiciously at the Su-K-en people, most never having met any before, but apparently they had no problem with the robots as they had some of their own, used for menial tasks around the home and work back on Gar-Too, nothing of the intelligence of Argo and the other AIs.

The Endari girls looked disdainfully at the humble abode until Da-Ee shoved them hard in the ribs, letting them know her disgust with their attitude.

Guy went directly over to Omera and scanned her body with his equipment. He looked at the readings and then spoke directly to Krisus, worry etched all over his face. "How long has she been like this?"

Krisus replied that it had been a couple of days.

Guy spoke again, "And how many people have been in contact with her since she fell ill?"

Krisus and the others began to feel uneasy.

"All of us here now and two more. I sent the others to stay elsewhere when she fell ill so she could have peace. Why?" Guy looked at the crew.

"Did any of you come close to her?" Guy asked urgently. Everyone shook their heads, looking extremely afraid now.

"Get away from this tent, she's contagious! " Guy ordered his colleagues. "Krisus, the two people that you say had contact with her, where are they now?" Guy demanded urgently.

"They are standing guard outside my tent." Krisus replied, his heart racing.

Bull and the others went to stand back outside the tent as the two guards were asked inside. Argo looked at the crew and felt their concern.

"Don't worry. You haven't been in there long enough to be affected, Guy was right to send us out." Argo stated calmly.

"But what about Guy himself?" asked Star worriedly. "He's now exposed to the contagion!" She looked to Bull then back to Argo.

"I'm sure Guy will have it all in hand. Let's not worry unnecessarily." Argo replied, trying to sound confident, although he was unsure if his comment was based on truth!

One of Krisus' soldiers came over to the wind-blown group and asked them to come with him out of the storm. He led them into his own tent nearby and they shook the debris that had blown onto them out of their hair and clothes.

"I am Kafaar, the second in command here, welcome." He reached out to shake hands with Bull. "Krisus tells me that you have brought us the most welcome news about Gar-Too. You don't know how much this means to us!" He indicated for them to sit down on the blankets that were draped in one part of the tent.

"I would offer you refreshments, but I'm afraid we have such short supplies, everything is rationed here." Kafaar stated unhappily.

"We have plenty of food supplies on our ship that's orbiting the planet." stated Argo reassuringly. "It would be no problem to stock your fleet up with provisions for your journey back to Gar-Too."

Kafaar was surprised to hear this news and a broad smile filled his dust smeared face.

" Krisus tells me you have a medic looking at his wife?"

He replied that Guy was hoping to help her but he wasn't sure if he had the right medicines or not, but that Guy would be sure to do his best.

As Helon re-appeared in Kafaar's tent Bull realised that everything was on short supply here and that seemed to include fresh water to enable the people to bathe properly too. He knew that in order to be able to make it back to Gar-Too alive these people would need some basic supplies first of all.

They would have to provide some of the food and water that they had on the Starfinder to these people. That would be a logistical nightmare, given the numbers of people here!

Helon confirmed that the Gar-Toyans would ally themselves with Earth and offer the help of their army in times of need if the robot army were prepared initially to help restore Gar-Too with them. Argo agreed. He would offer them their help for the first six weeks until they could begin to help themselves.

***

Bull and Argo thought the sooner that they could feed the people the better, then they could load up with supplies to their ships here on Cressus before leaving for Gar-Too. They conferred over rough numbers with Helon so that they could start as quickly as possible.

Ursu went over to the man and woman seated on the floor nearby.

"How long do these storms usually last over here?" Ursu inquired with interest, eager to be out collecting samples for her lab.

"Oh, not long, the storms usually last no more than a week at a time!" The woman replied.

"A week!" Ursu gasped. She didn't fancy being stuck here that long! "And how long has this current storm been going then?" she asked tentatively.

"Well, actually, this one has been going for eight days now! Quite unusual." the woman replied helpfully.

Ursu groaned, *This was going to be a waste of time,* she thought.

Lin looked over at Ursu and spoke. "Don't worry Ursu. It will be over in a few minutes!"

Ursu looked astounded at the child. By the roar of the wind outside it certainly didn't sound like it, but Lin was a shrewd kid, thought Ursu, she would wait and see.

The man laughed at her remark, shaking his head.

***

Guy stood beside Omera's own doctor, confirming the diagnosis, then he injected Omera with a serum that he hoped would help her. His face masked against the contagion, it made him think of the time they all wore masks back at home on Earth , when the air had been too polluted to walk outside without one. He scanned the others inside the tent and discovered that the two children had early signs of the illness too. Luckily none of the others had been exposed enough to be affected thus far, however, Guy would need to treat all of them to prevent the illness spreading.

The illness he'd heard about before. It rendered those affected with severe headaches, then fever, followed by convulsions and loss of life. He was sure that he'd arrived in time to prevent it advancing to its final stage, another day and it might have been different. He certainly thought that she had contracted the illness from living in these harsh conditions.

***

Ursu opened the tent's flap to reveal a blue sky with not a hint of breeze in it at all! Lin had been right! It had been three minutes since she had assured them it would cease soon!

The man and woman followed her out of the tent, completely overwhelmed by the accuracy of Lin's prediction. The rest of the people came out of the tent to survey the calm contrast to the vigorous storm they had just encountered.

Bull looked over towards the nearby city walls. It was easier to see now that there was no storm obstructing their view. To Bull it looked like the medieval castles of old that he'd read about in the Hub library. The crenellated walls, encompassing turreted stone built towers and vast buildings, stretched along the length of the encampment for hundreds of metres.

To one side was an arched gateway allowing entrance to the city, but a metal curtain filled the gap inside the doorway. There were guard turrets on either side of the gateway to protect it. It was hard to see from here how far the city extended as the walls were so high and because of the storm as they landed it had been hard to see its extent from the skies too. All around the Gar-Toyan encampment the army had created defence ditches to try and protect themselves as much as possible given the circumstances. Bull wondered how often they had to defend themselves here.

From what Argo gleaned from Helon, the people of Cressus were fairly primitive people, with no modern technology to speak of. It was only through visiting the planet that Troi-Kah's ambassador had managed to secure a place for them here, but on their arrival they had resented the Gar-Toyans' superior technology and turned against them over the years.

***

On Cressus

The Endari girls whizzed backwards and forwards at great speed looking for samples of rock and soil to take back to the lab, and the Gar-Toyans watched in astonishment at the speed the girls could move. They obviously had never encountered such a thing before! Professor Chase went in search of any medicinal plants growing in the spartan landscape, but found very little there.

Gale, Fay and Lin walked around the encampment with Finch and Star to protect them if needed. There were so many people here that they wondered how on earth they were all fed. Children ran in the dust and debris left by the storm, picking up fallen branches and making use of them as makeshift swords to form a pretend battle amongst themselves. Lin and Fay ran over to play with them under the watchful eye of Gale.

"How many of you are there in this encampment?" inquired Bull, wanting to figure out how long it would take to get them fed before their return to Gar-Too.

"We are three hundred thousand give or take a few." Helon replied tentatively. Bull whistled. A lot of bodies to feed!

"Well, I guess the sooner we get going with feeding you the better!" replied Argo , adding "We can set up a few feeding stations in a few hours here, and we'll get some of our fleet robots to ferry down supplies for your journey back to Gar-Too as soon as possible."

Kafaar and Helon nodded happily and went off to organise a few groups of refugees to help set up an area for the feeding stations. Helon and Kafaar came back in half an hour with news that four areas were being prepared for that purpose.

Argo told Kafaar that Guy would probably want to treat Omera and the infected on board the Starfinder in the medical bay as soon as possible, where isolation bays were available for such an event over there.

Kafaar went over to Krisus' tent to confirm that.

Argo called the Starfinder on his mic, asking the Bronzes to make ready enough food supplies for three hundred thousand people to return to Gar-Too. Also he asked them to bring down four feeding stations, ready supplied to feed the people here as soon as possible.

The Bronze commander said it would be no problem and they would bring down the feeding stations immediately, with enough robots to run them. He figured that three shuttles would bring down food supplies for their journey within the hour. He also thought it would be advisable to bring full water containers for the people to stock on their ships too.

Argo was proud to have such efficiency amongst his army. He went to tell Bull and Kafaar the news so they would be ready to receive the despatches.

"Do you have any other people who require medical services?" Argo asked Kafaar as an afterthought. Kafaar replied that there were a few elderly people who were suffering with stiffness from the cold nights on Cressus and could hardly walk, but that was all.

"I'll get our medic to give them injections before he leaves with the infected for our ship." Argo replied.

Kafaar thanked him and went to see the people concerned to let them know. Now, the main thing was to get the people fed and supplied, then they could begin their journey back to Gar-Too. Argo also thought it would probably be better for the contagious people to stay on the Starfinder until they were well and they could rejoin their people once the Starfinder met them on Gar-Too.

***

In an hour Guy and Gale were armed with enough ampoules to administer vital injections into the elderly with arthritic joints and supplied them with medicines to keep them mobile for a few months. They were extremely grateful to Guy and gave him a small gift as thanks for his help. When he opened the little box he found inside an intricately engraved silver torc. It was so beautiful Guy felt embarrassed to accept it, but the people insisted and so he wore it to please them. He then took the infected family via shuttle up to the Starfinder to treat them in the isolation bay. Krisus came along to watch over his family, grateful for Guy's care.

***

The feeding stations were set up in the allocated spaces by a large group of robots, carrying the equipment on hoverboards to their preferred site. A canopy was placed around the feeding area so that it kept out the elements. The Gar-Toyans provided boxed seating and tables in the space around the food service area as they would no longer need them with their tents. People busied themselves with packing away their temporary dwellings and making preparations to get their ships ready for flight again. They had their own service-bots that helped them out with such tasks Bull noted.

***

The first line of people were gathered by Kafaar to attend the feeding stations, the young and the elderly were called first, being the most needy. For some it was the first decent meal they had received in weeks, having previously lived on the scraps the Cressians sold them when they were allowed to enter the town gates. Up on the ramparts above the encampment a group of guards had gathered to view the activities taking place below them. Since the arrival of the supply shuttles there was much pointing and conferring going on up there Bull noticed. He saw too that Finch had realised there was trouble brewing on the horizon and he gave Bull a nod to confirm that he was watching the goings on over there.

Bull was relieved to see that Kafaar had organised their people well at the feeding stations and progress was steady as people went along the line to receive their food. Nobody showed impatience whilst they awaited their turn, so Bull went up to speak to Kafaar.

"I've noticed a lot of activity going on over on the ramparts over there. Are we likely to have trouble from the Cressians do you think?" Bull asked worriedly.

"Yes, I noticed that. So far the Cressians have not ventured into our camp demanding anything, but their attitude towards us is not exactly welcoming! It could possibly be a problem, but I'm not sure." Kafaar replied truthfully.

"How well armed are they?" Bull asked again, looking carefully to see if he could spot what kind of weapons they held.

Kafaar said that he'd only seen the guards with bows and spears on the ramparts and around the town the soldiers carried swords as well.

"No guns?" Bull inquired hopefully.

"I haven't seen any. I think they haven't yet been encountered here on Cressus! With a bit of luck we could easily hold our own against them if there was to be trouble." Bull hoped so, but he couldn't count on it. He went to inform the security team.

Chapter 14

The fight

It was the second day. Hours had passed and the feeding stations were working well. Dusk was beginning to fall and the temperature was dropping. Most of the people who had been fed were now stowed on board their ships, with all their tents and belongings packed away ready.

The encampment had large bare patches in it where the tents had previously been, for as soon as the people had been fed they packed up the remainder of their goods and took them to their allocated ships ready for the flight home. Their ships had been supplied with enough food and water and medicines to last the journey home by a relay of shuttles from the robots on the Starfinder. All that remained to be fed were the strongest, the soldiers of Gar-Too, but still numbering twenty-five thousand at least.

All of Bull's crew, bar his security team, had long since returned to the Starfinder. But, just in case there was trouble shuttles of Silvers and seven Argonauts had landed on Cressus on Argo's orders as a large gathering of troops had amassed on the ramparts along the city walls.

There had been a lot of noise coming from the city for hours, as though troops were deployed ready for a battle. Bull wondered what the Cressians could possibly want to fight about, he thought that they would be glad to see the Gar-Toyans leave their planet after the way they had treated them. All the robots eyed the ramparts for any signs of aggressive behaviour.

As the last of the men ate their long awaited meals a commotion was heard from the direction of the city gates. It was hard to see anything as darkness had fallen hours previously and only a few torches lit the area between the feeding stations and the ramparts. A metallic grating sound was heard coming from the gateway. The gate was being opened!

The robots formed a line between the remaining soldiers and the city walls. It was a formidable sight, almost like a white wall of warriors with red lighted eyes. Glowing in the dark were also the multi coloured buttons each robot displayed on each arm, ready for confrontation.

They all heard troops marching out of the gates towards them, with the clanking of metal echoing along as they walked. The Gar-Toyan soldiers got up from their tables to confront the Cressians alongside the robot line that stood in front of them. The Cressian troops halted around a hundred metres from the robot line, looking with interest at the strange wall of white.

Then two men stepped forward from the rest of the troops and headed a few metres closer to talk. One of them was a large burly man with a snake tattoo on his shaven head; he wore a necklace of teeth around his neck. They looked to be human teeth. The other man was smaller, with wiry unkempt hair and he kept looking anxiously at his neighbour as if he was afraid of him.

The burly man spoke. "I am Cardacius, head of the Cressian army and these are my troops." He looked to the wiry man to his left and the man nervously handed him a roll of parchment, which he then ceremoniously unrav-

elled. "I have a message to read from our leader to you."
He began to read the message on the parchment.

*"Any man wishing refuge on Cressus must pay the
Cressian emperor the sum of one hundred credits before
leaving his land. This is to compensate the emperor for
the care the refugee has received during his stay on Cressus.*

*By order of the Emperor Daionius, fifth Emperor of
Cressus."*

The man rolled up the parchment again and handed
it back to his aide, then continued his speech.

"By the emperor's reckoning, you number in excess
of two hundred thousand persons, therefore if you intend
to leave, as I see that by your preparations here you do,
then you may not leave until you have paid the emperor
the sum of twenty million credits!"

A deathly silence fell over the Gar-Toyan soldiers
as they digested the information, then Kafaar laughed at
the ridiculousness of the declaration. He stepped forward
to speak.

"I am Saiam Kafaar, leader of these people. You as-
tound me with your belated declaration! When we asked
for refuge here on Cressus there was no mention of such a
levy on our stay. In fact, we have received very little in
terms of care, as you put it, from your people! Everything
we have received we have paid extortionate prices for it.
Goods that were often unfit for human consumption! How
dare you demand anything more from us! You will receive nothing but our removal from your *caring* city! "
Kafaar stood defiantly in front of the troops.

The burly man, now enraged, grabbed his helmet

from his aide and before placing it on his head spoke just once more, full of hatred. "Then you will all die rather than leave this place!"

He brandished his sword and grabbed a shield from his aide and the whole army of Cressians spewed out of the gate of the city and ran towards them shouting and banging their shields as loud as they could! The horde were wild with blood lust and the Gar-Toyans began to shoot at them with their weapons as fast as they could. Their guns though would only last a limited time as their ammunition was already running low. Many bullets bounced off the enemy's shields.

***

Finch and Star fired a relay of bullets into the horde and several fell in their wake. Argo and the Silvers tried to encircle the human crew of the Starfinder to protect them as they fired into the Cressian army, but although the robots decimated the front runners of the Cressian army in their droves, the Cressians overran the front line, resulting in many of the crew battling it out in hand to hand combat. The Gar-Toyans also engaging in hand to hand combat as the Cressians overtook their ranks, but the robot army strode towards the bulk of the enemy, firing their deadly rays into the mob, decimating their ranks like they were a pack of cards falling over one by one! The Cressians who were yet to reach the front line saw the carnage in front of them as their comrades succumbed to the robots' deadly force!

The seven Argonauts then flew above the horde and blasted them with warning shots above their heads and disintegrating their metal shields. Their eyes wide with shock and fear, they began to run back towards the city gate in their hundreds, leaving behind them the last vestiges of their ineffectual army to be driven to the ground by the Gar-Toyan soldiers' line of defence.

Very soon the short battle was over, with the enemy left cowering behind their ramparts after discovering the might of the robot army. Despite the retreat, there were several mounds of bodies heaped along the front line, where the battle had been thickest. The Gar-Toyans began to help their wounded, retrieving them from the carnage.

***

Finch lifted Star up off the floor, where she had tripped over a fallen enemy's body as she had fought another bravely. She looked around at the piles of enemy bodies, lying in heaps along the blood-soaked terrain and recoiled in horror at the sheer numbers of dead fallen at her feet. She saw Meera lift herself off the floor a few paces away, holding her arm. She shouldn't have been there at all, but she and Kian had come to join the crew when they saw the gathering of the enemy on the ramparts, aiming to support their friends.

"Meera! Are you hurt?" Star leapt towards her, concerned.

"Oh, it's nothing! I just caught the edge of a sword as a man fell onto me, that's all." Meera replied, wiping her bloodied face with her sleeve. A Silver rushed to look at her arm and found it wasn't too deep; she'd be okay he advised, much to her relief.

"Where's Bull?" Finch asked Argo as he looked around him urgently. There was no sign of Bull anywhere!

"Where did anyone last see Bull?" Finch shouted to be heard.

People shook their heads. They hadn't noticed where he was fighting. Panic began to fill Finch and Star as they scanned the piles of bodies in front of them. They called out his name, but there was no sound to be heard in reply.

The Gar-Toyan soldiers began to lift up some of the bodies piled in front of them, fearing the worst! Star and Finch looked at each other, they could not lose their friend, it was beyond horrible to think of! Suddenly a Gar-Toyan soldier called out from the left flank of the piles of bodies in front of the encampment. He had found Bull in the middle of the pile at his feet!

***

The operation.

Argo ran over towards Bull's body before anyone had a chance to move, as his crew froze in horror at the thought that their friend and captain lay dead in front of them. He lifted Bull's bloodied body up and flew with him over to their shuttle to gasps of shock from the Gar-Toyans below.

Star, Finch, and Meera ran towards the shuttle, praying that Argo could save their friend. When they caught up with Argo inside the shuttle Bull had already been laid out on an emergency bed within. Star could see a knife jutting out from Bull's side, blood pouring from the wound! She sank to her knees and began to sob uncontrollably. Finch rested his hand on her shoulder, equally distraught, but trying to remain positive for Star's benefit.

"I'm sure Argo can help him Star, you know how fantastic their technology is!" Finch tried his best to suppress his fear that his friend was gone from him as Argo looked sombrely at the two of them.

"Tell Kafaar we have to go up to the Starfinder to save Bull immediately!" Argo told the Silver standing by the pilot. "You can come up in one of the other shuttles later." The Silver ran out of the shuttle to do exactly that, pressing the button to close the ramp on his way past. The pilot had the engines going in a second and the shuttle lifted off without further ado.

"Is there anything I can do?" Finch asked, looking at Bull's wound.

Argo got him to press on Bull's wound with a gauze pad whilst he sorted out an IV for him. There was no time to waste! The knife would have to stay in his side until Guy could operate on the wound properly. Bull barely had a pulse, he had lost a lot of blood already! It was fortunate that the soldier found him quite soon, or it might have been too late. The only option they would have had then was to clone him!

***

Argo was the epitome of efficiency as he set up the drip for Bull and dealt with pain relief for him, whilst Finch applied pressure to the wound. It was obvious from the angle of the knife that Bull had been struck from behind as he was probably grappling with another soldier at the time. Such cowardice he could not tolerate, war or not!

He changed the pressure pad for a dry one as the blood had soaked through already. Argo hailed the med lab and spoke to Guy to make sure that he was prepared for surgery when they arrived at the Starfinder. There was no time to lose. Bull's eyes flickered slightly as the pain relief kicked in, but his eyes closed again immediately after a few seconds as he lapsed into unconsciousness.

The shuttle had made it to the mother ship in record time, the Blue had given it all he had, concerned for his captain. At the docking bay Guy's assistants were ready with a hover stretcher to carry Bull straight to theatre, where Guy was scrubbed ready. Star and Finch watched him disappear out of their view as the robots hurried along with the hovering stretcher, not wasting any time.

***

Meera temporarily had her arm bandaged by a Silver on the shuttle after having her wound cleaned with a steri-swab. She felt no real pain so she felt she could wait to be seen properly once Bull was out of danger. The crew headed for the lounge, they could all do with a stiff drink after their battle! It wasn't every day you fought for your life after all!

Star and Finch didn't feel like drinking, all they could do was think of their friend. They passed Gale in the corridor all dressed up in hospital whites, she said that she was going to help Guy should he need it in surgery. Star thanked her, grateful at her offer to help.

In an hour Argo came to see how they were faring and sat down with them to give them an update on what he intended to do, It would be a few hours before Bull would be out of theatre, so he had no news about him yet. He had placed Kios in charge of the bridge in Bull's absence and he explained that the intention was for the fleet to leave in a few hours, along with the Gar-Toyans' fleet to head for the Corona gate and then on to Gar-Too.

When the gate was mentioned the crew's eyes showed their concern over the journey through it. They all still pondered over what happened to the rest of their fleet and nobody knew if they'd ever see them again. And what if more of their fleet were to disappear? What then? They were fearful of what could happen, but there was no option but to go through it. Argo had discussed the incident with Kafaar, but none of the Gar-Toyans had experienced any difficulty with the gate when they had gone through it and found it a complete mystery.

They all waited fearfully in the lounge, preferring each other's company whilst they awaited news on Bull. Ursu and Genai were comforting a distraught Da-Ee in one corner of the lounge, she really had deep feelings for Bull, Star realised. She wasn't sure how she felt about that, in one sense she felt a pang of jealousy towards her, but that was ridiculous she realised, her love was for Finch.

***

"Well, we've come a long way and we've achieved much of what we set out to do, and more." Meera remarked as she leant on Kian on the lounge chair. "We've practically formed alliances with the Scenarians, Gar-Toyans and the Coserai. Earth will be pleased with that!" Ursu interrupted from the corner next to them.

"Don't forget the people of Su-K-En! Our people would be glad to form an alliance with Earth I know. My father is the Head of State on our planet and I know he is always trying to build up alliances with other people."

Kian and Meera smiled at her response, then Kian spoke.

"We have also found new technology on our travels, thanks to you girls in many ways! Our cloaking system, the impenetrable metal to name but two. Now we are setting up a Hydroponics sector thanks to Professor Chase. Captain Grey will be proud of us." He hugged Meera again and the room went silent once more, apart from a few stifled sobs from Da-Ee.

Kios had just arrived from the bridge and he went to add his view. "Yes, we have achieved much. The people of Gar-Too will be home again and I'm sure they will waste no time in sorting out their cities, making them fit for habitation. The Scenarians are happily ensconced on Gley and the Coserai people I'm sure will benefit from their company. The Starfinder has become a veritable rescue ship!" He smiled at the thought of them as inter galactic do-gooders. But missions seemed to come their way that was for sure! Bull loved a challenge..

"I think I would like to come back with you to see your Earth." announced Da-Ee all of a sudden, which made the two Endaris think about it and decide they would like to as well.

Kios then nodded and agreed that he would like to see the beautiful planet he'd heard so much about from Bull and Kian..

"Well, you would all be very welcome to come back there with us." Finch announced gladly." Bull will be pleased to have Da-Ee come back with him I'm sure," he smiled directly at her, which caused Da-Ee to form a small smile briefly.

The silence returned as they all waited glumly for any news of Bull.

***

Result

The hours ticked by and everyone became nervous

at the length of time it was taking to operate on Bull. It would be unthinkable to lose him like this. Star paced backwards and forwards in the lounge, worried that things were going wrong.

"Why haven't we heard anything? It's been longer than Argo said! Something's wrong!" Star yelled bitterly. Finch came over to hold her in his arms to comfort her. Minutes passed, then a harassed looking Argo came into the lounge with news. They all stood up, craving to hear what was happening.

"Bull's lost a kidney. We had to clone him another one, which is why it took so long. He's lost a lot of blood. He had a lot of help from Gale, it was lucky she was a blood match and Guy used her for giving him a transfusion in the theatre. He is coming out of theatre now, but it will be a while before he regains consciousness."

Da-Ee stood in front of Argo and pleaded. "But he's going to be all right? He is going to recover isn't he?"

Argo looked at the awaiting crowd, realising how much Bull meant to them. "Time will tell, but Guy is hopeful of a full recovery," he replied, hoping it was true. The crew hugged each other with relief etched on their faces at last.

Da-Ee looked over at Star and knew her pain, for she felt the same.

***

"Kian and Kios, we need you back on the bridge to make preparations for the fleet's departure for the Corona Gate. My second in command, Pallas will cover my duties whilst I am occupied with other things, he awaits you on the bridge. The Gar-Toyans have almost completed their clear up of their encampment below us on Cressus and they will leave within the hour. They have no wish to linger on Cressus longer than necessary as you can well imagine."

Argo was relieved. He had himself worried that Bull might have to be cloned completely because of his injuries, but now it seemed he might well pull through. He had not wanted to let his friends know that they lost him once on the operating table. It was only through Guy's skill that he had been resuscitated.

***

Bull lay in the medi-bay, tied to drips and monitors, which were recording his every function. Da-Ee was allowed to visit him briefly, but he was unaware of her presence due to his sedated state. She held his hand lovingly and caressed his forehead, sweeping aside a few strands of golden hair from his eyes.

He looked so peaceful lying there she thought. She couldn't wait for him to wake up, but that wasn't to happen for a long while yet!

Guy came along to check on his vital signs and made a note on his i-pad. He told Da-Ee to come back in a few hours when he would be more likely to awaken, so she kissed his cheek and left to join the Endari girls who waited for her outside.

Guy moved over to the next cubicle to check on Meera's wound, but found that the Silver had made a good attempt at treating it. It didn't require more than a couple of steri strips to keep it together as it healed. The wound had been cleaned well and it should heal in no time at all he reported to Meera.

"How's our captain doing?" Meera nodded over towards the cubicle next to her, beyond the glider that separated them.

"He should be fine if the cloned kidney is accepted." Guy replied.

"And if it isn't?" Meera probed worriedly.

"Then we'll have to take him back to theatre and remove it." Guy answered, not wanting to reveal his fears over that procedure. "Okay! Your arm will be fine. You have my permission to return to the bridge," he added brusquely.

Meera got up and exited the medi-bay, looking over towards the stricken Bull as she passed the foot of his cubicle. He looked so pale she thought, and for once, helpless.

Across the room, in a sealed tented cubicle lay Omera and her two children, isolated from the main ward. She looked asleep and calm as her husband stroked her hair seated next to her and their two children.

Guy had a lot on his plate she realised, it was no wonder Gale went to help him in theatre. The bots were a help, obviously, but a human's touch is so different. Krisus looked up and saw her leave the ward and he gave a slight nod and smile at her before resuming his attention upon his family.

***

Lin rushed into the lounge with Fay, searching for her mother. She saw Gale sipping coffee next to Genai, so she went over to her mother and gave her a hug.

"You helped the captain." Lin stated with a satisfied look on her face.

Gale confirmed it and asked her if she needed her for anything, but Lin replied that she thought it would be good if she worked with Guy full time as he needed her help and that she needn't worry about her because Fay was looking after her and that she enjoyed playing with her very much. Gale looked at her daughter and smiled.

"Well, aren't you growing up fast!" Gale responded, marvelling at her daughter's perceptiveness. "Well, I guess that he could do with some help, perhaps I will!" Gale beamed at her daughter and gave her another hug.

As Gale prepared for her evening shift at the medi bay she could feel his presence nearby. She hadn't felt it this strongly since before Lin was born! Her body glowed inside with the warmth he was sending her. He was very near, she realised. Was he watching over her? Would he come back to see her? How she had longed for that. She hadn't realised how much until now.

***

The gate. Leaving Cressus.

The Gar-Toyan fleet headed off past the robot army's ships and made towards the Corona gate which lay some distance ahead. It was time to move once more. Kios took the comms instead of Bull and Pallas commanded the fleet to head towards the same gate, but leaving a respectable distance between them. In six days the fleet would be once more passing the Sventhri pirates home world, and they would have to remain cloaked to get by. Kios realised that they hadn't had time to ask the Gar-Toyans how they managed to pass the Sventhri without hassle on the way to Cressus. He would make sure to go and find out from Krisus before they left the gate the other end!

Omera was responding well to treatment and Guy reckoned that the family would be well recovered before they exited the gate at the other end. They hoped the same would happen with Bull. The countdown had begun and soon the Starfinder and its fleet of ships were travelling through the Corona gate, experiencing once again the annoying feeling of floating as they walked around the ship, doing their various jobs.

***

The next day, down in the medi-bay Star looked at Bull's pale face as he lay surrounded by bleeps and drips. He looked so different down here, like this, like a helpless child needing to be looked after. She was tempted to kiss his forehead, but instead held his hand. She was concerned that it felt clammy and cold.

"Guy! Can you take a look at Bull?" Star called out around the slider. Guy put down his notes and rushed over to the cubicle.

"Feel his hand." Star exclaimed worriedly. "It feels cold and clammy. It's not meant to be like that is it?" she asked worriedly. Guy scanned Bull's body immediately and pushed a button on the wall that set off an alarm, bringing three medi-bots to Bull's bedside in an instant.

"Prepare him for theatre!" Guy ordered his aides urgently, then he turned to Star and spoke. "Get Gale to prep for theatre, I need to operate, he's rejecting his new kidney!"

Star stood frozen for a second as she watched Bull being hauled past her on his way to theatre, then something clicked inside her and she hailed Gale to give her the message.

***

The agonising wait started again, as the crew prayed

for a good result on Bull's operation. Da-Ee and Star were the most affected by the news of his kidney rejection. Star had gone to Da-Ee's room to let her know about Bull's deterioration and she decided to wait with her until the operation was over as she was overwhelmed by her fears for him. They sat side by side on Da-Ee's settee, unable to contemplate eating or drinking anything until the op was over.

Ursu and Genai had come to see Da-Ee on hearing the bad news, but she told them she'd be fine waiting with Star while Guy performed his miracle! Ursu was reluctant to leave her, but Da-Ee insisted that they had wasted enough of their valuable scientific study time on waiting around with her already. She knew they had experiments to conduct down in the science lab and she felt guilty keeping them away from their work.

"She'll be fine with me." Star reassured the pair as she touched Da-Ee's shoulder comfortingly. So, reluctantly the Endari girls left to carry on with their work. The hours passed slowly and the girls spent it worriedly taking turns to pace the floor. Da-Ee stood leaning against her workstation, looking across the room at Star's distraught expression.

"You love him too, don't you?" Da-Ee uttered quietly. It was more of a statement than a question. Star looked up at her, unsure what to say.

"Sure, he.. he's like a brother to me, we grew up together. He's always looked out for me." Star tried to convince Da-Ee.

"It's all right, I won't reveal your secret. I can see how much he means to you.. He loves you too... only you." Da-Ee uttered quietly, turning her back on her companion to avoid letting her tears betray her.

Star was frantically thinking what she could say to convince her it wasn't true, but Star knew. She realised, it was true, she loved Bull very much!

Three hours had passed when the screen on Da-Ee's wall lit up and Guy's face filled the monitor. He was still dressed in his theatre gear, blood streaks strewn across his cover-all.

"Bull's fine. The operation was a success!" Guy smiled tiredly at them both. "You can see him soon, I'll let you know when." Guy's image disappeared from the screen as it went blank once more. The two girls burst into tears of joy and hugged each other. A few seconds later Genai and Ursu burst into the room and exclaimed excitedly that Bull was out of theatre. Star and Da-Ee laughed and said in unison,

"We know!"

***

An hour later the two stood beside Bull's bed looking down at his calm demeanour. He was no longer pale, colour was returning to his face, he just looked as if he were asleep.

"He's doing fine!" Guy spoke from behind the girls as he entered the cubicle. He went over to the drip and checked it, then told the girls he would be awake in a few hours so they could come back then. Da-Ee stroked his forehead lovingly and Star held his hand awkwardly, unsure if she should, with Da-Ee there, but Da-Ee smiled sadly and said simply "He needs us both."

***

Shock!

Bull woke to find Da-Ee and Star both by his bedside. As he opened his eyes he saw the fear in Star's eyes as she tried a smile. Da-Ee held his hand and held it to her cheek as Star looked on from behind her, unable to utter a word. She excused herself, mumbling something about letting them have some alone time, that she'd see him later.

For the next few days he enjoyed the attention he was receiving from his visits by the crew, but he noticed the frequency of Star's visits especially and he was unsure what to make of it. She had been visiting twice a day for the past few days, more if anything than Da-Ee had visited. He had given up on her feeling anything but friendship for him a while back, but this was odd.

He had received little gifts of fruit and chocolates from his visitors and was enjoying the rest. He had been ordered to stay in bed and not to stress about anything. Every time he asked about their progress through space Guy refused to let him know anything because it was off limits until he was better apparently!

Bull began to lose track of time as the days blurred into one and when he asked his visitors what day it was they refused to let him know! Highly annoying.

Krisus came over to see him a few times and he had informed Bull that his people had left for the gate ahead of them and they'd had no more trouble from the Cressians after their battle, all had got off the planet safely thanks to Bull's crew.

**

Apparently Krisus's family were now all well again and had been given rooms on the Starfinder until they met up with their own ships once more to be transferred back on board his own fleet. Bull was glad that they had made it out successfully and even more glad when Krisus pointed out that his people would be glad to form an alliance with Earth.

A few days later Bull was allowed to sit up, but not to over exert himself, no return to normal duties for at least ten days, to give time for his stitches to begin healing. As he sat on the bed to dress he felt slightly dizzy and remarked to Guy how light headed he felt. When he saw the expressions on Finch and Guy's faces as they stood beside the bed he began to suspect something was amiss.

"I am all right, aren't I?! Bull asked hesitantly. When Guy assured him he was fine Bull asked further. "Well, why do I feel odd, all light and floaty then?"

Guy cleared his throat and looked to Finch, unsure what to say, Then Finch decided to give him the bad news.

"Well, actually it's not just you, we all feel this way. we're still in the gate, we haven't come out yet!" Finch tried to look positive, but found it hard.

Bull looked slightly panicked. He tried to remember how long the journey through the gate was supposed to be, then he recalled it was meant to take around five days.

"How many days have we been in the gate?" Bull asked worriedly. The three of them looked at each other and Guy finally nodded, giving his consent to reveal the answer.

Finch replied "Nine days."

Bull fell back onto his bed in shock! They were stuck inside the gate, going nowhere!

******

The story continues with RETRIBUTION, the final book of the Trilogy.